SHADE OF LIGHT

BOOKS BY KIMBERLY GRYMES

Aevo Compendium Duology Series
Young Adult Science-Fantasy

Isoldesse

Fawness

The Red Umber Forest (a companion novella)

♦ ♦ ♦ ♦

Three Shades Trilogy
Young Adult Dark Fantasy

Shade of Light

PRAISE FOR SHADE OF LIGHT

"Dark fantasy with feeling! Shade of Light is full of redemption and vengeance, and friendships forged in fire that weave through the story." **—Liz Delton, author of the Realm of Camellia Series**

◆ ◆ ◆ ◆

"This book is fast-paced and full of hard questions and unseeable twists. A coming-of-age story in the tradition of Sarah J. Maas and Leigh Bardugo." **—A.E. Kincaid, author of the Widdershins Series**

◆ ◆ ◆ ◆

"Honoring the Dark Fantasy genre, Adele brings a refreshing twist to the morally grey character trope; goodness doesn't need to be sweet." **—Elisa Menz, author of Easy Guide to Escape Hell**

◆ ◆ ◆ ◆

"This is the kind of book that you not only can't put down; you become addicted to it." **—A. M. Dunnewin, author of All the Dark Souls Trilogy**

◆ ◆ ◆ ◆

"A MAGICAL and MIND GRIPPING fantasy! Grymes takes you on an adventure with unexpected twists that keep you on your toes. You'll fall in love with the characters and stay for this unique dark world. An absolute must read!" **—Adina Chiles, author of the Royal Blood series**

◆ ◆ ◆ ◆

SHADE OF LIGHT

BOOK ONE IN THE THREE SHADES TRILOGY

KIMBERLY GRYMES

TRACTOR BEAM PUBLISHING

ISBN: 978-1-7361793-69 (paperback)
ISBN: 978-1-7361793-76 (hardcover)
ISBN: 978-1-7361793-83 (special edition hardcover)
ASIN: B0C6LC4XLJ (Kindle eBook)

Cover Design and Interior Formatting by Kimberly Grymes
Character Artwork by Yves Muench | Fiverr.com/creatyves
Map by Angeline Trevena | Step-By-Step Worldbuilding
Chapter Title Illustrations from Depsoitphotos.com and Canva.com
'The Home for Me' song lyrics co-written by Kimberly Grymes and Audrey Weatherstone. Song recorded and sang by Audrey Weatherstone

Shade of Light is book one in the Three Shades Trilogy.
Genre: Dark Fantasy
Age Category: Young Adult (14+)

Trigger warnings: Medieval fantasy world violence including death, battle scenes, and torture through mind infiltration; all scenes appropriate for teen readers 14+ years.

Tractor Beam Publishing
P.O. Box 261, Rose Hill, KS 67133

For more information visit www.kimberlygrymes.com

To Abby,

You're not just my daughter, but also a friend,
and I know we'll always be there for each other.
I look forward to many more nights of binge-watching
TV shows, playing boardgames, and baking sweet
treats together!
I love you infinity plus one.

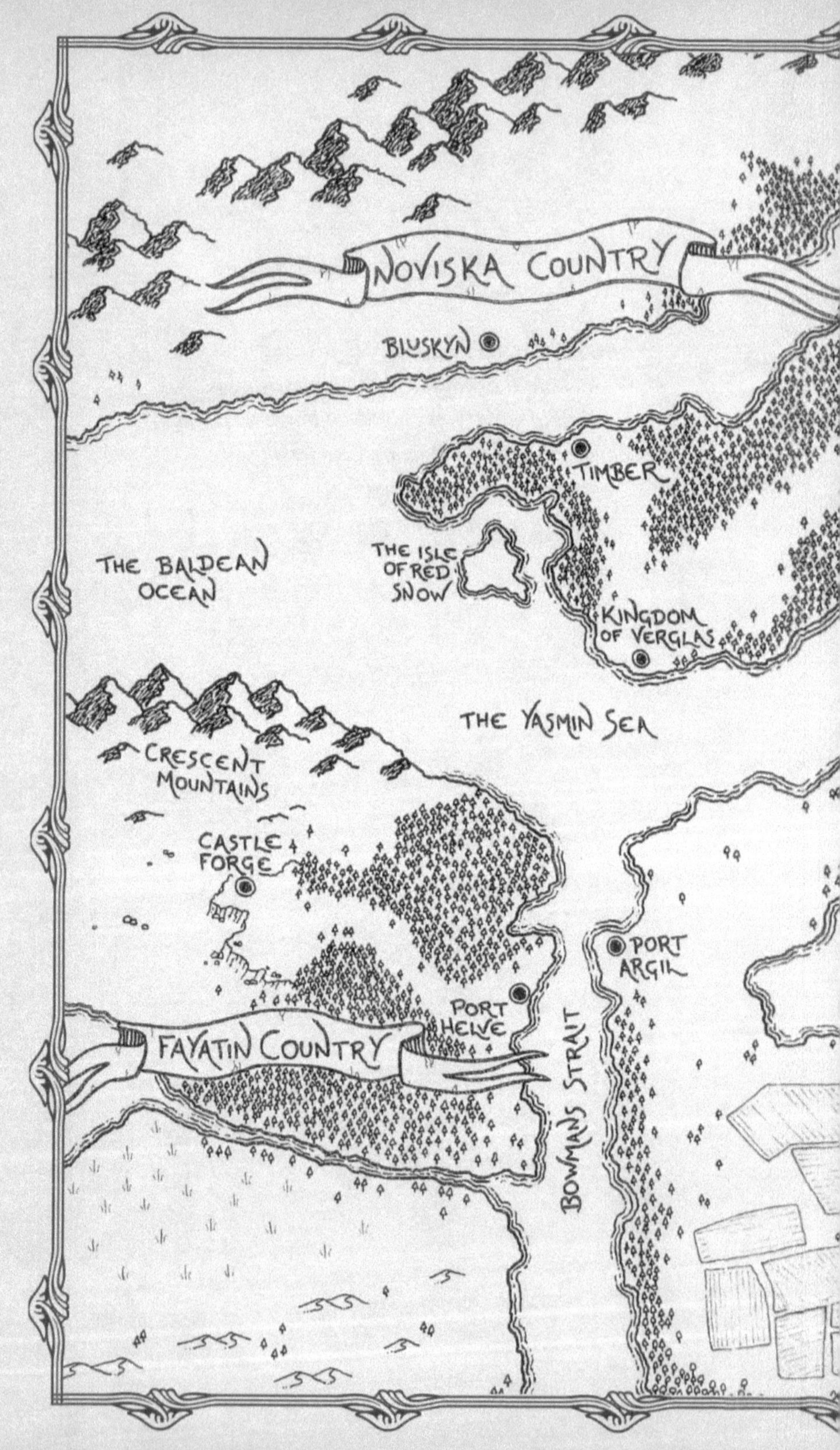

NOVISKA COUNTRY
BLUSKYN
TIMBER
THE BALDEAN OCEAN
THE ISLE OF RED SNOW
KINGDOM OF VERGLAS
THE YASMIN SEA
CRESCENT MOUNTAINS
CASTLE FORGE
PORT ARGIL
PORT HELVE
BOWMANS STRAIT
FAYATIN COUNTRY

N
THE ICEBROCK OCEAN
GAILSTEIN
BRICEN
UNDER REALM CAVE ENTRANCE
ARVESGROVE COUNTRY

PROLOGUE

GENERAL ONICA

The second the screaming erupts outside my door, I stand, knocking over my chair and bumping the edge of the table with my hip. One of the pillar candles tips, spilling hot wax onto the map I've been strategizing over. Red wax pools over the borderlines of Fayatin's neighboring country, Harvesgrove, and I can't help but smile at the symbolism. Blood will spill and my rule will expand.

Leaving the mess, I tuck my steel dagger into my waistband. With two long strides, I cross the room and grab my sword, which leans against the stone wall beneath the window. Stealing a quick glance outside, the moon hasn't peaked over the Crescent Mountains yet. It's still early.

More screams erupt.

With haste, I lift the iron latch and swing open my bedchamber door. Out in the hallway, a group of guards races by, armed with swords and daggers. At the end of the hall, Alister turns the corner, cheeks flushed as he marches toward me.

"What's going on?" I demand.

"Sorry to disturb you, General Onica, but she's escaped." He holds out a piece of parchment. "This was on her bed."

I unfold it and silently read the message:

I was never yours to keep.

More screams fill the halls of the castle. Closing my fist, I crumple the paper into a tight ball. "That little heathen." Every muscle in my body tenses with rage—with betrayal. Jaw clenched, I tell Alister, "Find her! She'll be traveling east, toward Harvesgrove Country. You'll have to cut her off before she reaches the port." Another group of guards run by. "I want her back in her chamber by midday tomorrow."

"Yes, ma'am."

"And Alister," I call out, stopping him before he turns the corner. "If she touches you or any of the soldiers"—I pull out the dagger from my waistband—"you know what you must do."

With a curt nod, Alister takes the blade and storms off, barking out orders to guards waiting for him at the end of the hall. They follow him, disappearing down the stone stairwell.

I stare at the crumpled ball of paper. There's only one person brave enough to go against army orders and teach one of my soldiers to read and write—Selene. "That treacherous, ungrateful pain in my ass!"

Another wave of tormented cries erupts from the grand room below. I toss the note aside, tighten my grip on the hilt of my sword, and head toward the stairs. There's only one way to end the suffering of those afflicted by that little heathen's touch.

CHAPTER 1

Bessie snorts, and I grip the reins tighter, leaning forward as she gallops through the forest. "Almost there, girl. You can do it. Hyah!" I'm sure she'd prefer to take the road, but it's too risky and going back isn't an option. Not until I get the answers I'm owed.

Twigs snap beneath Bessie's pounding hooves. Poor girl isn't fond of the night, but I'll make it up to her one day. She's an old mare and has never minded the longer journeys when there's no rush. It's the quick getaways she's always struggled with, which is probably why General Onica gave her to me.

After hours of riding, the end of the forest comes into view. I pull on the reins, slowing Bessie to a stop. With a gloved hand, I rub her neck before feeding her a few carrots from my bag. The forest opens to a narrow meadow and is the last obstacle before reaching the docks. Being on the outskirts of Port Helve gives me the best chance of staying out of sight and crossing Bowmans Strait.

I'm almost there. Harvesgrove Country is just beyond those waters—as is my freedom.

There's no looking back or dwelling on the cost others had to endure for me to get here. Embracing who I am was the only way to escape.

The dim light of the half-moon allows me to survey the narrow meadow, over to where the boats are tied up along the docks. At this late hour, there isn't supposed to be this many crew members guarding the shipyard, but I count a full detail, plus a few extra, standing on the main pier. Most of the men are focused on the dark waters, and after a few seconds I see why. A large barge breaks through the fog, drifting up to the main dock. It's carrying a group of Fayatin men surrounding an unmarked freight wagon. They're not wearing their red coats, the standard uniform for a Fayatin soldier, which means whatever they are doing requires anonymity.

There's peace between the three countries, but that's because an agreement was made decades ago that no one shall trespass into their neighboring country. And all three countries—Fayatin, Noviska, and Harvesgrove—have abided by this agreement, never crossing borders without permission. Though, General Onica rarely follows anyone's ruling but her own.

After the barge docks, the men work quickly to attach the freight wagon to a pair of horses. At the end of the pier, when the horses cross the threshold onto dry land, they inadvertently jostle the wagon. A deafening shriek echoes up into the night air accompanied by forceful blows from the inside. The wagon almost tips over, causing all four lanterns, hanging from the front and rear corners, to sway vigorously. Everyone rushes and circles the cargo hold doors, their swords drawn, ready to restrain whatever beast they've captured.

There's only one reason an unmarked freight of that size could be coming from either of the two neighboring countries. A reason I'm well familiar with. If it weren't for the piercing shrieks and violent blows coming from inside, I'd be tempted to see if my suspicions are right, if the general has acquired more laborers to mine her precious iron ore.

Whatever they've got, it's not worth risking getting caught to find out. Not this time. This time I escape and finally get answers about why I am the way I am.

"That, my old friend," I lean forward and remark to Bessie, "is the kind of attention we don't need right now. And exactly why we didn't travel the road. Now you understand and forgive me for taking the unbeaten path?"

Bessie shakes her white mane before dipping her head to nibble on a patch of tall grass.

I shift my attention from the freight to the thick fog creeping in over the line of boats. Weighing my options, I disregard the fishing ships and ferries and settle on a modest-sized rowboat far from the main dock. Swinging one leg over the backside of the mare, I slide off the saddle. "All I have to do is sneak over to the docks and borrow one of those—"

"The word 'borrow'…"—a woman's voice cuts me off—"…implies you'll have to return it."

I spin to see a horse and rider emerging from the shadows of the forest. The woman draws back the hood of her cloak, giving me a familiar smile that I've only ever seen through iron bars.

My imprisonment at Castle Forge might have been comfortable, but I was never allowed to roam the grounds. Only when the general requested my services for an interrogation or an escort to diplomatic meetings was I permitted to leave my room. Eventually, the general granted me access to a locked stairwell from within my chambers that led to an enclosed outdoor courtyard. It was there, a few years ago, that Selene discovered the courtyard, and me in it, while hiding from her tutors. Ever since then, she came to keep me company regardless of the two layers of iron fencing surrounding the courtyard.

"Selene! What are you doing here?"

Tilting forward, she tsks at me before saying, "You were going to leave without a goodbye." She holds one hand out to me. Reluctantly, I help her off her horse. With her hand in mine, I suddenly don't want to let go. We've been friends for years, yet this is the first time we've been within arm's reach. Silently, I curse to the stars that I'm forced to wear these dreadful gloves.

When she's got her footing, I release my grasp and ask, "How did you know where to find me?"

The moonlight shines over her rosy cheeks. "I helped you write the note to General Onica, remember?"

Selene has been teaching me to read and write these past few months. A secret request I made after returning home with the general from a trip up north to Noviska Country. I'm far from proficient, but all I need to know are the basics, like how to pronounce a village name or how to address someone in a letter.

"But I never said where I was going in the note." Bessie nudges my arm, also wanting some attention. I oblige and scratch her neck. Then, looking to Selene, I ask, "So, how did you know?"

After a drink from her waterskin, she says, "Come now. You rarely mention your past life over there"—she gestures toward the water—"and I want to believe you have unfinished business or family you wish to see again over in Harvesgrove, but when it comes to these long journeys with the general, like your recent expedition up north, I have other suspicions as to why you want to leave."

When I avert my gaze, she continues, "Adele, I didn't pry after you returned from Noviska, but I know something happened. I can always tell when you're upset."

"There's nothing new about my foul mood."

Selene tucks the waterskin into the satchel hanging from her horse's saddle, then faces me. Loose strands of brown hair have escaped her thick braid. That, and her flushed complexion, makes me wonder how fast she must've ridden to catch me. She's staring at me, waiting for me to give her an answer about what she assumes happened up north.

Something did happen up north—but there's no way my dear friend could possibly know what I witnessed. It was pure luck—me being in the right spot at the right time—that I saw someone from my past do something no one else can, sparking an obsessive need for answers.

"Fine," she says, breaking the silence and crossing her arms over the bodice of her dress. "If you won't tell me, then I'm going to make a guess about what I think happened." I'm about to cut her off and tell her to go home when she raises a finger. "The general made advances, which of course you didn't consent to. She might be our general, but that doesn't give her the right to—"

"Selene!" I shout, needing to stop her before she says something I don't want to hear. Out of the corner of my eye, I notice one of the soldiers shift his attention from the freight wagon to the open field. I quickly lead Selene closer to the tree line, out of sight of the Fayatin soldiers. "It's nothing like that."

"Are you sure?" she asks. "I've always had my suspicions that the general keeps you around for more than"—she points to my hands—"your special set of skills."

I can't help but crack a smile. "Jealous?" It's a playful taunt, which is rare for me. The lively girl I was before my time in Fayatin is long gone. Yet, whenever I'm around Selene, she tends to bring out the old me.

"Oh, please, it's not me who's jealous. I think it's that crazy woman who has an entire army at her command that's jealous of what we have."

We both know the general is aware of our friendship and the secret rendezvous in the courtyard, but she's never spoken of it to either of us. And we prefer it that way.

Selene moves closer, her expression softening. "Just tell me why you're leaving. What happened in Noviska that got you so riled up? I mean, I know you've always wanted to leave, but not like this—not with so many left to suffer."

"I…" My voice cracks, and I almost divulge the truth I've kept from her all these years. Selene knows there's something special about my touch, and that I'm the infamous Fayatin Interrogator; only a few people know the Interrogator's true identity. But she doesn't know everything. Like that I'm broken. A cursed soul that can't be trusted. And how I've only entertained her kindness and friendship because of the courtyard's iron barriers between us, keeping her safe from my touch.

"Please, Adele. Tell me what weighs on your mind. Maybe I can help."

This is not the time or the place to divulge the secrets I've kept from her. And I wish I could say that I escaped to try and make a better life with her in it, but I didn't. What kind of happiness could a tormentor with a cursed soul offer?

Since I cannot give her what she asks for, I offer up a piece of the truth about why I need to leave. "The general never touched me. She knows better." I fear no one, yet whenever Selene is nearby my insides knot up. I'm too afraid I might accidentally cause her pain.

"Go on," she says softly, gaze locked onto mine.

"While in Noviska, I saw someone from my past. Someone I thought was lost to me forever, and she did something that…" I stop mid-sentence. I'm crossing into territory that I don't want Selene to be a part of. I hold up my gloved hands, turning them over. After a moment, I drop them to my sides and continue, "This woman may know more about who I am." I hesitate to say my next words, and eventually they slip out as a whisper. "Or what I am."

Selene clasps her bare hands over my gloved ones. I try to pull away, but she tightens her hold. There's nothing but a thin layer of leather protecting her from all the horrible things I could do to her. But I would never. She's the last person in this entire messed-up world that I'd hurt.

Squeezing my hands, she forces me to look into her eyes. "You're not a 'what.' Do you hear me? And why didn't you tell me sooner about this person from your past?"

I reel in the urge to shove her to the ground. To tell her that her benevolence will get her killed one of these days. Instead, I say with a clenched jaw, "This is not your burden. It's mine." Slipping my hands free from hers, I step away, bumping into Bessie. "And you can't be here. I don't know how long I've got until the general realizes I've escaped."

"Oh, she knows. You left quite the mess. That's why I'm here. To warn you."

I recall the trail of castle guards I subdued in my path to the stables. With one touch I reached deep into their minds, seeking out the thing they feared most, and then used that fear to trap them in a mental prison. There was nothing I could do to silence their screams or wails. The only way would be to release them, and that wasn't happening. Not without the risk of being caught. I left them to the mercy of General Onica, who knew exactly what needed to be done to free their tormented souls. If you're going to keep monsters locked up in your home, then you better be prepared to handle the consequences when they break free.

At some point in my life, I must've been cursed. It's the only reasonable explanation. But why? And how? Crossing Bowmans Strait and traveling to my childhood village is how I will get the answers I'm owed. It's the only way I can move forward.

Selene shakes my arm. "Adele, did you hear me? Alister is en route."

"Bloody hell," I mutter. "I guess I could've been a bit more discreet in my escape."

"You think?" Selene answers, one brow raised.

I knew the general would send soldiers after me—she always does—but never has she sent her lapdog to retrieve me. Risky endeavor on her part.

I stare into Selene's eyes for a long moment, trying to gauge the danger I've put her in. For the last eight years, I've shut out everyone and everything. Attachments, or emotions, were a luxury I abandoned the moment I agreed to be General Onica's secret interrogator. The only two souls I ever allowed myself to feel anything for are here with me now—Selene and Bessie.

"Adele, what's going on in that head of yours? I know that look all too well."

"How much time do I have? I need to get to the docks."

Selene tilts her head to the night sky and then along the main road. "Not much. Alister is the fastest rider in Fayatin, and he's got half of the general's army with him."

"Only half?" I can't help but jest. For a split second, I imagine what that battle might look like, and feel sorry for all the fallen soldiers that would suffer in my victory.

She slaps my arm. "It's no time to be joking. You know the lengths the general will go to when it comes to *you*."

I flinch from her sudden contact, but quickly focus my thoughts. This isn't the time to be dwelling on insecurities like boundaries because she's right—there's an urgency to the situation.

"Yes—yes. But you need to go," I say, pointing to the forest. "I don't want Alister or any of the soldiers seeing you here."

"I can help!" she insists.

"No, you can't. This isn't a time to be throwing around your noble connections. Your uncle may be one of the more powerful Fayatin lords, but even he won't be able to save you from General Onica's wrath if you're caught, and I can't lose…" My words trail off.

She closes the space between us and whispers, "You'll never lose me." Her eyes lock onto mine. "You will always be my dearest and closest friend."

I stumble backward along the uneven ground, turn away from her, and unstrap my quiver from Bessie's saddle. Selene is of noble blood. Her place is with the lords and others from noble bloodlines. She would never be permitted to befriend or be seen with someone like me—someone with evil coursing through their veins.

She's quiet, and it's a first. Normally, she rebuts everything without losing a breath between retorts. Unbuckling my bag from the saddle, I tell her, "You're the only friend who means anything to me." I shoulder my bag, then unlatch my bow from the saddle. Then, after I've whispered my goodbyes to Bessie, I face Selene. She lunges forward, wrapping her arms around my neck. My entire body goes rigid.

"You mean the world to me too." Our proximity has me nervous, and I'm about to push away, when she pulls me in closer. Wavy dark hair brushes against my face, smelling like rose petals and lavender. "I wish I could come with you."

"I wish you could too."

A few men holler something from the road, and we break apart. The soldiers have clustered by the rear of the freight wagon, swords drawn again. When I realize their outburst wasn't because of us, I look to Selene, who is watching the road. Every part of my body urges me to bring her with me— to protect her. But I can't. I don't know what awaits across the strait in Harvesgrove Country.

I loop my quiver's leather strap over my head and tell her with a stern tone, "You need to go." No more games and no more conversations. She needs to leave before that brute, Alister, finds her.

Returning her attention to me, she hesitantly nods. Then, before I can react, she leans in and plants a soft kiss on my cheek. "We are family, Adele. Sisters for life."

I expect a barrage of visions—or memories—to flash in my mind, but nothing happens. I've never let anyone touch me before, always assuming my entire body has the ability to create that bridge of invasion. But nothing happens.

Selene plucks a narrow hairpin from within her braid. With one finger, she rubs the three small rubies affixed to the top. Then, after wiping her damp cheek, she gently sticks the hairpin into my braid. "I want you to borrow this."

"Borrowing would imply…" I whisper, but she cuts me off.

"I know what it implies." More tears fall.

I can't bring myself to express the heartfelt words I want to say. That her declaration of sisterhood means the world to me. Instead, I offer her a weak smile, hoping it provides enough reassurance. I hand her Bessie's reins and tell her, "I will come back…for both of you." The second she takes my horse, I turn and run, crouching low as I go.

There's a loud commotion on the road by the freight wagon, and the pier workers posted at the entrance of the main dock rush to assist. Not wasting the distraction the stars have bestowed, I hurry and climb into one of the rowboats, untie its rope from the post, and let the gentle current carry me away from Fayatin. I'm one step closer to getting the answers owed to me, even if it means using certain methods of persuasion on people I once called family.

CHAPTER 2

It's midmorning by the time my small boat drifts toward the shoreline. The second I set foot on dry land, I peel off my damp red overcoat and stash it beneath a bush. For the past eight years, I've imagined what this day might look like—to return to my homeland—and now I'm here.

With my coat discarded, I glance down at my white shirt. A thread from one of the embroidered red stars circling a black capital F has come loose. But that's not what concerns me. Even if the people of Harvesgrove Country don't recognize the insignia indicating my high-ranking status, they'll know it's a symbol of Fayatin. A sure sign that I don't belong on this side of the strait.

I quickly realize I should've brought some extra clothes and was too hasty in my escape. Though, I've never been good at keeping my patience in check or making proper plans.

I stay hidden by the river's edge, but with a clear view of the main road that's twenty to thirty paces straight through the wooded area. While unpinning my hair and storing Selene's hairpin in my satchel, I observe the travelers passing by. They're mostly women, children, and a few older men. Nothing I couldn't handle if confronted.

Combing my fingers through my long blonde hair, I sweep it forward, covering the insignia. It'll do for now.

With my bow in one hand, my bag across one shoulder, and my quiver strapped across my back, I jog toward the edge of town. As I pass the last house, before leaving the port town behind, a strong wind from the north hits me. Harvesgrove Country doesn't have the Crescent Mountain range that Fayatin has, blocking the northern winds from Noviska. Here, everything is flat farmlands or dense forests. I have a good chance of freezing to death if I don't find something to keep me warm. And I have no intention of leaving this world as a cold, lifeless stiff just because I forgot to pack a blanket. Actually, I didn't think to pack a lot of things.

After backtracking a few houses along the water, I sneak into the yard that has a line full of clothes hung to dry. Instead of grabbing a fresh shirt, I snatch a worn leather lace-up vest. Then a pair of thick wool socks and a long brown cloak. With everything rolled up into my arms, I wait until I'm at least five minutes from the port town before donning the vest over my shirt and draping the cloak over my shoulders. I stash the socks inside my bag in case my feet get cold later.

Continuing east, I keep my head low and stay off to the side while walking the dirt road. Whenever travelers do pass by, I pretend to be coughing or sneezing. No one ever stops to talk to someone if they think they're afflicted with an illness. Well, no one in Fayatin, that is. This tactic doesn't seem to work here. There've been quite a few people who've stopped and asked me if I need water, food, or a place to rest. At first, their hospitality catches me off guard, and I wave them away while grumbling, "Leave me be." These people wouldn't last more than a day in my country. Their kindness would be seen as weakness or an opportunity to swindle them out of everything they own.

Once I make it past the farming fields, it isn't long before I reach the forest. While I walk beneath the canopy of leafy branches shielding me from the afternoon sun, my thoughts drift to what kind of welcome I'll receive when I reach Bricen. Will the villagers who knew me recognize me now? Or maybe they've forgotten about me. I mean, no one ever came looking for me. Not even my mum's sister, my Aunt Lauren. But then again, why would they? Not after what I did.

Everywhere I go, I cause pain. I'm convinced that's part of my curse. Not only because of what I can do with a simple touch but also because of the rash decisions I make—impulsive decisions that get people killed. People like my mum.

Slowing to a stop, I squeeze my eyes shut, tilt my head back, and raise my chin to the sky. There's comfort in knowing that even though I can't see the stars during the day, I know they're there. That one doesn't have to see something to believe in something. I have my doubts that angels exist—that there are celestial beings living comfortable lives in a world beyond the stars—listening and answering the prayers of mortals. But because I believe in balance, and because I know there's evil in this world, I have to hope there's goodness out there too. So, I pray to the stars, hoping whoever's up there hears my pleas to keep Selene safe.

"Do you have any spare food?" A young man's voice cuts through my prayers.

Opening my eyes, I look at the slender boy, maybe eleven or twelve years of age, standing before me. A few missing teeth and dirty cheeks are the least of this kid's problems. He looks as though he could use a hearty meal or two…or ten.

Gripping my bow, I sidestep past him while grumbling, "Nothing to spare. Now, get going." With long strides, I put some distance between us.

"Hey!" he shouts, jogging up beside me. He's trying to match my pace while talking. "Are you one of those hero-wannabes looking for death?"

I skid to a stop, pebbles sliding beneath my boots. Grabbing the kid's shoulder, I force him to face me. "Are you threatening me?"

He wiggles free but doesn't run. "No, I'm not threatening you. I'm only wondering why you're heading east." He points a dirty finger down the road. "If you keep going that way, there's a good chance you won't survive the night."

"I'll manage."

I'm about to shuffle past him again when he blocks my path. "And you're going at it alone?"

The muscles in my jaw tense, and I inhale a deep breath because my patience is wearing thin. "I prefer it that way."

"That's too bad." He briefly glances toward the empty road stretching out ahead, then tells me, "'Strength in numbers' is what my pa used to say. And that 'a lonely life isn't a life worth living,' but then again, maybe he was wrong, and a lonely life is the only way to live—to survive."

Surely, he can't be out here alone. Glancing down the road behind me, I search for any traveling companions. No one. A branch snaps and a chorus of shushes floats out from within the woods. There's movement and I make out four or five pint-size, mangy mops and dirty faces watching us from behind thick trees, fallen logs, and moss-covered boulders.

Returning my attention to the wild-looking boy, I ask, "Where are your parents?"

"Dead." His reply comes too quick, and lacking sorrow. As if much time has passed and he's come to terms with their absence.

Pressing my lips together, I make a *hmm* sound while digesting his words. After a long moment, I shift the conversation. "Okay, so tell me. What exactly is going to kill me?"

He looks me over, as if I've asked him the oddest question in the world. Pale blue eyes scan over my clothes, bag, and bow, like he's trying to figure out my story or an explanation as to who I am. Observant little bugger.

"You're being serious. You don't know."

"Listen here, kid. I don't have time for your games." His narrowed gaze has me wondering if there's some truth to his warning. Shifting my weight, I grip the leather strap of my bag crossing my chest and ask, "Where's your village?"

His gaze dips and his hands go straight into his pants pockets. Kicking a rock on the road, he tells me, "I used to live in Gailstein, but now the forest is my home."

Gailstein… I remember that quaint village. It was half a day's walk from Bricen. Mum used to travel there to visit an elderly woman and would often bring me and my friend Kit with her. We'd sit outside picking the sweetest blueberries, filling our baskets to the brim, while Mum had a healing session with her client.

An ache pinches inside my chest. Over the years, the memory of her has become increasingly difficult to hold on to. Now that I'm older, I can't help but feel I'm nothing like her, except for the wheat-colored locks and deep brown eyes. A thought surfaces, and I can't help but wonder if things had gone differently that fateful day…if the attack never happened and I never left Bricen…would I be different than I am now? Would I be more like my mum—kind and able to love? Or would this curse coursing through my veins have found me regardless of where I went?

"You know the place? Have you been to Gailstein?" the kid asks, breaking me from my thoughts. He shoots a quick side glance over at his hidden gang watching from the woods, before scrunching his brows at me. Before I can answer him, he jumps in and asks me, "You're not from around here, are you?"

My skills as an interrogator aren't shining at the moment, letting this pint-size nugget ask all the questions. But I can't stop thinking about his warning. *Are you one of those hero-wannabes looking for death?* Who or what has been terrorizing this part of Harvesgrove Country?

It can't be…

No.

Even if the threat is what I suspect it is, at least I know Aunt Lauren's alive. She's the reason I risked everything and escaped from Castle Forge. The reason I'm dredging up old memories and revisiting a home that may not even remember my name. But after spotting my aunt up in Noviska Country over three months ago and seeing how she healed a child with a drop of her blood, I knew she'd been keeping secrets from me—possibly from my mum, too.

It's all I've been thinking about since the general, Alister, and I returned from Noviska Country. I deserve to know the truth. And I will get the truth from her one way or another.

Ignoring the kid's presence, I press on. But he persists, walking alongside me with an outstretched open palm. "So, no spare food?"

"What? No! Now, get lost!" I pull out a knife from inside the waistband of my pants. The second the boy sees the gleam along the polished blade, his eyes go wide, and he takes off running into the woods. Several children burst out from their hiding spots and take off after him. Their hoots and hollers fade as they retreat away from the direction I'm heading.

For stars' sake… I forgot to get a straight answer about what's going to kill me. Or, at least, what's going to *try* to kill me. Yet again, my impulsiveness has gotten the better of me.

CHAPTER 3

ADELE

After making camp and using my sleeping tonic to keep the nightmares at bay, I got somewhat of a decent night's sleep. Whatever was supposed to come and kill me never showed up. One thing I've learned from the general is to never let your guard down, so for the time being, I keep the kid's warning of death fresh in my mind.

Before heading out, I head over to the creek to refill my waterskin. Not wanting to ruin or lose my gloves, I set them on a smooth rock away from the water's edge. The chill of the cold current flowing over my hands is a nice relief from constantly being sheathed in leather.

The forest grounds and Harvesgrove Country's gusty winds have taken a toll on my hair, so when I'm finished filling my waterskin, I take a minute to redo my braid. After tying off the end, I retrieve Selene's hairpin from my bag and secure it in the top of my braid. Once I'm done, I gather my belongings and make my way to the road.

As I walk the empty road, the overcast sky has me concerned. Dark clouds linger off on the distant horizon. A sure sign rain is coming. It also makes it hard to tell the time of day, but I assume it's around midmorning. This means I should reach Bricen by late afternoon. Then, hopefully, I'll be heading back to Fayatin by nightfall.

I don't know if it's the dreariness of the day or the anticipation of returning to a home that may not welcome me, but I can't stop thinking about my last day in Bricen—that fateful day of the attack.

The day started like any other. I was playing outside our cottage home with my friend Kit and her younger brother, Elijah, when the screaming started. Kit dropped the bucket of frogs, and we all ran to see what the commotion was, but it was hard to tell because everyone was running in every direction. Kit and Elijah's mum ran up to us, grabbing each one by the arm and dragging them off, leaving me behind. I screamed and cried for either my mum or my aunt, hoping one of them would come and carry me off to safety. But neither came.

More villagers cried out. Scared, I took off running, weaving through the chaos, eventually making my way toward Goslings. Mum liked to meet her clients at the tavern, so I hoped and prayed to the stars that she was there.

Out in front of Goslings, as the dust cloud settled, that's when I saw them. Strange men and women with shaved heads and even stranger clothes—tattered strips of black fabric wrapping their arms, legs, and bodies—casually standing about, watching the villagers scatter like frightened beetles. More strangers in tattered black disappeared into the forest with villagers over their shoulders. I opened my mouth, wanting to call out and see if they had my mum or auntie, but Kit and Elijah's older sister, Alya, grabbed me, one hand over my mouth. She dragged me beneath the porch of Goslings, where a bunch of other people lay hiding.

"Who are they, and what do they want?" I asked, my voice low, quivering with each word. We peered out from the tight crawlspace. All I could see from our hiding spot were the strangers' legs, wrapped in that strange black fabric, and their bare feet, coated in dirt.

Alya quickly covered my mouth with her hand. Her fingers smelled of damp soil and fresh herbs. She must've come from the gardens near the front gate. Pressing a finger to her lips, Alya shook her head, silently pleading with me to stay quiet. Understanding, I nodded, but the second I saw the hem of my mum's blue dress as she gracefully stepped off the porch step of Goslings, and out onto the dusty road, I scrambled to break free from Alya's embrace. But the older girl held me tight.

"You're not welcome here," Mum said. A mixture of severity and sternness emphasized her words. "Turn around, leave, and never return to this—"

Hands tugged at my waist, dragging my body farther back beneath the porch. My attention shifted from Mum to Alya, who was trying to shimmy us closer to two other women hiding beneath the porch. Rocks and sticks poked at my legs and arms. I tried to wriggle free, but Alya's fingers grasped the fabric of my dress. "Adele! You're too close! They'll see you!" she anxiously whispered.

I remember the fear and panic on the features of the two women hiding under the porch with us. They clung to one another, chins pressed into the dry dirt, arms hooked, and hands clasped with one another. They didn't even acknowledge the black beetles crawling around the dead leaves, inches from their faces.

After a forceful kick, Alya's hands released me. I wasn't sure where my foot connected, but it didn't matter—I needed to see my mum. Hurrying, I crawled closer to the edge of the underside of the porch. Mum had moved farther out onto the street. The strangers surrounded her from the left and right sides, but they didn't advance. They only stood staring at her.

"You heard me!" Mum shouted. "I know who you are and where you come from, and you will not harm these people! You will—" Her words were cut off by a hand from behind, covering her mouth. She yelled, but her efforts were short-lived. One of the strangers had snuck up from behind her, and the instant his hand fully clasped over her face, she slumped forward like a rag doll.

I didn't understand what was happening. Bricen had never been under attack or threatened before. My heart pounded against the hard ground, and something inside me snapped. The moment the attacker lifted my mother, tossing her limp body over his shoulder, I let out a piercing scream.

While the man carrying my mum trudged away from the village, the others like him stalked toward Goslings. I wasn't thinking straight and didn't care that I'd revealed our hiding spot. All that mattered was getting to my mum.

Alya tried to grab me again—tried to drag me back under the porch—but I scrambled out, desperately wanting to get to my mum. By the time I got to my feet, she was gone. All I could think was they'd taken her to the forest like the others, so I ran. From behind, Alya screamed, along with so many others.

I know what I did was reckless, and looking back, I wish I'd done things differently, but the past is the past and there's no changing that. Alya and the other women hiding under the porch were probably killed, leaving Kit and Elijah without an older sister. But I lost more than my mum that day. I also lost a home. Trying to find my mum, I kept running and running until my legs gave out and my lungs were too exhausted to inhale any more air. I woke the next day, tied up in the back of a freight wagon on a barge, crossing Bowmans Strait toward Fayatin. Never to set foot in Harvesgrove Country ever again—until now.

By late afternoon, I hadn't seen a single drop of rain or another soul traveling the road. The only company is a few crows, perched up in the trees and cawing their hellos as I pass by.

I know it was eight years ago, but I don't recall this road ever being so vacant. There were always trappers, merchants, and lumbermen bustling about from village to village, trading their goods and mingling with the locals. And with Bricen being the last village along the main road, Goslings Tavern was always lively with tradespeople, regardless of the season.

Yet here I am. The only soul for miles.

My suspicions grow stronger that the attack on Bricen might not have been a one-time incident.

Caw, caw, caw.

I glance up at the large, silky black bird. Its beady eyes track me as I walk beneath an outstretched branch. "Except for you, my new friend!" I yell up to the beast of a bird. "Do you know where everyone is?" The bird cocks its head before spreading its wings and flying off.

"Fine, be that way. I didn't want your company, anyway."

The boy's warning about death comes to mind, along with a daunting thought that Bricen won't be the same village I once knew. It's understandable that the village will look different. Eight years is a long time, plus I was a naïve kid who saw beauty and merit in everything. But I'm not a kid anymore. And I've seen things…done things…that age me well past my eighteen years.

The wind picks up, and a chill travels over my face and neck. After adjusting the strap of my quiver, I grip the wool cloak tighter across my chest. I passed Gailstein three hours ago, so Bricen isn't too much farther. This stretch of road is vaguely familiar, but I can't be sure.

A sweet scent drifting in the air catches my attention. My stomach approves with a grumble, and I slide down the shallow embankment to a small clearing where there's a bush full of wild blueberries. One handful after another, I eat my fill. I'm about to make my way to the road when one of the crows dives straight at me. Within seconds, a sharp pain sears along my scalp. Yelping, I toss the handful of berries at my attacker then swat both hands through the air until it stops.

"Wretched bird!" Cursing under my breath, I press one hand to the top of my head and cringe. There's no blood on my glove, so it's only a scratch. But still. Ow. When a loud *caw* cries out, I tilt my head up. Its black wings are spread wide as it circles above. Two seconds before it flies off into the forest, something clutched in its talon sparkles red.

Selene's hairpin.

"Wait! No! That's mine!"

Running into the woods, I leap over a fallen log, dodge a massive spiderweb, and shove my way between two low branches until I'm met by an enormous oak tree. I search for the thief up in the branches, while being careful not to trip over the large roots. A loud *caw* draws my attention to the back side of the tree. As I come around, four crows are perched on a low branch. One of them is holding Selene's hairpin.

I draw an arrow, then deftly nock it and pull back the bowstring, my muscles tensing as I aim at the pesky thief. I'm about to release the arrow when all four birds take flight. Their *caw*s echo up into the treetops, causing more birds to join their swarm. I crouch down, tucking my head to my chest, and wait. When the birds' calls fade, I stand and glimpse the last of them flying down a narrow path obscured by the dense overgrowth. Without hesitation, I sprint down the winding trail, my feet pounding against the packed dirt of the steep path. It winds around the large oak tree and descends to a dirt clearing alongside a lively river. The current churns and froths as it smashes against jagged rocks.

Most of the birds soar over the water while the four troublesome crows veer left. I spot a glint of red as the hairpin falls from the bird's grasp, then lands in a pile of pine needles. After retrieving the sentimental piece, I store it in my bag rather than return it to my braid.

"I should end your thieving ways right now!" I shout as they watch me from a nearby tree. "Annoying birds. You've wasted enough of my time."

I turn to head back to the road, but something in the air tugs at my attention—a lure that I cannot see or hear. It lingers at the edge of my mind. The feeling vaguely resembles warm sunny days and picnics with my mum.

"What is that?" I say, searching out the source. When a small cave comes into view, my curiosity peaks. The narrow opening is tucked beneath the overhang from the forest ground above. Fibrous roots from the underside of the soil cling to the rocks forming the mouth of the cave. I've seen my share of caves, as I often accompanied General Onica to the mining caves of the Crescent Mountains, north of Castle Forge, but never anything like this. This one is so small, and perfectly hidden.

Then it dawns on me that I know this place. I came here many times as a child with Kit and Elijah. We'd play here for hours. Moving closer, I brace one hand along the top before entering. It's not a big space. Enough to fit four or five adults inside. There's a stream of daylight, allowing me to see the shallow cavern, which is good. I'd hate to twist an ankle, bump my head, or injure myself in some other way this close to Bricen.

Thinking about the memories I made in this cave reminds me that the people of Bricen will know me as Adele, the lost kid returning home and not Adele, the infamous Interrogator of Fayatin. And I'm hoping to keep it that way. I can't imagine what kind of welcome I'd get if they knew the truth about who I've become. General Onica exploited my abilities, while keeping my identity a secret, to instill fear in those who questioned her rule. And I let her.

Besides the general, Alister, and Selene, the only others to learn the truth about who the Interrogator was were the ones sent to me for questioning. I found amusement in how they always expected a strong, ferocious man and never a young, blonde-haired girl. They'd laugh and jest, not believing I could be the Interrogator. But their naïve perceptions changed the second my fingers grazed their skin.

Invading their minds—seeking out their traumas and fears—I hated all of it. It didn't matter if they knew the truth about who the Interrogator was because once I finished getting whatever information General Onica wanted, she'd order me to bind their sanity in a mental prison. Forcing them to relive whatever trauma or fear haunted their minds.

Dragging my gloved hand across the cave wall, I whisper, "Only someone with a cursed soul could cause that kind of evil."

Not wanting to fall into a somber mood, I remind myself that even though I was locked away at Castle Forge, I was never a captive, not truly. I could've left at any time, but I chose to stay. All those years, I convinced myself that everyone sent to me for interrogations had committed crimes against the general, such as theft or sabotage of the mining operation. I even convinced myself that I wouldn't find a more comfortable living out in the world on my own. However, deep down inside, I knew I was only making excuses for staying, avoiding the truth that I was too afraid to leave—too afraid of never seeing the one person who treated me like a real person and not the cursed soul I am. Selene was my family now. She needed me as much as I needed her. Glancing out the cave entrance, I can't help but feel obligated to return to Selene—to protect my dear friend from that treacherous place.

I return to Bricen for knowledge. Not to reconnect with family or rekindle friendships. The plan is to find my aunt, get my answers, and be done with my past once and for all. Though, I have no idea where to go once I return to Fayatin. Selene's of noble blood and would never leave the castle grounds. How can I protect her and avoid being captured by the general? Standing in the opening, I peer inside the cave and push the question from my thoughts. I'll worry about that problem when it's staring me in the face.

There's nothing more to see and I need to get going. Though the moment I turn away, that strange lure tugs at my mind again, beckoning me from somewhere inside the cave. I scan the dimly lit interior one more time and discover a shallow alcove discreetly set out of daylight's reach, tucked behind a jagged boulder. Inside the nook is a large obsidian slab, the size of a door embedded in the cave wall.

"What's this?" I ask, touching a hand to the unfamiliar section of cave wall. It's warm, I can tell that, but it's hard to feel anything more while wearing my gloves. After removing one glove, I press my palm to the smooth rock. The second my skin comes into contact with the obsidian, the surface transforms, resembling more glass than stone. On the other side is another small cave, except beyond the cave entrance isn't like anything I've ever seen before. The ground is a desolate land, covered in crevices glowing red along the seams. From above, thunder rumbles across the midnight sky, which is completely void of any clouds, stars, or even a moon.

"What is this place? And"—I lean closer—"is that a voice?"

Facing one ear to the wall, I swear someone is speaking—a woman—chanting words I can't decipher. The soothing sound of her voice sinks deeper into my mind, slowly growing louder and louder, but I still can't understand what she's saying. I'm about to shuffle closer, to decipher what she's saying, when those annoying crows do a flyby outside the cave entrance, cawing loud enough to wake the dead. Startled, I stumble backward, then trip and land on my side. Regaining my balance, I press my hand to the obsidian slab again, waiting for the strange dark world to reappear, but nothing happens.

Did I imagine the whole thing?

It wouldn't surprise me if I were losing my mind. Every mind has its limits and will eventually break, and I presume that truth to include me. After everything I've witnessed, through my own doing and through the minds of others, I don't know how much more my sanity will take before it fractures. Staring at the obsidian slab, and the strange world it showed me, I can't help but wonder if something inside me has already cracked.

CHAPTER 4

Leaving the cave behind, I continue toward Bricen. I hoped to make it to the village before the rain, but what starts out as a light sprinkle quickly becomes a downpour. Covering my head with the hood of my cloak and adjusting the strap of my quiver, I pick up my pace. My boots splash in the deep puddles forming. The last time I ran down this road, I was running away from Bricen, trying to find my mum. I never found her. Instead, I passed out from exhaustion and woke on the barge heading for Fayatin.

I forge ahead at a steady pace despite the rain. The hood of my cloak keeps most of the rain from hitting my eyes. While walking, I think about the early days when my abilities manifested.

I'd been an orphan on the streets of Fayatin for a few weeks, trying to survive, when an old woman grabbed me.

She kept blabbering on about how I'd be worth a lot of coin, wanting to sell me to one of the masters or lords. I feared for my life, causing something inside me to snap. I shoved my hand to her face, trying to free myself from her hold, when it happened. It was as if my hand moved through her, even though it didn't. My fingers reached into her mind. I remember screaming as moments of time—memories that weren't my own—filled my head. Horrible things that a ten-year-old shouldn't see.

Eventually, the old woman toppled over. Her mouth stretched wide, and her eyes opened to their fullest, staring off at nothing. I ran from the alley, never looking back.

It took a few days, but eventually I embraced this new gift, using it to steal food and provisions to make my life as an orphan more comfortable. It also helped me stay out of the hands of masters and lords. That was until General Onica caught me subduing a bread baker twice my size. Impressed by her kindness and her promises of a life of luxury and protection, I accepted her offer to come "work" and live at Castle Forge. My naïvety got the better of me, and over time, I realized I'd inadvertently walked straight into captivity.

Biggest regret of my life.

Except for the part where I met Selene.

I guess I can't have one without the other.

I've never been able to figure out how or why I'm able to infiltrate a person's mind. Or why it's easiest to access emotions or memories associated with fear and pain. A question I'm hoping will be answered once I reach Bricen.

The rain isn't letting up, so I shift my brisk walk into a jog. After rounding the bend in the road, I slide to a stop. Mud splashes over my boots and halfway up both legs, splotching dark stains along my fitted pants. I stand there and stare at what lies ahead, while rain pelts my hood and shoulders.

When did Bricen put up a protective barrier around the village? And not just any fence—it's a seriously high, keep-the-hell-out kind of wall. Eyeing the surrounding forest, I recall the boy's warning: *Are you one of those hero-wannabes looking for death?*

Something's not right. Keeping a watchful eye on the road and the forest it cuts through, I make my way toward the enormous wall. Why would a peaceful village like Bricen need to protect itself? Lifting my gaze, I notice the sharp tips of the logs pointing into the sky. They must've used some of the tallest trees from the woods, as the top reaches well over ten feet.

I'm still trying to understand the reason for such a wall when it suddenly comes to me at the same time a bolt of lightning crosses the gray sky. This must mean the incident eight years ago wasn't a one-time attack. That Bricen has been in trouble all these years.

When I reach the front entrance, a set of heavy wooden doors wide enough to fit a horse-drawn cart through, I swing my bow off my shoulder and hold it at my side. I come in peace, but that doesn't mean I won't defend myself if attacked.

With one hand raised and ready to knock, I shout, "Hello? I need to speak with—" but my sentence is cut off by a whizzing sound followed by a *thwump*. I turn to the line of trees behind me when two more arrows fly by, sinking deep into one of the logs lining the barrier. I pluck one arrow free, removing a sizable chunk of dead wood with it, then walk over to the forest's edge.

It's not the black feathers of the vane that give away the archer's identity, but the white paint decorating the shaft below the worn arrow tip.

Elijah.

"Your aim hasn't gotten any better over the years," I yell over the heavy rain, but no one answers. My patience is growing thin, and my clothes are now drenched. I drop the homemade arrow, grab one from my quiver, nock it, and release it up into the treetops. Unlike his nicked and scratched arrowhead, my sharp steel tip slices through the leaves. A few seconds later, a branch snaps and someone yelps. There are more cries as the tree rustles with a cascading ripple, ending with someone landing in a large puddle. He clutches his chest with one hand, while gasping to catch his breath.

"Ow, that hurt," he whines from beneath a red scarf covering the lower half of his face. I slowly approach him and only stop when his attention shifts from the pain in his chest to me. Dark eyes lock onto me from over the edge of the red fabric while rain drips over his short hair and down his forehead. He holds his gaze to mine while frantically searching the muddy water.

I lower my bow. "There's no need to—"

My words are cut short when his hand, covered in mud, emerges, holding one of his broken arrows—the jagged tip pointing straight at me. Using his free hand, he scoots along the ground, trying to put some distance between us. His voice trembles as he shouts from behind the thin layers of his scarf, "Keep your distance!"

Over the rain, I say, "Hello, Elijah."

He pauses in his retreat, and his arm holding the arrow wavers momentarily. Familiar brown eyes narrow in confusion, searching for an identity beneath my cloak's hood. "How do you know my name?" When I don't answer, he gets to his feet, scrambling to adjust the empty quiver hanging askew over one shoulder. His wool pants are sodden with muddy water while the rain continues to drench his tunic, making the fabric stick to his chest. When he's done fixing himself, he takes a step closer, broken arrow still clutched in one hand. "I can't let you pass if you don't tell me how you know my name, stranger."

"I'm no stranger," I say, then lift back my hood. The rain immediately soaks through my braid, chilling my scalp. The water trickles along my forehead and into my eyes, but I keep them open. I want him to recognize me.

Elijah lowers his hand, letting the broken arrow fall from his fingers. His brows pinch as he scans me up and down. "Adele?"

He remembers me. Good.

"How's Kit?" I ask, turning back to the gate's entrance. "And what's with the wall?"

He runs up and stands in front of me, forcing me to stop. "Is it really you?" he asks, eyeing me from head to toe.

I nod. "The one and only."

"What are you doing here? And where have you been all these years?"

I hold out a hand, gesturing to the barrier doors, water collecting in the crevice of my glove. "How about we talk inside…somewhere where we aren't getting soaked?"

"Of course. It's just good to see you." He leans in, arms open wide, and I quickly raise my bow, blocking him from embracing me. Shuffling back, he lowers his arms. Heavy drops of rain fill the awkward silence lingering between us. For a second, I think he's going to turn me away due to my lack of enthusiasm. Even if he does refuse me, there's no way I'm leaving without speaking to Aunt Lauren. But eventually he nods and meanders over to the front entrance. The heavy old planks of the wide door rattle with each knock. He pounds three times, then pauses for a beat before pounding three more times. From behind, boards are being removed and iron latches released.

While we wait, he tells me, "All visitors must check in with Trevor."

"Trevor? The huntsman who used to pass through just before the winter season. The guy with the softest furs and tastiest dried meats?"

"Yes. Though, he's not a huntsman anymore, nor is he the same man from ten years ago."

"Eight," I correct.

Elijah shuffles his feet, looking off to the side as if he's trying to count the years since that day. Without looking at me, he agrees, "I guess it has been eight. Seems longer than that."

The doors open, and we're about to continue in when he presses one hand to my shoulder. The physical contact catches me off guard and with one swift swing, I knock his hand away with my bow. Staggering away, he clutches his wrist. The shock in his eyes shifts, almost as if he's too exhausted to react. Then, from beneath his scarf, he tells me, "If Trevor says go, you gotta go, Adele. And"—he shakes his head—"I'm pretty sure he's going to tell you to go. You're too much of a risk."

His words sting. I mean, I know we're not close anymore. Hell, I'm the reason he lost his older sister, Alya. But to hear him say how much of a risk I am hurts. But he's not wrong either. I am a risk, which is more of a reason to get in and get out. These people might have been friends and family to me at one time, but that time has come and gone.

"I'm not staying long. I just need to talk with Lauren, then I'll be on my way."

His gaze dips, water dripping off his long eyelashes, and he nods. "Come on," he says, turning and waving for me to follow. "Trevor will be at Goslings."

Trevor was a giant the last time I saw him. But then again, I was much smaller than I am now, and most adults towered over me back then. But I do remember the huntsman. He was probably the broadest and strongest man I ever saw. Arms twice the size of most men. But it doesn't matter now how big he is, because all I need to do is remove my glove and he'll be begging me to spare his life.

CHAPTER 5

The barrier wall surrounding Bricen isn't the only thing that's changed. Once inside, I can't believe this is the same village I spent most of my childhood years in. Even on rainy days, this place was filled with color through its gardens and greenery, but that layer of life has been stripped away, leaving behind only dirt and weeds.

Following the road into the village, we pass three homes, each enclosed by run-down fences. There are no lit lanterns inside or smoke from the chimneys. Looking closer, there are also missing boards along the roofs, broken muntins in the windows, and most of the front doors hang off their hinges.

"What happened here?" I ask, yelling over the rain.

"A lot has changed since you ran away." The scarf muffling his voice doesn't hide his grief, and I can't help but wonder how much suffering Bricen has endured over the years. If only he knew the truth…that I didn't intentionally leave. Holding one hand out, but careful not to touch me again, he gestures to wait on asking anything else. "Trevor will answer your questions. Now, come on."

"And if he doesn't?"

He doesn't answer and continues toward the tavern without another word. Rain hails down, bouncing off his shoulders and the top of his head. When we were kids, his thick, curly brown hair sprang out in all directions, catching clumps of mud and grass burrs whenever we'd played outside. His mother would be livid with us because washing and picking his hair clean was no simple task. But now, the curls were cut short, almost to the scalp, making him appear well past his seventeen years.

It's not just the row of empty homes that catches my attention. Across the road, there's a small stretch of workshops that appear empty and abandoned. One in particular, nestled between the butcher's shop and Goslings, is the smithy. There wasn't a day when Bricen's blacksmith wasn't working the fire, forging horseshoes, and sharpening tools. To see a cold firepit is a sure sign something is wrong. That, and the butcher shop has boards nailed up over its windows and front door. I saw depraved villages in Fayatin in better condition than this place.

A series of dull metal *dings* fills the air, drawing my attention to the roof of the tavern. Affixed to the overhang is a bell. The crack along the bottom edge doesn't keep it from chiming as heavy raindrops pelt its leaden sides. Looking over my shoulder and behind me, I spot several more. Each one was the size of a large melon. If not attached to a roof, they were affixed to tall poles with ropes long enough for a child to reach.

My suspicions about Bricen's troubles are still only assumptions—that the attackers are still at large. Regardless, whatever's happening here, Harvesgrove has been kept quiet and contained within the country's borders.

"What's with the excessive alarm system?" I ask while walking by one of the poles planted in the middle of the road, a bell hanging off the top.

"You shouldn't have come back" is the answer he gives me. Which isn't an answer at all but a jab… A subtle reminder that I'm a risk and shouldn't be here. From the other side of the wood gate, iron chains clank and boards bang against wood. Glancing back to the entrance, two older girls, an old man, and a young man hurry to secure the barrier gate.

"Hey, keep up!" Elijah calls to me.

At least now I know this place isn't completely abandoned. We're almost to Goslings when my gaze instinctively shifts and follows the road past the line of buildings. It ends at the base of a small hill. There at the top, tucked behind overgrown trees and bushes, is a single cottage—Aunt Lauren's place—and my old home.

Besides its bleak appearance, everything seems intact. No signs of broken windows or doors hanging off their hinges. My heart pounds with anticipation, because the one person who may know more about why I am the way I am is less than two hundred paces from where I stand.

"Adele." Elijah says my name with a hint of warning. He's standing at the top of the steps, beneath the overhang covering the front porch of the tavern. My gaze dips to the dark crawlspace beneath the porch—where Alya dragged me to hide that dreadful day Bricen was attacked.

"Trevor first, then Lauren," he says, loosening the red scarf from around his head. His cheeks have lost their chubbiness and are more defined beneath a light scruff along his chin. But other than that, he hasn't changed too much from the young boy I used to chase squirrels and build forts with.

The front door of Goslings opens, and a man walks out. Elijah steps aside, making room for the walking stick that's guiding the old man toward the end of the porch. His cloudy eyes look past me as he leans on the polished staff.

"Trevor?" I'm half guessing and half sure this is the huntsman who used to tower over me. There's some resemblance but barely, especially without his thick beard that used to make all the single women swoon. Now, his face resembles that of the starved miners from the Crescent Mountains. General Onica would often have me interrogate the ones she suspected of stealing extra rations or pocketing fragments of iron ore. Those unfortunate souls had the same haggard features around their eyes and cheeks as the man before me now.

"It's been a long time," he says with shallow breaths. "Come inside, out of the rain." His haggard breathing makes it hard to hear, but I get the gist of what he's saying when he waves for me to follow.

Climbing the front steps to Goslings, I stop at the top and ask Elijah, "That's Trevor?"

"I told you things have changed—he's changed." He stops as we're about to enter the building. A frown crosses his face. "I've changed too, Adele. We all have, in order to survive."

The irritation swelling in my gut at not knowing what the hell is going on isn't getting any better. Walking across the porch, withered boards creaking beneath my boots, I follow Trevor into the tavern.

The main hall of Goslings remains the same, except for the dark blue tapestries hanging on the wall, decorating the sides of the fireplace. Most of the tables and chairs spaced out in the center of the room are about where I remember, except with less patrons. This place was always packed with lively villagers and traveling tradesmen. Seeing it empty now causes an unnatural chill along my spine.

What the stars is going on?

Trevor leans against the worn wood of the bar counter, his staff resting in the crook of his elbow. From behind the bar, which stretches the entire back side of the tavern, a young woman with the same brown skin as Elijah pours two drinks. I lick my lips. It's exactly what I need to ease the frustration humming beneath my skin. After crossing the room, I pick up the metal tumbler even before it's offered to me and swallow the contents in one gulp. Slamming the empty cup on the counter, brows pinched, I wipe my mouth with my glove before asking with a hint of disappointment,

"It's water?" When the old man nods, I turn to the young barkeep. "How about something a bit stronger?"

"Sorry. Only water." The young woman's brown eyes hold my gaze. An unsaid challenge of who-can-look-away-first forms between us.

"What kind of tavern only stocks water?"

"The kind that needs people to keep their minds alert," Trevor answers.

I hear him, but I'm also too focused on the stare-down between me and this girl. "You've got a problem?" I ask, leaning one elbow on the countertop, silently hoping she pushes me too far.

"No problems here," she answers, and then stands tall, looks away, and resumes wiping out the glasses behind the counter.

The corner of my mouth curls up, and I revel in my victory. After a moment, she notices me still staring and picks up my glass, then refills it with another helping of water. Meanwhile, Trevor's talking with Elijah, and I catch the end of their conversation. "Go and see if Lauren is available." Elijah nods, then makes his way out the front. Trevor waits until the door latches before resting his staff against the counter's edge and then searching with wandering hands for the nearest barstool. It takes him some time to get comfortable.

Honestly, I don't know why I'm wasting my time waiting for this old man to get comfortable when I could march right up to Lauren's cottage and find her myself. I don't need his permission. I don't need anyone's permission.

"Why are you here, Adele?"

I give the old man the benefit of my company instead of charging out the front door. Maybe he can clue me in to what has happened here. His eyes find mine, except he's not looking at me. A thin veil of white covers his pupils. Testing my suspicions, I wave a hand in front of his face. No reaction. How has Trevor's health diminished so gravely over these past eight years?

"Adele, you need to tell me why you're here." He's not quite demanding but his tone is strong enough for me to read the room. He's concerned about something. Is it me? Has word already crossed the borders about who the Interrogator is?

Needing more time to think about what to do next, I reach for the water, but then stop. My hand hovers off to the side. Glancing up at the woman, who smirks at me, I drop my hand to the wooden counter.

For stars' sake… How did I already let my guard down? I drank that water without questioning if they—

"It's only water," Trevor says, cutting through my thoughts. "We're not trying to poison you, if that's what you're thinking."

"How do you know what I'm thinking, old man? And how can you see what I'm doing if you're blind?"

A crooked smirk appears, adding more creases to his withered face. "I can't. But you, of all people, should know there's more than one way to *see* a person."

He's not wrong, which raises more questions. I mean, I know that looking into the minds of others allows me to see people for who they really are, but how does he know that—if that's what he means. Not wanting to dive into who I am, I keep the conversation focused on him. "You use your other senses to help you see?" It's more of a question than a statement, and he picks up on that with a shrug.

"Something like that."

The village leader continues to drink his water while I assess the room.

Thirty seconds.

That's all I'd need to subdue both the old man and the barkeep. I don't know what game the old man is playing, but I'm not in the mood to be wasting time like this. All I need is thirty seconds to slip off my glove and search his mind for the answers to my questions—if I want.

Flexing my fingers, tempted to take the easy way, I watch the barkeep moving away from us when Trevor's hand rests over my gloved one. "That won't be necessary, child. I'll tell you whatever it is you want to know about your kinfolk. Starting with the one who started this whole mess."

I'm too focused on his words to register the weight of his frail hand, and he withdraws it before I can react. Wanting clarification, I ask, "Started what mess? Was it Aunt Lauren? Because I know she's not like other people."

"You don't know anything, and it's not my place to tell you about your aunt. I'm talking about Sara."

"My mum? You knew her?"

He nods.

It doesn't surprise me. Everyone knew my mum. Her healing sessions were widely known throughout the villages of Harvesgrove. What piques my interest is how he made it sound as if he knew her from more than just her healing services.

A grin forms while he continues to stare blindly over my head. "Oh, yes. Sara and I had a few encounters over the years. They weren't exactly pleasant ones, but not bad ones either. We had a mutual understanding of one another."

"I don't understand."

The front door of the tavern flies open, slamming against the wall. A petite woman in a long blue dress stands in the doorway. She immediately spots me, a wide smile spreading. "It really is you!"

Lauren's skirt grazes the hardwood as she swiftly weaves between the aged tables. The flour dusting her cheeks and forehead brings back old memories of the many mornings I'd woken up to help her roll out bread dough. With her as the village baker, our home always smelled of fresh bread, savory rolls, or sweet pastries.

For the first time in a long time, I don't know how to react. The general had Alister privately train me in my secret courtyard like one of his soldiers—to be strong and think fast in any difficult situation. But my mind is paralyzed. I don't know what to think, say, or do as she crosses the room, arms wide and face beaming with joy. It's as if I'm ten years old all over again, lost and confused.

The muscles in my arms go rigid when she embraces me, and surprisingly, I don't push her away. Physical contact is something I've happily avoided during my years at Castle Forge. And something I don't foresee changing for the entirety of my life. A safe practice for me and the rest of the world.

After a long moment, Aunt Lauren leans away, but doesn't release her grasp on my arms. I'm at least a head taller than her, which is strange since the last time I was this close to her, I was the one looking up at her. Bright eyes stare up at me, and she asks, "Are you hurt? Injured in any way? What about hungry? Has anyone fed you yet?"

"I'm fine." Turning to the barkeep, I add, "Though I could use something stronger."

Lauren pulls me in again, squeezing tighter. "I can't believe it's you." She then steps back, one hand grasping my wrist, the white linen of my shirt pressed between her skin and mine. She looks at Trevor. "Let her stay, please? One night."

"She's too much of a risk, and you know it," he answers.

"I'm not planning on staying long," I assure them both. "I only need to talk with my aunt…in private…about Noviska Country. Then I'll be on my way."

She releases my wrist, bringing her hand to her mouth. Tears well beneath brown eyes rimmed with amber. "You saw me up north and didn't find me then?"

"I couldn't." There's no reason to get into the details of why. Things might get ugly if they know I'm a Fayatin. Instead, I'm about to ask her if there's somewhere private we can talk when one of the bells rings outside. Everyone turns and faces the front door. A few seconds later, a second bell rings. Then a third.

Trevor leans on his walking stick and shuffles across the room to the window. Elijah and Lauren follow. I wait behind, wanting to see what the commotion is before getting involved. Trevor whispers something to Elijah, who rushes out the front door. The old huntsman turns to me, his gaze still looking up at the ceiling, and says, "Kit, stay here with Adele and Lauren. We'll take care of the others."

As Elijah and Trevor leave Goslings, my attention shifts from the urgency outside the door to the other end of the bar. "Kit?"

"Hello, Adele. It's about damn time you found your way home."

CHAPTER 6

ADELE

The barkeep, the girl with the same brown skin as Elijah, is my old childhood friend Kit. She's shed a lot of weight, but I can see it now. That rebellious gleam in her eyes. The same one that often got the three of us in mounds of trouble.

Kit hurries out from behind the bar, a few tight brown curls spring out from the edge of her braid. "Quick, over here!" After pulling aside a tapestry hanging next to the fireplace, she lifts a wooden latch attached to a panel in the wall, revealing a secret closet. Then, she waves for me to come.

"What's going on?" I ask, coming up behind her.

She opens her mouth to answer but is cut off by a sudden band of shrieks coming from outside. The high-pitched cries are vaguely familiar, but I can't place where I've heard them before.

"Lauren!" I shout. "Move!" Sprinting into action, I rush to the front door. As my hand goes to slam it shut, a group of birds swoops inside. Turning to Kit, I yell, "Watch out for the crows!"

Kit reaches behind the bar and emerges with a shortsword. "They are NOT crows! They're something evil—something not of this world!"

Stepping to the center of the room, I eye the creatures flying around us. Kit is right. They are definitely not crows. They have beady red eyes and black smoke wafting from their semitranslucent bodies.

If they're not crows, then what are they?

But there's no time to ask.

One of the creatures dives for Kit, sharp black talons splayed wide. Quickly, I unshoulder my bow, nock an arrow, aim, and release. Archery was one of my favorite ways to pass the time at Castle Forge, other than talking with Selene out in the courtyard. I know my aim is true, yet when the arrow lands, the creature disappears into a thick cloud of black smoke.

"What the hell?" I curse under my breath. From behind, Lauren is screaming as the last two swarm her. Their shrieks are overpowering my senses, causing my vision to blur momentarily. It's hard to pinpoint their position while they're making that deafening sound. Trying to focus, I look to my aunt. Blood-red claw marks crisscross her arms and face.

I react quickly and bellow a scream, hoping to draw their attention to me.

It works.

Their screeching stops, and I quickly draw another arrow from my quiver, aim, and shoot, taking out another one. Again, it turns into a black cloud of smoke, dissipating in the air.

Kit appears at my left side, jumping onto a chair, then running across the tabletops. Leaping off the last table, she swings her sword through the air, slicing the creature in half. It, too, turns to smoke.

Kit doesn't hesitate after her kill and rushes to close the front door to the tavern. I hurry to Lauren, who struggles to stay on her feet, and catch her before she collapses.

"I got you!" I say, carefully lowering her to the hardwood.

She grabs the front of my leather vest, struggling to hold her head up. Eyes wide, she tells me, "I'm sorry I...I didn't...come for you. I couldn't..." She pauses, wincing while catching her breath.

"Hold on," I plea, pulling her into my lap. "We'll get you help!"

"Adele!" My aunt tugs on my vest, drawing me in closer. "Don't...don't listen to her!" she coughs, eyes fluttering shut as her words trail off. "You...you have a choice. Don't..." Her eyelids drop and her body goes limp, head lolling back against my arm.

"Auntie! No!" I shake her shoulders, hoping to wake her. To save her somehow. Not only because I haven't gotten my answers yet, but also because I realize that even though we're not close, she's still family. The only kin I have left, and I don't want to lose her.

No matter how hard I shake her shoulders, Aunt Lauren's eyelids remain shut. The deep scratches along her arms and face swell red. Then, from the edges, dark red veins sprout, branching outward beneath her skin.

"Hey, how about some help over here?" I shout to Kit over the nonstop shrieking coming from the chaos outside. She doesn't move from the window. Her fingers flex over the hilt of her sword. Trying again, I shout, "Hey! I'm talking to you!"

Kit surveys outside a second longer before hurrying over to help me. Kneeling at Lauren's feet, she slides her arms beneath her legs and says, "We need to move her." Together we lift and carry her across the room, then rest her slouching body on the floor inside the secret closet. "She'll be safe in here," Kit says, arranging Lauren's skirt to cover her legs.

If it weren't for the scratches covering her arms, neck, and face, she could've been mistaken as a drunkard passed out in the back of a closet. I turn, about to ask what the hell is going on, when Kit raises a hand to me, stopping me from following.

"I'm coming to help," I tell her, holding up my bow.

"No. You need to stay here with her—protect her until we can get help."

Briefly glancing over to Lauren, then back to Kit, I shake my head. "I'm not hiding. I can fight."

"I have no doubt you can, but right now, she needs you. Because if they find her—" A sequence of loud *thud*s slams against the exterior wall of Goslings.

We turn to see the creatures slamming their bodies against the glass panes of the front windows. Each one that hits explodes into a thick cloud of black smoke. Within seconds, the barrage of shrieks from outside ceases. The silence is so sudden it gives me chills.

"Oh no. We're out of time." Then, all in one motion, Kit faces me and pushes me hard, using the length of her forearm, forcing me to stumble into the closet.

"Don't touch me!" I've had about enough of whatever the hell is going on. No one is telling me anything. My anger amplifies, humming beneath my skin. I'm two seconds away from releasing that anger on Kit, but then we hear someone screaming. They're not crying out from pain but warning everyone with a single word: *hide*.

Kit's mouth drops open. "They're here."

"Who's here?"

"Please, Adele!" Kit gestures to the closet with her shortsword. "Stay with her. There's no point in following me because I'm only going to hide over there." She points to the other side of the fireplace where a second decorative tapestry hangs. "I highly doubt we'll both fit comfortably."

I glance over to the nearby blue drapery and wonder why she's hiding. I just saw her fight, so it's clear she can handle a sword.

"Lauren needs you."

"Fine," I say, then drape my bow over my shoulder and shuffle back into the closet. She closes the door and I watch as the wooden latch drops into the "lock" position. There's comfort in knowing I can unlock the door from this side. Within seconds, the tapestry swings down. Soft fabric brushes against the door, concealing our whereabouts. What I'm not expecting is the fabric to be worn thin in the perfect spot over a wide gap between two of the horizontal planks, giving me a view out into the open room.

Kit takes a step toward the fireplace, heading to the second secret closet, as the front door swings open. She freezes where she stands and slowly raises her sword, gripping it with both hands. When two men stride into the tavern, Kit slowly retreats toward the bar. There's no urgency to their entrance, or emotion in their expressions.

My breath hitches the second I see their shaved heads and strange clothes—tattered black strips of fabric wrapping their bodies from ankles to neck. Their shaved heads and faces are covered in a thin layer of dirt, as if they haven't bathed in weeks.

Seeing them confirms my suspicions. The people who attacked my mum and Alya have been terrorizing Bricen all these years.

"In here," one of the men says, facing the open door. He returns his attention to Kit.

Kit holds her sword out across her body, ready to strike. "You'll not take me alive, you vile monsters!"

"How did we miss this one?" the man closest to Kit says.

"She is strong," says the second man, who is now circling the front, coming toward the fireplace.

"Merigoth will be pleased," the first man says.

"That she will."

Through the hole in the fabric, I continue to watch. There are only two. If they do attack, I could jump out and take them both down before either knows what hit them.

"Come on! Let's do this!" Kit yells, swinging her sword at both intruders as they slowly surround her.

I'm about to lift the latch when Kit subtly glances in my direction. The muscles in her jaw tense, and I don't know if the strangers take notice, but I catch the slightest shake of her head, silently telling me to stay put. It's killing me to remain and do nothing, but she's right—I need to keep Aunt Lauren safe.

The men don't attack. They only cock their heads and stare. It isn't until a girl, maybe a year younger than me, walks into the tavern and gives the command—a nod of her head—that they advance. Their movements are effortless and they're somehow predicting Kit's strikes and preventing her blade from connecting with either of them.

While Kit's fighting off the men, I briefly shift my attention to the girl. I gasp the second our eyes lock. The girl has a shaved head and grimy skin like the men, but unlike them, she has black smudges streaking beneath her eyes along the tops of her cheeks. And the strips of black fabric cover her top-half and bottom-half, leaving her midriff bare. At first, I think I'm mistaken, and that she can't be looking at me, but then she turns her body away from the fight and faces my direction. There's no question—she knows someone's hiding behind the tapestry.

Silently, I curse while slowly withdrawing my dagger from inside my waistband. Holding it to my side, I'm ready to strike whenever the door swings open. But the strange girl doesn't move. Instead, she turns her attention to the fight with Kit. I do the same, but also keep an eye on the girl.

Kit's waving her sword out in front of her, trying to fend off one of the men, when the other one sneaks up from behind and presses a hand over her forehead. Her eyes go wide, and her arms drop to her sides. The sword slips from her hand. The blade clanks to the hardwood and the room goes silent.

The fear trembling within Kit's eyes is something I'm quite familiar with. It's a look I see every time I infiltrate a mind. My breach causes a person's will to fall at my command, locking their muscles into a tense state of shock. I'm not exactly sure that's what is happening to Kit, but it sure as hell looks that way.

How is this possible?

It takes everything in me to resist charging out of the closet. Not only to save Kit, but also to find out more about who these people are and where they come from.

When the man finally withdraws his hand from my old friend's face, he drags it along the strips of tattered black fabric wrapping his leg. Then, without speaking, he makes his way past the tables and chairs, exiting the tavern. The others silently follow, and so does Kit.

CHAPTER 7

Opening the door isn't an option. Not yet at least. I don't know if the attackers are still in Bricen, and I can't risk revealing our position, putting my aunt in danger. After seeing what that man did to Kit, I'm not sure I can protect her.

After tucking the knife into my waistband, I rest my shoulder against the wall and wait. The silence gives me time to think about what I witnessed. What that man did to Kit and why that girl didn't reveal my hiding spot have me stumped. It seems the attacker and I share a similar ability. But I do not possess the ability to command actions and behaviors as that man did.

So, it seems I'm not the only one cursed with evil.

When the door to Goslings bursts open, slamming against the wall, I give up on trying to understand the *how* of what just happened and focus on Elijah running into the main room of the tavern.

I lift the latch, then open the door and step out of the closet. "Where are they?"

"Gone," he answers. "We don't know how they get into the village, but they always leave through the front gate."

I duck back into the closet, then drag Lauren's limp body out while saying, "It sounds like they've found a weak spot in your wall. Somewhere they can slip inside."

He unwinds his scarf from around his neck, the fabric wearing thin in several spots, and places it beneath Lauren's head. Then, while inspecting the wounds, he tells me, "After each attack, I check the perimeter, and it's the same each time. Absolutely nothing. No broken logs or giant holes dug beneath the base. It's an ongoing mystery how they get in, and the reason we have such an elaborate alarm system."

"This is bad," he says, pointing to the multiple lacerations along my aunt's arms, neck, and face. "The others don't have these markings."

My gaze follows his finger as it hovers over the dark red veins spreading outward from the swollen edges of her slashed skin. Kneeling across from Elijah, I ask, "What others?"

He stands and heads to the bar. As he fills up a large wooden bowl, he answers, "There are at least six more injured."

"Is everyone all right in here?" Trevor's voice floats in from the front door.

Elijah comes out from behind the bar, the bowl of water in one hand and a rag in the other. "You're bleeding!"

He walks right past my aunt and over to the huntsman. "Hey!" I shout, "He's barely bleeding." Unlike Aunt Lauren's wounds. But I bite back that last part.

The old man waves Elijah away. "I'm fine, boy. It's the others outside that'll need your help." He sits in a nearby chair, holding his staff close, leaning on it for support.

Shifting my weight from one knee to the other, I point out the window where a dark residue remains from when those things crashed into the glass. "What the hell were those things? I've never seen gashes like this before."

"Gashes? What happened?" Trevor inquires while breathing heavily through his nose.

"Those creature-things attacked Lauren. And now she's lying on the floor unconscious."

"But Lauren's wounds aren't like anything I've ever seen," Elijah explains as he dips his head, checking out Trevor's bleeding chin. "She's got these thin dark veins, like poison or a reaction of some sort, sprawled out beneath her skin."

Shoving the boy's hand away, Trevor grumbles, "I said I'm fine. Go and tend to Lauren, and then the others. We'll need to get everyone inside Goslings to watch them."

It pains me to see my aunt's body torn into like this. The edges of the wounds starting to pucker a bruising shade of reddish-purple. Is this the kind of pain that awaits Kit wherever she's being taken?

After resting Aunt Lauren's arm over her stomach, I look up to Elijah. He's about to kneel and tend to my aunt with the bowl of water but stops when I say, "I'm sorry about Kit."

He freezes, eyes wide. "What do you mean, you're sorry? Where is she?"

"I thought you knew, since she left with them—"

A loud clatter cuts me off. The wooden bowl Elijah held now spins upside down next to Lauren, spilled water soaking the bottom of her dress.

Trevor blindly reaches out to his side, bony fingers grasping at air. "Elijah! No!" but Elijah's already running for the door.

"I thought you would've seen her!" I yell, feeling slightly bad for springing the news like that.

"Adele!" Trevor shouts. He's struggling to stand, using his staff for support. "He'll get himself killed if he catches up to them! Please, go after him!"

Grabbing my bow, I race out the door. Elijah's running down the muddy road, but instead of going to the front gates, which are now locked, he veers left and disappears behind the row of run-down homes. Hurrying down the porch steps of Goslings, I chase after him. I round the corner of the last home, and I'm met by overgrown bushes clustered with thorny vines. There's a narrow gap between the side of the house and the bush. Using my cloak, I shield my arm and face from the prickly spikes, following him to the rear of the home.

"I don't need your help," Elijah snaps.

He grabs hold of a rope attached to the barrier wall. I'm surprised this rope hasn't snapped yet with all the frayed pieces broken away from the main line. With a hard tug, he removes a small section that consists of two adjacent logs. The secret hatch drops to the ground, landing in a pile of dead leaves.

"Where are they taking her?" I ask.

"I don't know," he admits, dragging a weary hand across his forehead. "I only know the general direction." He slips through and is about to pull the rope to close the passage when I block him with my bow.

"I think I know where they're going," I say in a low voice.

This stops him from closing the passage. The hatch falls to the ground again and he waves for me to come. Ducking low, I crawl through with my bow.

After he seals it, we take off running down the road. At least it's stopped raining. That's one thing going in our favor.

"The small cave by the river," I explain between panting breaths. "The one we used to play in as kids. I saw some kind of doorway, or window—I know it sounds crazy—to another world. I think they're going there."

"Another world? Are you sure?"

"No, but have you got any other ideas as to where they'd go?"

Shaking his head, he makes a sharp turn into the woods, abandoning the road. "This way! I know a shortcut!"

CHAPTER 8

One foot in front of the other.

Keep moving forward.

Do not fall out of step.

Our orders repeat in my mind: *Stay together, search out the strong, and return right after.*

Arriving at the river, Marcellus leads the procession toward the cave entrance. I take up the rear, as usual. It's my responsibility to make sure everyone follows. But no one ever tries to run. Not after being compelled by Marcellus. His touch is as powerful as Merigoth's lure.

"Rune, keep up," Evander calls from the cave entrance.

Evander is like me. As are all the Shades serving Queen Merigoth. All but Marcellus. He's one of the original three Shades born with Queen Merigoth's blessed blood running through his veins. No one knows what happened to the other two.

Evander ducks his head and follows the last offering into the cave. Merigoth will be pleased with this group of humans and surely reward us with an extra blessing of her bliss.

As I walk closer to the cave, I try and block out the distractions of this world and focus on her words, which grow louder in my head. However, the obtrusive sound of the river makes it hard to concentrate. Despite my determination not to disappoint, I find myself torn between Merigoth's voice beckoning me to come home and the overpowering drone of the river currents.

I shuffle my bare feet off the dirt path and onto a bed of dead pine needles. With my hands clasped over my ears, I try to block out the distractions, but my efforts fail. The roaring sound of water overpowers her persuasive tone, momentarily freeing my consciousness from its binds.

Squinting, I look to the cave. I know it's where I must go, but there's something I feel as though I need to do first. I can't recall what it is, but something out here—in this world—means something to me.

I look up into the trees.

No. Not the trees—but the dimming sky beyond.

Daylight is fading fast, and I'm not sure what I'm looking for, but then it appears. A single speck of light dotting the evening sky. Once my eyes adjust, more peek through the thin layer of overcast clouds.

Stars.

I want nothing more than to stay right here and watch them grow brighter.

"Rune." A woman's angry voice invades my thoughts. *"Where are you?"*

Ignoring the invisible string tugging within me, I stare up, trying to memorize where each twinkling star sits. One in particular shines brighter than the others, and I know that's it. That's the star that means something…but I don't remember what it is…or how I know that it's important.

"Rune! Come to me, now!" Merigoth's voice commands again, and this time I feel the weight of a powerful hook sinking deeper into my mind.

"I'm sorry. I won't let it happen again," I plead, shuffling away from the embankment. I rush up the dirt path leading to the cave entrance. With each step closer, the sounds of the human world diminish and Merigoth's binds return, subduing my thoughts. I'm no longer concerned with…

Uh… What was I doing again?

The second I enter the cave, my confusion vanishes from existence. A familiar cadence amplifies from behind the doorway of the Under Realm. Without hesitating, I repeat the words, "My will is her will, and she is all that matters."

As I step through the obsidian doorway, a warm energy embraces me from within, saturating my soul with bliss.

"Stray again and you will no longer feel my blessings."

Why would I stray? Her warning makes no sense. I don't remember wandering off. I let the warm haze enveloping me take control. The emptiness of my mind comforts me in knowing she's looking after me—looking after all of us.

"Close the door," she commands.

"As you wish." Turning to the doorway, I raise my hand to the obsidian slab. But before my hand reaches the smooth surface, voices shout out from the human world: "This way! It's over here!" Two humans run into the cave and make their way toward the doorway. Above me, thunder rumbles from within an everlasting, angry sky—a sky void of everything but darkness.

"She's in there!" A girl's anxious voice fills the small cavern.

"I see nothing," a boy says, narrowing his eyes and trying to look through the doorway between our worlds. "It's just a slab of black rock."

"What do you mean? She's right there!" The girl with the blonde braid trailing over one shoulder shouts, pointing at me.

Cocking my head, I stare, unsure of how she can see this world while the boy cannot. Unwilling to move, I watch them, even as Merigoth calls to me.

The girl locks eyes with me. "I see you," she says in a low grumble, jabbing her gloved finger against the barrier.

"Rune, come to me." The command rakes through my senses, too painful to ignore any longer. I press one hand to the obsidian slab, activating the Under Realm doorway. A gentle wave caresses over the surface, fading the doorway back to its original stone. I turn and walk away, leaving the two humans to bicker over what is and isn't real.

CHAPTER 9

It's real. The dark world I saw earlier has reappeared, showing a flat desolate land covered in thin cracks that glow red. Looming above is a midnight sky void of everything but darkness. Though this time, one of the attackers is standing there, staring at us. It's the young girl from the tavern. A thick layer of soot smudges the tops of her cheeks, below dark eyes glaring at me.

"What now?" Elijah demands, cutting through my thoughts.

Glancing between him and the otherworldly girl, I ask, "What do you mean? She's right there!"

He searches the cave wall where I'm pointing. "I don't see anything!"

Inching closer, I poke one finger to the obsidian slab, though at the moment it resembles thick glass rather than black stone. I don't know how she got over there, but I'm starting to think that over there is where I'll find my answers. "I see you," I say in a low voice. The girl's gaze flicks between me and Elijah. Seconds pass, and she suddenly straightens, turns, and leaves the shallow cave, taking the dark world with her.

After multiple attempts to revive the mysterious doorway with my bare hand, I eventually tell Elijah, "She's gone."

"Are you sure?" he says, moving closer, peering into the stone as if it were a dirty window.

Slipping my glove on, I tell him, "Whatever that place is, it's not of this world." Stepping back, I take in the entire slab from top to bottom. "And I think this is some kind of door, but I don't know how to get through."

"I can't lose her, Adele. Not Kit." He slaps his palm against the cave wall. "She's all I have left."

There's not much I can say to make him feel better. I'm good at causing emotional pain, not comforting it. Even though I haven't seen him in years, something in my chest twists. I might not feel her loss as he does, but Kit used to be a friend—someone who cared about me. They both did.

Shadows shroud Elijah's features as daylight dwindles. Shouldering my bow, I shuffle closer to the cave's opening. "I think we should head back. There's nothing more we can do here."

He presses his forehead to the wall. "I will find you. I promise." With one last sniffle, he walks out of the cave.

I follow him to the river's edge. The harsh currents are no longer threatening, probably because dusk has fallen, making it harder to see the jagged rocks. Keeping some distance between us, but close enough to see the scowl on his face, I tell him, "You shouldn't make promises you can't keep."

"And you should leave. Return to wherever you came from."

Maybe he's right. Maybe I should go.

But what if Kit is still alive?

What if all the people I thought were dead aren't actually dead?

"I want to help." The second the words leave my mouth, a sharp ache pulses from behind my temples, as if my brain is protesting. This isn't why I came here. I should get back to Selene. If General Onica suspects Selene had anything to do with my escape, she'll punish her. And it won't be locking her up in her room for days or a simple backhand slap across her cheek. No. I'm positive the general will do her worst and make Selene suffer.

I gasp as an idea forms.

"If I stay and help, I'll need a favor in return."

"There's no point in helping Bricen," he mutters. "There's barely anyone left."

Pivoting, I face him. "I know you didn't see what I saw in there," I say, pointing up toward the cave. "But that doesn't mean it's not there. That is where they go—whoever *they* are." He doesn't answer, so I continue, "But again, I'll need a favor first. Then, I'll stay and help Bricen."

With a sniff, he lifts his head to the sky, sighing while rubbing the top of his head. "That's not my call to make, Adele. But…" He moves past me and starts for the forest. "I'm sure Trevor will hear your request."

That's good enough for me. I follow him toward the tree line without another word, because silence is the best thing I can offer while he grieves.

At some point, Elijah took the lead, which was fine since nighttime came upon us faster than I expected. Adjusting my bow over my shoulder, I use the time to think about my options. If Trevor denies my request, then I'll leave.

I have to.

Selene may need me.

Or… She may not and be perfectly safe.

What if I leave and miss the opportunity to learn more about the mysterious attackers and their abilities? Or the chance to rescue Kit—and possibly others.

Hope is a dangerous thing. I know this. Yet, I cannot help but hope that maybe my mum is alive.

We've almost reached the road when a branch snaps, catching my attention. I freeze. Elijah must have heard it, too, because he's slowly walking backward toward me. When he reaches my side, he whispers, "We're not alone."

"Is it them? Do you think they've returned?" I ask, scanning between the silhouettes of trees. I'm done playing games and lean my bow up against a large rock.

"What are you doing? We need to be ready to run."

I'm about to shush him when a low chuckle floats through the night air. We spin around to see three men walking up to us. The center fella, a lanky man, holds up a torch. The two well-fed men at his sides crack their knuckles and roll their necks. The weasel leading the group *tsk*s at us before he says, "What do we have here?"

"We don't want any problems, Heathrow," Elijah says, taking a step away from the men. I, on the other hand, hold my position. "Come on, Adele. Trevor is waiting for us at the gate."

"Oh, is that right?" Heathrow says more than asks, snickering while slapping the man to his right. "Big ol' Trevor is waiting for you, aye?" The two brutes flanking this oaf laugh. "You's a bit aways from Bricen, now aren't cha?" He emphasizes his words, hinting at what's coming.

Elijah clears his throat. "Bricen was attacked."

"That's a bloody shame," Heathrow mocks.

"They took Kit."

"Aww." The light from the torch flicks across his face, and it sickens me when his smile spreads wide. "Poor, poor Kit." He feigns grief, pressing his free hand across his heart, but quickly shrugs it off. "I rather enjoyed running into that feisty sister of yours now and then." The two men grunt, crooked grins crossing their faces.

Heathrow then turns his attention from Elijah to me. "I haven't seen you around these parts. What'd the lad say your name was? Adele? That's a pretty name for a pretty girl." He hands the torch to the thug on his left, then steps closer, reaching for my face. I stand perfectly still, eyes locked onto him like a fox waiting for the right moment before striking and feasting on its prey. The idea that this imbecile thinks he's going to bully me makes my insides roll, and I can't help the chuckle that escapes.

"Are you amused?" He looks over his shoulder to his men. "I think the lass wants to get to know us better."

"Oh, that I do," I say in a low, teasing voice, stepping closer.

"Adele!" Elijah tugs at my sleeve. "What are you doing? They're not playing."

Heathrow shakes his head. "Put it away, boy," he warns, and Elijah slides the small knife into its sheath hanging from his waistband. "Let the girl have a little fun." Heathrow's gaze slowly sweeps over me. "She's new to these parts, and we'll need to break her in at some point."

He reaches up and wraps a bony finger around a loose strand of my blonde hair. "You should know that after dusk, we claim these woods and whatever's in it." His breath is thick with ale, mixed with a stench comparable to spoiled potatoes. He draws back, quickly raises both hands out to his sides, and bellows, "It's what we agreed on—the almighty Trevor and me." Lowering his voice, he adds, "Not my fault. You twos are out here past your curfew."

I've had about enough of this unruly man's babbling nonsense. Crossing my arms behind my back, I slip off one glove and then the other, letting them fall to the ground. As Heathrow opens his mouth to continue rambling on, I reach out and grab him by the neck. He gasps and his body goes rigid, arms out like a bird, fingers splayed. I know he feels the weight of my reach extending past my fingers and into his mind.

I raise my free hand, warning the other two. "Come any closer and he dies."

Elijah gasps and moves to my peripheral. His mouth hangs open and his eyes are just as wide, intently watching me. I'll deal with him after. Right now, I'm eager to have a little fun.

Fingers digging into the man's grimy skin, I pull him closer. Both eyes have rolled back into his head, revealing tiny blood vessels stretching up from beneath his lower lids. "You weren't wrong about one thing. I do want to get to know you better."

And with that, I force a mental command directly into his mind. *"Show me your greatest fears."*

Closing my eyes, I welcome the flurry of remembrances—memories of moments from his life—playing out in my mind. I've perfected this invasion over the years and know exactly how to sort through the memories associated with the emotion I've commanded to come forth. This time, something happens that has never happened before. In addition to his fears, I see the fear he's bestowed upon others. The horrible things he's done and the pleasure it brings him.

"And I thought I was the monster," I say in a low seething tone, glimpsing one horrible act after another.

"Adele," Elijah says, interrupting my search. "Let him go."

Opening my eyes, I tell him, "Not yet."

"She's one of them! A demon born of sorcery!" One of the broad men drops the torch and takes off running after his companion, disappearing between the trees of the dark forest.

Elijah rushes over, picks up the torch, and stomps the ground where the dead leaves have caught fire. With the torch in hand, he raises it over his head, illuminating the small clearing. "They're gone! You can stop now!"

One might take offense to being called a *demon born of sorcery*, but not me. I know there's evil inside me. And Elijah's probably right too. I should release Heathrow, but I don't. This miscreant needs to be taught a lesson, and I know exactly how he'll pay his consequential dues.

Constructing mental prisons has become second nature to me, courtesy of the general and how frequently she calls upon my services. I once described it to Selene as creating a bubble inside someone's mind, forcing them—and whatever memory I choose—to remain inside.

Drool trickles out from the corner of Heathrow's mouth. Inhaling a deep breath, I bind his consciousness into a memory loop of the moment he snuck up on his brother and drowned him in the river. Except, in this scenario, a second before his brother goes under the water, I amend the memory and swap in Heathrow for the man being drowned, so he can feel the pain and heartache his brother felt.

From beneath my fingers clutching his neck, Heathrow makes a gurgling sound as foamy saliva spills out over his bottom lip. He's at the drowning part. I release my hold on him, and he drops to his knees, sucking in air and whimpering apologies to a man that no longer has a beating heart.

We stand over him, and Elijah's about to say something when Heathrow's body frantically writhes along the forest's floor, kicking up dead leaves and fallen branches. His arms are straight as a board, pulling behind his body, while his fingers spread wide. Every muscle in his body is tense from the shock of his temporary death. A strangled wheezing sound escapes his gaping mouth. I pick up my gloves and slip them on. A few seconds later, Heathrow is frantically gasping for air. In his mind, the drowning has ended, but death doesn't come. Not yet. He'll remain in his mental prison, the memory loop I've created, until his heart gives out. A suitable and lengthy death for a wicked man.

Torch in hand, Elijah crouches and reaches out for Heathrow.

"Leave him be," I say, grabbing my bow. I turn and head back to Bricen.

He jogs up to me, pinched brows scrunching his face in concern, and asks, "Is he going to die?"

"Probably."

Looking over his shoulder, breathing heavily, he objects, "Adele! We can't leave him there to die." He stops and starts back for Heathrow, boots stomping.

"Hey!" I call.

Elijah turns. The light from the torch flicks across his face. His lips are pursed, and with each heavy breath, his nostrils flare.

"That man would've left you for dead," I say, striding toward him. "And probably done worse to me." He doesn't respond, but his stance relaxes. "You're not the only one who has changed these past years."

His gaze dips to my gloved hands. "You kill people now?"

"I do what I need to do to survive."

"And how is it you did that—" He turns and gestures to the darkness. We can't see Heathrow, but we can hear the leaves rustling and faint gasping sounds.

When he steps closer, I take a step back. "Look," I say with a stern frankness, "I want to tell you everything, but I need to talk to Trevor first. About that favor. Deal?"

There's a long moment of silence before he concedes with a nod.

We walk the remaining way to Bricen in silence. I know Elijah has questions, but there's no point in explaining who I am or what I can do if my request to send a message to Selene is denied. And if that happens, then I will leave, holding no regrets.

Bricen be damned—literally.

CHAPTER 10

Reaching the barrier wall, we decide to enter through the front gates rather than the secret panel hidden behind the run-down homes. While waiting, Elijah softly says, "I'm sorry. I shouldn't have assumed we were the only ones whose lives were upended and changed after that day."

"I didn't return to Bricen for pity."

"Why did you come back?" The torch is dying, but there's enough moonlight for me to see his face. He's eyeing me over. Not like earlier when he was trying to identify me as the lost little girl he once knew. No, now he's trying to figure out who I've become.

When one of the barrier gates creaks open, I move, pushing the oversized wooden door inward, speeding up our entry into Bricen. Nearby, two torches are staked into the ground while two older boys stand by, waiting to close and lock the gate. Elijah matches my pace, glances over at me, waiting for me to answer his question. "You know why I'm here. I needed to talk to my aunt."

"And now that you can't talk to Lauren, will you leave?"

"Let's just find Trevor." I pick up my pace.

The village is dark. The Bricen of my childhood was lit up at night with wood and cast-iron braziers at every home. The only flames lit tonight are outside of Goslings. I climb the tavern's porch steps, two by two, Elijah on my heels, and stop when loud voices float out from the open door. Creeping closer, I try to listen to what they're saying. Elijah thwarts that plan, rushing past me with long strides and disappearing into the tavern.

"There you are!" Trevor's voice stands out among the other loud voices, all talking over one another. "Did you catch up to the Shades? Were you able to find Kit?" There's a pause, and I assume Elijah is answering with a shake of his head. Trevor then asks, "Where's Adele?"

Hearing my name, I enter the tavern. All the tables have been pushed to one side of the room, a few turned over and stacked on top of the others, making space for the afflicted on the floor. Gray- and white-haired women crouch next to each of the six unconscious villagers—one of them being Aunt Lauren.

"Did you find the doorway?" Trevor steps up to me, clouded eyes staring over my head. His knobby knuckles bulge as his fingers wrap around his walking stick. Dotting his temples are dark sunspots, which I swear weren't there before we left.

He slams the end of his staff against the wood floor, demanding my attention. "Did you find the doorway?"

I want to answer his question with more questions, like why he looks as if he's aged five years since we left and how he knows about the doorway. But instead, I answer with a simple *yes*.

Elijah jumps in. "Supposedly, it's inside the old cave by the rapids."

Laying my bow on one of the overturned tables, I clarify, "Not supposedly. It's there."

Trevor adjusts his grip on his staff while nodding. "Ah, yes. I know the place." He shuffles his feet in a circle, to better face the makeshift infirmary. "There were many nights I took shelter inside that little cave while traveling between villages. It was a good place to keep my pelts and meats dry from the rain, and safe from pillagers or wild beasts. Though, I don't recall there being anything out of the ordinary inside it."

"It's a bit hidden, in a shallow nook at the rear of the cave. A giant slab of black rock embedded in the wall." Elijah briefly shifts his attention to an approaching old woman. She hands him his red scarf, and he thanks her. "Can I get anything to help?" he asks. Politely, she shakes her head before returning to the injured.

They've replaced Elijah's scarf beneath Lauren's head with a folded-up blanket. The woman tending to her stands and crosses the room to the bar, where she washes her hands in a large metal basin.

I approach Lauren and crouch to one knee by her side. The gashes along her arms, neck, and face don't look as red and swollen as they did before. And the dark red veins sprouting from the wounds have slightly receded.

"What did you give her?" I ask Trevor. When he doesn't respond, I look over my shoulder to see he's gone. "Where'd he go?" I ask Elijah, getting to my feet.

He points at an open door tucked in the back corner, hidden beneath the shadows of a slanted ceiling. Weaving through the injured and the women helping them, I head toward the door. Outside, Trevor is standing in a stretch of grass between Goslings and a small shed.

Trotting down the steps, I go straight to the question that's weighing heaviest on my mind. "How did you know it was a doorway?"

He makes a *mmh* sound, as if he doesn't understand my question.

"You asked if we found the doorway. How did you know they travel through a doorway and don't have a camp or small village somewhere?"

He lifts his chin higher, and I swear if he weren't blind, I'd say he was staring at the stars. "They call themselves the Shades, and they are obviously not of this world. That information came fairly early on during their attacks. We learned to take cover and hide rather than fight an opponent with unworldly abilities."

"The Shades, huh?"

He confirms with a soft affirmative hum.

Well, at least I know what to call them now. "That's how these Shade people took Kit. One of them touched her, and she just stopped fighting and left with them. It's some kind of mind control."

Trevor nods. "That's how it works, and it's why we hide. There's no point in going up against them."

"Do they all possess that ability?" I ask him, thinking of my own.

The silence grows and I worry his thoughts are clouded. It's a struggle to sort through the many memories when forced to interrogate the elderly. Time eludes them, creating a jumbled mess of their memories. And I fear Trevor's mind may be slipping, too.

I sigh, changing the subject. "I need to send a message. Do you have any carriers to spare?"

He inhales a deep breath, chin still lifted to the night sky. "Why do you stay?"

"I have my reasons." My answer comes quicker than I would've liked. It makes me look suspicious.

The moonlight shines over his head, his eyes hooded by straggly white brows. "And that reason can no longer answer your questions. So, I ask again, why stay?"

He's right. There's no reason for me to stay now that Lauren is unable to tell me what I want to know. It was nice to see Elijah, and even Kit for the briefest moments, but I hold no allegiance to them. My allegiance is to my only friend, back in Fayatin Country. Yet, I'm drawn to the mystery of these Shade beings and the connection between them and me.

I don't give Trevor this answer. Instead, I tell him what I think he wants to hear. "I'd like to make sure my aunt's okay before I return home." Then, with a modest level of sincerity, I add, "Plus, I'd like to offer my services, to help protect the village whilst I'm here."

"Services?" Trevor asks with an inquisitive tone. His head shifts slightly in my direction, yet he still stares up at the stars.

I lift my bow, then when he doesn't respond, I say, "Right, blind. Sorry." Lowering my bow, I explain, "I'm an excellent archer."

Gripping his staff tighter while nodding, he tells me, "I can spare a carrier."

Relief washes through me at his approval. Instinctively, I think about the villagers I've seen so far. There aren't many that could fair the journey. I predict Trevor will call on one of the two young men standing guard at the front gates for the task.

Facing me, Trevor asks, "And where might you be sending a message to?"

The waning moon briefly ducks behind a lingering rain cloud, but then reemerges, providing enough light for me to see the deep lines of his face. "I'll tell the messenger where to go. The details aren't important."

Shuffling forward, he rests his walking stick against the shed, and then drags one hand along the front until he finds the wooden latch. Slowly, he opens the narrow double doors, revealing a dark space inside. He disappears into the shed, and I follow. Being surrounded by darkness is the least of my fears.

With a dragged-out *creak*, another wooden latch lifts from somewhere within the shed. Slowly, he swings open two oversized wooden shutters until the oversized window is completely open along the back side of the shed. Soft moonlight fills the small space.

"What are we doing in here?" I ask. That's when I notice there's nothing inside the shed. Nothing hanging on the walls or in the rafters above, and nothing stashed in the corners or on the floor.

Across the window frame is a thick iron bar. Trevor wraps one hand over the bar while holding his staff in the other.

A loud *caw* comes from outside.

It can't be.

There's no way it's the same… Searching the night sky, I see nothing but the silhouette of sharpened logs forming the barrier wall. Wings flap and four large crows, one by one, land on the bar. I stumble back, almost tripping over my own feet.

Trevor leans in closer, moving past each one, whispering words I can't hear. He stops speaking when I come up next to him.

From within his pocket, he pulls out a long, narrow strip of parchment. I take it from him. Then, from his other pocket, he withdraws a slim glass jar filled with black ink. "Write your message and one of my friends here will deliver it for you."

The moment he says the word *friends*, all four crows shake their feathers vigorously. "You'll need one of those," he tells me, and I bend to pick up one of the fallen feathers.

I was hoping to tell my message to a person, and not have to *write* any words, because Selene's lessons only taught me what I needed to make my escape. A note that I hoped would be enough to sever ties with the general, but unfortunately, according to Selene, it only fueled her anger. That pain in my ass, Alister, is probably still searching all of Fayatin for my whereabouts.

Holding up the parchment, I confess, "I don't know how to write."

He nods in understanding. "Well, if you want to send a message, then I guess you'll have to tell me what to write."

Defeated, I give in. "Fine. But how will you write the message if—"

"Ah, don't worry," he cuts me off. "I don't need my eyes to write your words. I've only been blind for a few years!" Not arguing with him, I hand him the paper and the feather, then uncork the glass bottle. After he dips the tip of the crow feather into the ink, he gestures for me to relay my message.

I keep it short, knowing I've only got to the end of the narrow strip of parchment.

I'm needed in Bricen a bit longer.
Reply that you're okay. Stay strong.

He rolls the paper up tightly, then tucks it into the smallest leather pouch I've ever seen. He loops the string over one of the crows' necks, like a necklace. "And who are we sending the message to?"

I inhale a deep breath. The moment of truth. After this, Trevor will know where I came from. "To Lord Caldridge's daughter of Castle Forge. Her name is Selene, and she resides at the top of the eastern tower."

"You'll have to tell me one day how you ended up across Bowmans Straight, and in the heart of Fayatin."

"Maybe," I offer, instead of a flat *no*. Shutting him down may deter him from sending my message.

Leaning closer, he presses his lips to the top of the crow's head. Again, he mutters words I don't understand, and the second he steps away, the bird takes flight, my message in tow around its neck.

Trevor whispers something to the three remaining crows and they, too, fly off. Then, he draws the window boards closed, leaving us in darkness again. I follow him outside and wait as he latches the shed doors shut.

"Your message will reach your friend sometime tomorrow morning."

"You're sure the bird knows where to go? Like, the exact location? What if—"

"Barclay is the strongest and fastest of the four. He will make it. He's trained to travel long distances and find specific locations."

I have no idea how people train messenger birds, but I'm glad Trevor does. "Thank you."

"Yes, yes. I guess this means," he says, hobbling toward the back steps of Goslings, "you'll be needing a place to stay."

"If you have a room to spare, then yes. Otherwise, I'm content to make camp outdoors."

He stands in the doorway, his body outlined by the glow from inside the tavern. Holding the doorframe for support, he points the end of his walking stick out, toward the hill—Lauren's cottage. "You can stay there if you'd like. It is your home, too."

"I'd rather not."

"Nonsense. We'll watch over your aunt. Go and get some rest." He heads inside, yelling back to me, "We can talk more in the morning."

Trevor shuts the back door, and I make my way around the outside of Goslings, toward the road. I tell myself it's only for a few nights. And it's not the anticipation of what memories may surface from being inside my old home that weighs on my thoughts. No. All I can think about is how Barclay better survive the journey to Fayatin Country and deliver my message to Selene.

CHAPTER 11

Staying changes nothing. My goal is the same: to get answers about who—or what—I am, and then leave. To do so, I'm going to need more information about these Shade people and that doorway in the cave. There's got to be a way to cross over.

Breathing in the crisp night air, I follow the road away from Goslings. With my bow slung over my shoulder, I pass another short row of abandoned homes. There's no smoke from the chimneys or candlelight in the windows, yet now that I understand Bricen's situation better, the empty-looking homes may not actually be empty. The homes' disarray is the perfect disguise to hide behind.

A yawn slips free, and for once, I'm eager to get some sleep. To let the problems of today roll into the problems of tomorrow. Focusing straight ahead, I notice a small glow of light from inside the front window of my aunt's cottage. When the dirt road ends, I continue trudging up through the wet leaves littering the hillside. I'm trying to list off what I need to do to prepare for bed, but the memory of Kit's abduction nudges my thoughts. The events I witnessed from behind the tavern tapestry made me realize there's more to my past than whatever Aunt Lauren's hiding. How did he—that Shade man—subdue Kit and then command her to leave with them?

Invading a person's mind, I can do that.

Trapping them in a mental prison, that I can also do.

But forcing a person to blindly follow my commands, like a puppet? That's beyond my capabilities.

A dreadful thought crosses my mind. I don't know if all the Shades possess such power, but if General Onica ever got her hands on one of them… A chill rattles my spine at the idea. Status wouldn't matter—noble blood, commoner, or one of servants mining the Crescent Mountains—no one would be safe from the general's reach.

Not even Selene.

I can't help but curse under my breath, thinking about how that damn bird better make it to Castle Forge with my message. I need her to reply and let me know everything's okay. No matter the many reasons we shouldn't be friends—our differing statuses or the fact that I'm cursed and she's not—I refuse to let that stop us from being friends. She's the closest family I've got, and I need to make sure she's safe. Another reason to make sure the Shades never reach Fayatin soil.

Another thought pushes its way to the forefront of my mind about how those Shades didn't kill Kit. They took her.

Does that mean they've spared others too? It's doubtful that my mum, Alya, and whoever else has been taken over the years are still alive… But what if they are?

Reaching the front door to the old cottage, I'm about to lift the iron latch and let myself in when one of Trevor's pets *caw*s at me from a nearby low-hanging branch. The cluster of leaves blocks out the moonlight, making it hard to see the crow with its ebony feathers. I can't tell if it's one or all three of the remaining crows.

"What do you want?" I call out. It's ridiculous to think the animal understands me, yet if Trevor has trained these birds, then maybe they do. Pointing the tip of my bow up, I say, "Your friend better make the long journey."

Caw! The bird rustles its feathers, giving away its position.

I peer at the dark silhouette. "Did Trevor send you to watch over me?"

Caw! Caw!

A soft yellow light flickers from behind the dingy front window, diverting my attention from the winged spy. It seems no matter where I go, I'm kept under close watch.

After knocking, I lift the iron latch, step inside, and call out, "Hello? Is anyone in here?"

A cool breeze greets me, escaping out the door. The flame in the pillar candle next to the window resists being snuffed out, dancing low along the wick. Only after I shut the door does it settle.

With one hand on the latch and the other pressed to the door, I inhale a deep breath before turning to face the open room of the cottage. It's exactly how I remember it. From the savory aroma of rising dough to the mismatched furniture—everything in its place. Another breeze sweeps in, and I spot the source. After crossing the main living area in less than ten strides, I close the wooden shutters to a small window tucked between two oversized cupboards. Facing the room again, I realize my bedchamber at Castle Forge was twice the size of this cottage.

In the front corner is Mum's old rocking chair. Much of the red paint has worn off, exposing the warm oak tones underneath. She'd sit there for hours, sewing her quilts as she watched Aunt Lauren work. And my aunt was always working, baking bread and sweet desserts for the village. It seems that, too, hasn't changed. A long wood table stretches the center of the room, a faded rug covering the hardwood beneath it. At the far end of the table is a cutting board, dusted with flour. An open sack filled with flour rests next to the board. Lauren must've been getting ready to make bread for the morning.

There's a lingering chill in the air, causing a sudden shiver to run across my shoulders. If I'm sleeping here, then I might as well get a fire going. Inside the fireplace is a single log, its life down to the embers. Moving to the end of the table that's not dusted with flour, I rest my bow against the edge. Then, after setting my quiver and shoulder bag on the rocker, I grab a few logs from a nearby stack. It doesn't take long for the fire to grow, bringing light and warmth with it.

In the opposite front corner of the room is a blue curtain hanging from a thin rope. As I draw it open, I accidentally hook my finger on one of the many metal rings sewn into the side along the hem. Unsure of their purpose, I brush it off and continue to draw open the curtain. I would've thought the cozy space might've changed over the years, but nope—it's exactly as I remember it. Two single beds with a simple wood table between them. The same blue quilts my mum sewed cover each one. I remember the day Mum asked me to help her dye the fabric using the blooms of purple irises. My fingers were stained indigo for weeks.

Mum and Aunt Lauren were the closest of friends, and they raised me to embrace friendship wherever I could find it. They'd never met people like General Onica or Alister.

Although the quilts are worn and frayed at the seams, the memories of all those nights I spent snuggled in bed with Mum come flooding back. She might've been known for her healing sessions throughout the eastern side of Harvesgrove, but in our house, she was known for her stories. She had a way of spinning the most captivating tales, full of magical creatures, heroes, and villains.

Drawing the curtain closed, I swallow the lump forming in my throat. Good things aren't meant to last. Well, not for people like me.

Moving on, I climb the narrow ladder against the wall and peek over the joist boards to the loft. The entire space spans the length of my outstretched arms. The mattress lies on the withered planks lining the loft's floor. Bits of wood shavings spill out from a few holes alongside the seams. The blanket is gone, and in the place where my pillow should've been, is an old friend, propped up as if waiting for my return.

"It's been a long time, Tato," I say, picking up the potato-like stuffed toy. The light from the fireplace casts shadows over the low wall enclosing the loft area, highlighting Tato's mismatched button eyes. Besides the slight mildew stench, he's exactly how I remember him. Returning Tato to his spot on the mattress, I tell him, "Sorry you got left behind, old friend."

There's nothing more I can do tonight but rest. After climbing down from the rafters, I remove my cloak and vest and drape them over the top of a wooden chair. It wobbles from the additional weight. I'm tempted to sleep in my shirt, but don't want to risk anyone stopping by and seeing the Fayatin emblem sewn on the front. That, and I'm starting to smell a bit ripe. The earlier downpour combined with the intense chase for Kit has my shirt needing a good wash.

After finding a nightshirt in the linen cupboard, I set it aside on one of the beds. I want to take my sleeping tonic before changing. I grab my shoulder bag from the chair and rummage through it, searching for the amber bottle. But I find nothing. My mouth goes dry, and I dump the contents out onto the table. There's dried meat, wool socks, a compact waterskin, and Selene's hairpin. But no tonic.

"Bloody hell! Where did it go?" I don't know how it fell out, but it did. My heart races. The second I fall asleep the bombardment of nightmares will come haunting. How can I sleep now?

I need to make more, and fast.

The ingredients are fairly common, and I'm hoping my aunt has what I need. Leaving my things on the table, I hurry to the larger of the two cupboards and search through her stock of dried herbs and cooking ingredients. The first thing I grab is an amber bottle that's almost empty.

It'll have to do, I think while popping out the cork and dumping the pale green leafy remnants into the fireplace. The dried herb gives off a faint citrus scent as it burns. Now that I have an empty bottle, I search out the tonic's ingredients: crushed lavender, dried moonflower petals, honey, and lemon extract. The only thing not stored in the cupboard—and, of course, the most important one—is mistletoe.

There's no debate. I'd rather push through my exhaustion and search the dark woods than face the onslaught of nightmares.

With haste, I wrap my cloak over my shoulders before grabbing my empty bag. Forgoing my bow, I double-check my steel dagger is secure beneath my waistband. Now that I know the whereabouts of Elijah's secret escape hatch in the barrier wall, I should be able to sneak out, get the mistletoe, and be back before anyone realizes I'm gone.

Lifting the iron latch, I open the front door. Standing outside is Elijah. He's got one fist up, as if he's about to knock. In his other hand is a wood plate partially filled with boiled potatoes and a meager piece of bread.

"I thought you might be hungry."

The second I smell the warm potatoes, my stomach rumbles. Food does sound nice, but I also need to find the mistletoe.

His gaze dips and lingers over my shirt. Glancing down, I realize the strap of my shoulder bag has gotten caught on my cloak, exposing the emblem embroidered over my collarbone. Quickly I adjust the strap, tugging the cloak free.

Brows pinched, he asks, "You're a Fayatin soldier?"

"I don't have time for this." As I push past him, he grabs my wrist. His fingers wrap over the white fabric of my sleeve. Instinctively, I go for my dagger and press the blade to his throat. The sharp steel isn't angled to where it'll cut him, but it's pressed hard enough to make my point. "I thought I made it clear. I don't like being touched."

Without releasing his grip, he leans closer, ignoring the blade. His face is inches from mine when he asks, "Is that because you can kill a person just by touching them?"

"Do you want to find out?"

Slowly, he loosens his fingers from my wrist. Then, instead of putting some distance between us, he hands me the plate. "You should eat."

I lower the knife, tucking it into my waistband. "I don't have time to eat. I've got to go find something… Out in the woods."

Elijah pops one of the potatoes into his mouth. "I don't think that's a good idea. Not at night."

When he eats another one, my mouth starts to water. I reach for the plate and pop two fingerlings into my mouth, savoring every bit of the warm, semisweet potatoes. My body demands more, so I take the plate from him. After I swallow, I tell him, "You should stay here. I can handle myself."

"Can you at least tell me what you're looking for?"

I grab the last of the potatoes, then hand him the plate and usher him outside. Once the door latches, I turn and reluctantly say, "I need some mistletoe."

"Mistletoe? What for?"

I make my way down the hillside, kicking up wet leaves as I go. Elijah's on my heels, still asking questions. "Isn't mistletoe poisonous?"

"In high doses, yes. But a small amount helps me sleep." The faint sound of him breathing lingers between us. He trudges through the leaves behind me. I abruptly stop and face him. "I don't need your help, but if you insist on following me, you can at least point me in the direction of where I can find mistletoe. Then—"

"Then what? Let you wander the woods alone where the Shades can find you and—"

It was my turn to cut him off. "I said I can handle myself."

"No, you can't. Not against the Shades."

"Let them try and take me," I say, leaning closer. When he says nothing, I release an exasperated huff before continuing along the road, away from him, toward the line of run-down homes near the entrance.

His persistence used to drive Kit mad. She would force me to be mean to him and shove him until he looked ready to cry. When Kit stormed away, I would always crouch low and whisper apologies. But I wasn't going to apologize today, especially if knocking him on his ass is the only way to get him to leave me alone.

For a moment, there's silence, and I think he's veered off toward Goslings, but two seconds later, there's gravel crunching, and I know he's nearby. He jogs up next to me and says, "I know where to find some mistletoe. And I'll take you there, but only if you promise to tell me about the Fayatin emblem on your shirt and how you did what you did to Heathrow."

"No."

"No, to what?"

"No to both."

He holds out his arm, trying to block my path. When I do stop, he immediately retracts his hand. "Sorry, I know—I know. Don't touch you. But you promised me that if Trevor heard your request, you'd explain what happened in the forest—what you did to Heathrow. And now I find out you've been living across Bowmans Straight over in enemy territory all these years." He pauses, rubbing a hand over his short hair. "I searched those woods every day for more than a fortnight looking for you."

"Great. Thanks," I grumble. Then, because I want to get this night over with, I try a different approach. With a more appeasing tone, hoping he'll give in and leave, I say, "Look. The past is in the past. I've moved on, and so should you." Picking up my pace, I hurry ahead, reaching the last home at the end of the row. I use a gloved hand to push aside the thorny vines while squeezing between the overgrown shrub and the edge of the abandoned home. When I reach the hatch in the barrier wall, I turn to see him standing behind me. "Persistent, aren't you? How about you just tell me where the mistletoe is, then go home and get some sleep? I'm tired and I've had an extremely long day. Meaning, I'd like to get this done as fast as possible. And that's not going to happen if you're tagging along."

He shuffles by me and grips the frayed rope handle that's attached to the cut section of the barrier wall. With a determined pull, he yanks on the handle and the two logs bound together come free with a dull scrape. The hatch falls to the ground, landing in the same pile of dead leaves as before. Turning to me, he says, "I'm coming with you whether you like it or not."

"Fine, whatever." I duck my head low through the short passage and start down the road, not waiting for him. It doesn't take him long to catch up to me. He doesn't say anything, and we continue in silence.

A few minutes later, he tells me, "There's a vine cluster not too far from the cave."

Exhausted, I let Elijah take the lead. It's not worth sending him home now, and even though I'd never admit it out loud, I'm glad for the company. Because without him, it would've taken me all night to find the white berries. As we walk, the crisp air caresses my face, giving me the extra wake-up I need after a long, stressful day. All I care about right now is finding the mistletoe, making my tonic, and then curling up in my mum's old bed. And I swear if anyone keeps me from getting a good night's sleep, there'll be hell to pay.

CHAPTER 12

RUNE

"*Rune. Open your eyes.*"

I open them as commanded. A thunderous dark sky looms above. Sitting up in my designated hole, I listen and wait for further instructions. From the corner of my eye, a shiny black bug wiggles its way out of the packed dirt. It's been a long time since I've seen a living creature wandering the desolate lands of the Under Realm. It's far from home, wherever it came from. Curious, I pick at the dirt beneath it, trying to assist its escape. At first, it retreats into the soil, but then slowly it reemerges, reaching its tiny, jointed forelegs out as if desperate for a lifeline. I move my finger closer, and it latches on, pulling free from the dirt. It's a long critter, about the size of my finger, with an armor-like shell running the full length of its body.

"Where did you come from?" I ask, holding it at eye level for inspection.

Long antennae perk upright before it skitters along my finger, then my hand, and eventually down my arm. It momentarily disappears, blending in with the dark strips of fabric wrapping my arm. But then I see it race across the dirt that surrounds me. My attention is focused on this rare occurrence, watching the bug crawl up and over the side of my hole. The second it's gone, Merigoth calls to me.

"Rune! Why aren't you answering me?"

"There was a bug," I confess through my mind.

"You mean a distraction." I'm about to offer my apologies when she speaks again. This time her tone is less harsh, but there's a hint of annoyance laced into her words. *"Never mind that. You're to open a new doorway for Marcellus."*

Without hesitating, I stand and climb out of my assigned resting hole. *"Yes, my queen."*

I pause because she never fails to reward those who comply with her wishes. And I'm overdue for one of her blessings. I strive to stay obedient like Marcellus and Evander, or the others, but it's hard. My attention is easily distracted, and I don't know why.

The wait is over and her blessing hits me like an invisible arrow into my skull. If there was any pain, I don't remember it. The bliss that blooms in the center of my head consumes my mind, then spreads throughout my body, caressing me from the inside.

I stagger forward along the path, bits of gravel rolling beneath my bare feet. My elation subsides. Despite its brevity, I silently thank our queen for her blessing. The side entrance to Merigoth's mountain fortress comes into view. My orders to meet Marcellus in the cave and open a new doorway surface, and I will oblige because *my will is her will.*

To my left are thousands of rectangular pits, identical to my resting hole. Some are empty, but most are occupied by other dormant Shades or one of Merigoth's Reborn creatures. Off to my right, a sudden flock of demon spirits flits past. An acrid, burned stench lingers in the dry air in the monsters' wake. They soar over the barren field covered in cracks filled with molten magma. Without the fiery glow of the lava fields, the realm would be consumed by darkness. Circling back around, they fly by again. Their wings fume black smoke, and their beady red eyes remain open, never closing—always searching for a body to inhabit. They are loyal to Queen Merigoth, and in return for carrying out her wishes, they only ask for a second chance at life. The offerings we collect from the Human Realm give these phantom creatures the second life they seek—thus creating the Reborns.

The Reborns are vile and savage. We avoid them and they avoid the Shades.

A series of low groans draws my attention away from the cave entrance ahead. Shuffling to a stop, I lower my gaze to my bare feet. The unfamiliar sound unhinges my train of thought.

What was I doing?

More miserable cries fill the silent air of the Under Realm, and I turn to see our latest offering to Merigoth writhing in agony in one of the pits. Her eyes are tightly shut while her head and hands jerk uncontrollably.

Her groans grow louder.

She's fighting Marcellus's touch.

How interesting.

I want to climb into the shallow hole and see what she's seeing. But that is not my ability. My gift is creating passages. But still, I'm curious to see what mental prison Marcellus has forced her to relive while she waits for Merigoth's blessing to become a Reborn.

Evander's voice interrupts me. "What are you doing?"

Facing him, I point to the girl and ask, "Where is she?"

Briefly, he looks at the girl and then at me. "What does it matter? What is your will?"

"Her will," I answer.

Without another word, he pivots and strides toward the cave at the end of the trail.

I give the girl one more glance before pursuing my fellow Shade. Ahead, the rocky base of the mountain fortress is visible, shrouded in a glow of red. When I've caught up to Evander, I try again, wanting to understand why I care, and he does not. "Do you not wonder—"

"No, Rune. I do not *wonder* anything," he cuts me off and stops before reaching the cave's entrance. Instead of looking at me, he faces the magma fields. "One of these days, Merigoth isn't going to be so merciful. You must do better." He walks away, disappearing into the narrow passage of the mountainside.

After a long moment, I pass beneath the jagged black rocks framing the mouth of the cave. The magma field from outside casts a soft light inside the cave. Evander stands off to the side, waiting for me. Dragging one hand along the rocky surface, I feel for the smoothest spot to open this new doorway. My fingers linger over the smooth surface where I open our usual doorway—the one that leads to the river and the forest.

"My orders are for a new location. Not the village in the forest," Evander explains. He points to another semi-flat surface, farther toward the back. "Here is good."

As I approach, the red glow from outside barely reaches this far into the cave. Yet, there's enough light to see his expression. The same docile look he always wears. Not wanting to disappoint Evander, I silently repeat, *My will is her will, and she is all that matters.* My thoughts about the bug I saw earlier or the girl writhing about in her hole fade away. All I wish is to feel her blessing once again, and to do so I need to open this doorway.

I think that's what I want.

"Rune, are you ready?"

I nod and he moves to stand behind me. I press both palms flat against the spot he's chosen and wait. The tips of his fingers slide along the sides of my face, halting over my temples.

"This is where I need to go." His words float into my mind, igniting the connection between us. Behind closed lids, I'm able to see his destination. It's as if I'm there, standing off in the distance on a grassy hill, looking out to the stone castle. Four high towers stand at the corners, each one with a red flag waving from the tips of their pitched roofs. A series of mountain peaks looms behind the castle, spanning a great distance.

"Do you see it?" he asks.

"I see it."

Arching my shoulder blades, hands still in contact with the cave wall, I inhale a deep breath, waking an ancient power from within my core. My shoulders tense as a sharp pain stabs my spine, but I don't scream. I'm used to it. An unknown force rustles beneath my skin, wanting to be released, yet I don't know how to release it. So, I endure the pain spiking along the bones of my back.

Once I've gathered enough power in my core, I focus on the destination—the castle—while redirecting the energy out of my body through my palms. The cave wall around my hands glows a bright white and continues to expand outward until the shape of a doorway forms. When the shape is complete and filled with light, I step away. The light fades, leaving a smooth surface and a new doorway in its place. The window-like surface wavers with a gentle ripple before settling flat. On the other side is the castle.

Marcellus comes up from behind us and tells me, "You should return to your resting state." He disappears through the doorway. I didn't even hear him enter the cave.

Before Evander follows, he says, "Remember, what is your will?"

I lift my chin high and answer proudly, "Her will."

Dark eyes silently plead with me to behave. "Good."

Behind Evander, the doorway frames the Human Realm. Marcellus walks through a stony field toward the castle in the distance. The sun is setting on the horizon. My energy wavers, and I hunch in on myself, striking an arm out to steady my stance. "What is your purpose over there?" I ask Evander before he goes through.

"Rune," he says with a warning tone. He sighs, flicking his gaze to the doorway and back to me. "The humans have captured a demon spirit. I don't know how they did it, but this particular one means a great deal to Merigoth. She's commanded that we retrieve it." Then he steps away from the doorway, closing the space between us. I'm still winded, but I try to stand tall and hear him out. "Close the door behind me. When Marcellus and I are ready to return, Merigoth will call upon you."

"Understood."

Once he's through, he picks up his pace to catch up with Marcellus. When he's far enough away, I do as he says and close the passage, which drains even more of my energy. With one hand on the cave wall for support, I slowly head toward the exit. As I pass the doorway leading to the forest village, I stop and listen. There are voices. Familiar voices. With my head resting against the smooth obsidian, my thoughts wander to the world beyond, and I picture the Human Realm with its verdant forest and noisy river. Then, not meaning to, I inadvertently open the doorway and fall through, leaving the Under Realm behind.

As I stumble into the Human Realm, my legs are wobbly, and my mind is foggy. I need sleep, and soon. The sound of rushing river water overwhelms my senses, muffling the serenade of her will. The haze clouding my mind fades, and I remember the stars. Shuffling along, my body still recovering from the recent power drain, I make my way toward the river's edge. I don't know why, but a heavy heartache tugs at my chest when the stars come into view.

I wish I could remember.

Familiar voices coming from within the forest interrupt my moment with the stars. Parting ways with the night sky, I stalk deeper into the woods until I find them. The shadows of the forest hide me as I peer around a tree. It's the same girl and boy from earlier—the ones who followed us into the cave. There was something different about that girl. She was able to see the Under Realm, whereas the boy couldn't.

Knowing my time outside Merigoth's will is short, I intently survey the pair from behind the tree. What makes this girl able to see into the Under Realm? How does she have the Sight?

"Is that enough?" the boy asks.

"Probably, but keep looking," the girl answers.

They're standing on the outskirts of a small clearing, moonlight highlighting their backs. The boy tugs on a low-hanging branch, then with his free hand, searches the leaves above.

Next to him, the girl takes a few steps back and raises her chin to the night sky. What is she doing? Do the stars call to her as well?

"How did you end up over in Fayatin, anyway?" the boy asks.

With a deep sigh, the girl steps over to another tree. Searching one of the branches, she answers, "It's in the past. You don't need the details."

"I can't imagine what that must've been like for you, living in that horrid country."

"You really want to know?" she snaps and releases the branch. "Life isn't fair. That's what happened. I think about that day…" Her voice trails off, and if she says any more, I can't hear it.

But the boy's words are loud and clear. "Adele, I don't blame you for what happened to Alya that day. It wasn't your fault."

The girl ignores him, continuing to search the low-hanging branches.

"I know we were once friends," he says, "and I hope that we can be again."

She sidesteps farther from him. "I'm not looking for any new friends."

Their conversation is longer than any I've ever had with other Shades, even Evander. It's fascinating. I try to hold my attention to them, but Merigoth's voice floats in the far back of my mind.

I'm not ready to go back.

I shuffle closer, using their words as an anchor to this realm where I still have free will.

The girl tugs at another branch, pulling free a long vine. She stuffs the plant into the bag slung over her shoulder.

"Fayatin isn't like here. I mean, I know things are looking pretty dreadful with these Shade beings tormenting Bricen, and other villages I suppose, but you still have it easier than the people of Fayatin. They haven't taken your freedom."

The boy steps away from the tree. His hands are up, clutching the red scarf wrapped around his neck. "You're talking about General Onica."

"You know of her?"

"Only rumors, but yes."

"Well, I'm sure whatever rumors you heard are true. Life over there is about survival. I did what I had to do in order to stay alive. That includes joining the Fayatin army and following orders from a despotic general." Then, barely above a whisper, she adds, "I was young and naïve and…alone."

"You didn't have anyone over there? Someone to confide in—to spend your time with?"

The boy is blocking my view, so I can't see her reaction. But the compassion confuses me… Merigoth says emotions make you weak.

The girl sits on a large fallen tree. "Forming attachments is a luxury I don't have. Anyway," she says, swinging her legs over the trunk. She leaves the small clearing and without the moonlight, I can't see her. From within the darkness, she says, "Stay here. I'll be right back. I've got to relieve myself."

"What? Where are you going?"

"I said," she shouts from somewhere behind the trees, "I have to pee!"

At first, I think he'll disregard her instructions and follow, but he eventually returns to his task of searching the tree branches. "Fine. But hurry up. I don't like being out here after dark."

I can't see her, but she's somewhere peeing behind the trees, whatever peeing is. Abruptly, a force tugs at my mind, trying to hook itself into my consciousness. I turn away from the clearing and focus on staying in control. Merigoth's lure is strong, beckoning me to return to the cave—to return to the Under Realm. Using all my might, I ignore it, then wince at the pain that accompanies my resistance. I'm still weak from conjuring the doorway, and I know I won't be able to resist much longer.

"Hey, are you almost done?" the boy shouts. "We need to get back before Trevor realizes we've snuck out."

Wanting one more glance, I roll my back against the tree, turning to look out at the clearing again. But I'm met with a punch to the face. The force throws me backward, and I land on the forest floor. Before I can get up, the girl is on top of me, her knees pinning my arms to the ground. With a wide sweep of her arm, she hits me over the head with something hard like a rock. The pain throbs, spiking into my temple. I should fight back, or at least be vengeful for the pain, but I don't and I'm not. I do, however, crack a smile because I can no longer feel the lure of Merigoth.

The moonlight behind the girl's body grows dim, everything goes dark, and I welcome sleep.

CHAPTER 13

I nudge open the door to Aunt Lauren's cottage with my back, hefting up the Shade girl's arms. Elijah's got ahold of her ankles. We stumble awkwardly through the doorway, and once we're inside he lets go of the girl's bare feet. They hit the hardwood with a *thump* as he quickly turns to shut then lock the front door. After the iron latch is secure, he wipes his hands on his pants as if he's touched something poisonous.

"This is a bad idea," he says, panic in his voice. He makes for the window, his wild gaze searching outside. "If Trevor finds out—"

"He won't find out," I cut him off. I run my hands over the girl, checking for weapons, careful not to touch her skin. "She's clean."

Elijah adds a log to the fire, then glances over his shoulder and grumbles, "That girl is anything but clean. She looks filthy to me."

"That's not what I meant." Although, he's not wrong. The layer of dirt dusting her face makes it hard to gauge her age, but I can definitely tell she's not much older than me or Elijah. She lacks the markings of a grown woman—wrinkles, sunspots, or leathery skin. "Hey," I call to him. When he turns away from the fireplace, I ask, "Do you have any rope we can tie her up with?"

"I have something better." He comes around from the other side of the table and drags away the two chairs nestled beneath. After crouching to one knee, he rolls back the rug, pushing it against the table legs. There's an iron ring embedded into the floor.

"That wasn't there before."

He slides the hatch door away from the floor.

"Yeah, well, we've had to make a bunch of these hidey-holes since you left. It's how most of us have survived the Shade attacks."

The dirt hole beneath the floorboards reminds me of a grave. It pains me to imagine Aunt Lauren lying in there while the Shades pilfered the village, taking people over food and coin. I should've come sooner. Bricen might not be in such disarray if I'd only… I stop myself and refocus. I shake off the unexpected lapse of guilt and jump into the hole. The hole is halfway beneath the table, and I'm careful not to bump my head against the edge as I stand there waiting for Elijah to bring me the girl.

"All right, let's hurry this up before she wakes up." I wave for him to hurry up. As he's dragging her toward me, I ask, "Do you have one of these holes in your home too?"

When the girl is close enough, I roll her body into my arms, then lower her onto the packed dirt. Elijah gives me space while I climb out, and explains, "Everyone does. There's two in our house. One for me and one for…" His words hitch and he doesn't finish, but that's fine. I know who he means. He grumbles, "Let's just finish things up here. I'm tired, and I imagine you are too." When I'm out of the way, he slides the hatch cover into place.

Sleep beckons behind my lids, but I can't give in yet. I still have to make my tonic. After he fixes the rug into place, he stands and marches out the door, leaving it open behind him. I set my bag on the table and take out the mistletoe we collected, then inspect the condition of the white berries. A cool breeze drifts in from the open door and before I begin, I go to close it. The moment the door's about to connect with the frame, a boot appears, preventing the door from shutting.

It's Elijah. He has two large rocks, one in each hand. "Just in case," he tells me, setting them on top of the rug. He then returns both chairs to their position nestled under the table. "There. That should keep her secure for the night. And if she does try and escape, well, we should have enough time to grab our weapons."

"What do you mean *we*?"

Removing his scarf, he gets comfortable in the corner rocking chair.

Crossing my arms, I tell him, "Oh, no. You're not staying here tonight."

With his eyes closed, he starts rocking. "I'm already half-asleep. Best you get some too."

I'm too tired to argue, so I remove my cloak and drape it over the chair. It doesn't matter if Elijah can see the large black F embroidered on my shirt. He's already seen it, so there's no point in trying to hide it now. Moving to the other side of the table, closer to the fireplace, I sort through the ingredients Aunt Lauren did have. Then, I get busy making my tonic. While the water heats up in a cast-iron pot over the fire, I pluck two of the mistletoe berries from the vines we collected. With a mortar and pestle from the cupboard, I grind the berries together with the other ingredients: crushed lavender, dried moonflower petals, honey, and lemon extract. When a paste has formed, I ladle one cupful of hot water into the mortar. With the end of a wooden spoon, I gently stir the tonic until it's cooled enough to transfer into the empty bottle.

"That's it?" Elijah asks, one eye open, watching me from his seat in the corner.

"Yeah, that's it."

"And it helps you sleep?"

Lifting the mortar to my nose, I inhale. The familiar scents of lavender, honey, and lemon overpower the faint aromas of moonflower and mistletoe. And from that one whiff, my anxiety subsides. My mind knows it'll be a nightmare-free night.

"Adele?" Elijah asks again. "That there"—he eyes the amber bottle in my hand—"will help you sleep?"

"Yes. It'll help me sleep but may kill you. I don't recommend trying it." With a wood funnel from the cupboard, I transfer the tonic into the empty bottle. Then, before corking it, I take two swigs. The sweetness of the honey and the tanginess of the lemon extract coat my throat. The effects of the mistletoe aren't immediate, but nonetheless, I feel better already.

After crossing the narrow room, I draw open the blue curtain to the nook where the two beds reside. I could offer the other bed to Elijah, but if he wanted it, I assume he'd ask. Plus, I'd feel more comfortable with a bit of privacy, leaving him in the chair—or better yet, at his own home. "You should go sleep in your own bed. She's not going anywhere."

He tucks his hands under his arms, acting as if he's too cozy to go anywhere. "Good night, Adele."

Sitting on the end of the single bed, I remove my boots before drawing the curtain closed. The metal rings I saw earlier, the ones sewn into the side of the fabric, line up to wooden pegs hammered into the side of the wall. With a simple hook, I secure each metal ring over its peg. It's a clever design. Another trick the village must use to alert them to intruders.

With the added level of security and my tonic kicking in, numbing my mind, I'm ready to let sleep take over. I slip beneath my mum's old quilt and hug the edges, thinking about the nights I'd lie here and listen to her stories.

I wonder what kind of story the girl will spin when I interrogate her tomorrow. I'll need to ask what happened to Kit, and if there's a way to heal my aunt and the other villagers.

More importantly, I want to know why her kind and I share similar abilities.

If all goes as planned, the Shade girl will enlighten us with everything she knows, leaving no question unanswered, and then I can decide what to do with her.

I'd like to think everything will be resolved by the end of the day so I can be on my way back to Fayatin—back to Selene—but I have a feeling my time in Bricen is far from done.

CHAPTER 14

The sound of wood hitting something hard followed by feet dancing across the floor wakes me. But I resist opening my eyes, because waking up means I'll have to leave this comfortable bed that has an intoxicating scent of vanilla and fresh bread.

"Adele!" Elijah's harsh voice cuts into my mind. Ignoring him, I curl my legs up beneath my mum's quilt. He calls to me again, this time with more urgency. "ADELE! Get out here, now!"

Slowly sitting up, I unhook the metal rings, freeing the curtain from the wall. Then, with one gloved hand shielding my eyes from the morning sunlight, I look to Elijah standing between the two cupboards at the back of the room. He's holding up one of my aunt's rolling pins.

"What is it?" I ask, shaking off the lingering haze the mistletoe has left me in. Something catches my attention over by the rocking chair, and now I see why he's panicking. The Shade girl is standing a few feet from me, staring out the front window.

Scrambling out of bed, fully alert, I pull out the knife tucked in my waistband. The Shade girl doesn't react, still staring out the window with her hands limp at her sides.

I edge out of the nook, keeping my back to the wall. The rocks Elijah placed over the hatch appear untouched. I watch the girl closely. "How the hell did she get out?"

His wide eyes lock onto the girl. "I don't know." Even though she's nowhere near him, he stands ready to strike with my aunt's rolling pin. His chest moves fast, too fast. I can see the blind panic in his eyes as his breathing turns to hyperventilating.

"Try to calm yourself," I say, taking a half-step toward him. I've seen plenty of people fall victim to their own doings before I've even laid a hand on them. It's not the Interrogator's methods they fear, because most don't know what happens behind closed doors, but the myths and rumors they've heard about how those who are sent to be interrogated are never seen again.

He closes his mouth and nods. His chest rises and falls in a slow, deliberate breath. Then, in a calmer tone, he says, "Adele, we've got to alert the village."

I hold a palm up to him, hoping he trusts me enough to handle the situation. "Not yet. Let me try talking to her first. This one seems different." Gripping the hilt of my knife, I keep it ready while looking the girl over. Her dark hair is sheared to the scalp, blending in with the thin layer of dirt coating her skin. Instead of clothes, she's wrapped in strips of black fabric, thick like leather. Her whole body is wrapped in them, except for an exposed midriff. She stands there, with no boots or slippers on her feet, only dirt caked between her toes.

After a long moment of silence, she slowly turns her gaze to me. There's a vacancy to her expression as she points to the window. "Where does the light come from?"

"What do you mean?" I ask, cocking my head while slightly lowering my knife.

Why would she be wondering about the daylight? Then I recall the dark world I saw through the cave wall—the otherworldly place she comes from. Pointing the tip of my knife to the window, I tell her, "That's sunlight…"

"Sun. Light." She looks out the window to the sky. "Light from the…sun?"

I shuffle closer. "Do you…not have sunlight where you're from?"

She shakes her head, attention glued to the bright world outside. Noting her relaxed stance and lack of interest in our presence, I lower my blade. She doesn't seem upset about being locked up beneath the floor. Actually, I'd say she's more curious than vengeful. But why? She and her kind have been attacking Bricen for years. It's not as though it's her first time in the village.

"Adele. We have to alert the others," Elijah repeats, rolling pin still clutched in one hand.

Cautiously, I wave the tip of my knife in front of her, urging her to move away from the window. "That's enough. We can't have anyone seeing you."

She obliges and steps away. For a fleeting moment, her gaze finds the knife in my hand, but she doesn't react. Elijah slinks along the wall, away from the cupboard, making sure to keep a good distance between him and the girl. I, on the other hand, remain within arm's reach.

"Why were you out in the woods last night?" I begin.

Some people you can be more personable with, while for others it's best to just get to the point. This is one of those times where I skip the small talk. Truth be told, I don't have to waste my time talking at all, but I don't actually enjoy torturing people. If I can get the answers I'm looking for without invading her mind, then it's worth the extra few minutes to try.

"I heard your voices from the Under Realm, and I was curious."

"The Under Realm, is that what you call your world?"

Unblinking, she searches my face with narrowed eyes. The dark smudges beneath her eyes are fading. With a slight tilt of her head, she says, "You're not like the others."

"No. I am not." I probably shouldn't give her any information, but she brings up a valid observation. "How can you tell?"

Instead of answering, she cries out, pressing her hands to the sides of her head. Her feet stumble backward, and she lands in my mum's old rocker. Startled, I raise my knife in case she lunges. I know all too well that deception goes hand in hand with any escape plan.

But she doesn't.

She's good. I'll give her that. Whether her expression is true or not, it's one I've seen many times these past years. It's the face of someone fearing for their life.

"It's too quiet!" she whimpers, pressing her hands to her shaved head. "She'll find me!" She lifts her gaze, her dark eyes finding mine. "Please! Don't let her find me!" Abruptly the Shade girl stands, the rocking chair vigorously swaying in her wake. She rushes toward door.

I beat her to the front of the room, blocking her path. "You're not going anywhere. Not yet."

"I must! I shouldn't have left. You're in danger if I stay." She shuffles back, her hands to her head again, and mutters, "My will is her will. My will is her will."

Then, the second I look at Elijah, the girl charges for the door. Her strength is unlike anything I've ever encountered. Before she can lift the iron latch, I've stripped away one of my gloves and pressed my palm to her cheek.

Her skin's cold, like that of someone who's been traveling Noviska's snowy lands without proper protection from the frigid wind. But it's not the chill that startles me. It's the barrage of images—thousands of them—flashing behind closed lids. One after another, they overlap, each wanting a turn to share whatever memory they hold. I don't recognize where the memories take place or who's present, but I do feel the deep longing that accompanies each one. A strange yearning to be reunited with…something. It's a powerful sensation, and thrums through my mind, growing stronger by the second.

Gasping, I'm unable to pull myself away. I want to, but I can't.

The Shade girl's eyes go wide and her face twists as if she, too, feels the pain of my invasion.

My hand finally breaks free from her face, and I stumble away. I try to regain my balance, but I can't because a powerful wind rushes at me from behind. My body falls backward and the cottage around me disappears into pitch darkness.

When the nothingness that surrounds me changes to a midnight sky with thunder rumbling in the distance, I realize it's not wind coming at me from behind—it's me plummeting to my death. I'm falling through the air.

But luckily, my body never hits the ground, and I continue to fall for what seems like hours. The more time that passes, the hazier my thoughts become. I can't recall where I was before this, or why rubies are so important to me. Nothing makes any sense.

I stop worrying about what I can't remember and embrace the enveloping warmth numbing my body and mind. I may not remember much, but something inside me knows it's been forever since I've felt this content. My body continues to cut through the air, but I don't care. My lips spread wide, and I can't help but laugh, something I thought I'd never do again.

Whatever is happening to me, I don't want it to stop. But then something wiggles its way into my bliss. A woman's voice calls to me. *"I've been searching a long time for you,"* she says, her voice soft and enticing. *"And now it seems you have something of mine. Bring her to me and all will be forgiven. For you… For Rune… And for your mother."*

"You know my mum?" I shout into the dark empty sky. Is my mum alive? I shake my head vigorously, pushing away the warmth and letting the happiness go.

Somehow, in my efforts, a different voice emerges—my voice—and it's saying, *My will is her will, and she is all that matters.* The words repeat in the back of my mind, soft and sweet like a lullaby a mother would sing to her children. There's a dangerous weight to these words as they try to permanently pierce their way into my mind.

"This isn't right. I shouldn't be here!" I resist, not only because I want answers about my mum, but also because I realize I can't stay here. This place isn't real and the joy I feel isn't real either. My happiness, if I'm ever to find it, is waiting for me out in the real world.

A stabbing pain pushes against my skull. The woman's voice seethes as she warns, *"Bring me what's mine or lose those you love forever."*

With everything I've got, I force the woman from my thoughts. In the back of my mind, there's a muffled voice. It's Elijah. I focus on him, picture his red scarf, and pray to the stars I find my way back home.

Blinking, I jolt upright. I'm on the cottage floor near the rocking chair. A shadow passes by and I look over to see Elijah walking in from outside.

My glove lays close by on the floor. With an annoyed sigh, I grab it and slip it onto my hand then adjust the fit with a forceful tug. "How long was I out?"

"Almost an hour." A soft grunt escapes his mouth as he lowers two large rocks on top of the rug, next to a pile he's brought in from outside. The whole hatch is barricaded with rocks. Some are covered in damp dirt, as if he dug them up solely for this purpose. "There. That should keep her from escaping again." He closes the front door and helps me to my feet. "Trevor's been asking to see you."

"What did you tell him?" I cross the room and pour myself a cup of water from the metal pitcher. My heart is still racing in the aftermath of whatever just happened. That place... Those voices... Was it real or a head trip from touching that Shade girl?

"Nothing," Elijah says. "But I should've told him everything!" There's a tremble to his voice.

"You did the right thing by keeping your mouth shut." I set the wooden cup on the table, then open one of the cupboards and search for a clean shirt. Aunt Lauren has a smaller frame than me, so I try to find the largest tunic she owns. Pulling a clean white garment out, I turn to Elijah. "I appreciate you not saying anything to Trevor." He's staring at me with a tense expression. I can tell he's weighing his options, so I add, "Do you really think Trevor would let her stay?"

Elijah closes his eyes and dips his chin beneath the red scarf wrapping his neck. After a short moment, he exhales and says, "No. Probably not."

"Right. Then we lose the chance to get some real answers."

His dark brows lift, and he leans against the wall, his gaze darting to the pile of rocks. "And you want to interrogate the Shade girl without Trevor here?"

"I do." I'm starting to regret letting Elijah come with me last night to fetch the mistletoe. If I went alone, I wouldn't have to deal with these insistent questions or that stupid glare he's giving me.

"If we have an opportunity to find Kit," I say, the clean shirt swinging from my hand, "and maybe to learn more about what they're doing with the people they've taken, then don't you think we should? Plus, the girl might know how to cure my aunt and the others." It's not completely a lie, but I also want to know more about their powers. This might be the only chance I get to talk with one of these Shades.

He pushes off the wall and starts pacing the room. "We should at least tell Trevor."

He continues to ramble off reasons why we should talk to Trevor, and I have no interest in hearing any of them. We're not telling the old man. My mind is set. Stepping into the small nook, I remove my Fayatin shirt and toss it on the floor between the beds.

"Hey! What are you doing?" Elijah shouts. He scrambles to draw the curtain closed.

"I didn't take you for being bashful," I say loudly through the blue curtain. "We used to change in front of each other all the time."

"When we were kids, Adele. Not now."

After slipping the clean shirt over my head, taking in the scent of herbs and flour, I tuck the ends into my pants. Then when I'm done, I duck out from behind the curtain and pick up my vest draped over the back of one of the chairs.

Standing and staring out the window, Elijah shifts his feet. With a cautious glance over his shoulder, he eventually turns and says with a scowl, "A little warning next time. I'm happy to give you some privacy."

"So noble of you." I come up next to him, but careful not to make contact, and lean closer to the window. The overcast is moderate and lighter in color, meaning no storms on the horizon. I spot only a few people outside. A gray-haired woman walking toward Gosling and then a small group of people conversing by the village gate. I don't see Trevor and take that as a good thing.

Backing away from the window, I finish working the leather laces of my borrowed vest, and tell him, "I promise we'll tell Trevor... After we talk to her first." He doesn't respond. Instead, he stabs the charred logs burning in the fireplace with the iron poker. The wood cracks and the fire burns brighter. I let him mope while I unbraid my hair, using my fingers to comb through the snarls.

I'm halfway into re-braiding my hair when under his breath, he gives in, turning away from the fireplace to face me. "Okay. We'll do it your way, but then we tell Trevor."

"Thank you," I say, trying to show some appreciation. My job as the Fayatin Interrogator is a solo job, which means I've never had to plan out or discuss what needs to be done with someone else. It's frustrating. And yet, it does keep me from acting on impulse.

Lifting my shoulder bag from the floor, I rest it on the tabletop before searching out Selene's hairpin. I find it at the bottom. With the sentimental piece in hand, I rub my thumb over the small rubies. I can only hope my closest friend is well, and that she's received my message. Pushing the ends of the hairpin into the top section of my braid, I feel the prongs slide into place against my scalp. Then, once it's tightly secure, I close my bag and focus on what to do next.

"That's pretty," Elijah says, resting the iron poker against the stone of the fireplace.

I ignore him because acknowledging it will only lead to more questions, and there's no need to get into a conversation about who the true owner is or my life in Fayatin. Grabbing one of my boots, noting the dried mud on the bottom isn't as bad as I thought it would've been after yesterday's downpour, and I tell him, "Listen. Before our guest wakes up again, how about you go and walk the barrier? Double-check for any broken logs while I go talk to Trevor."

"You're going to talk to him?"

"Sure. I—unlike you—have no problem lying." I slip the boot over my foot, and then grab the second one.

Elijah picks up the empty plate he brought over last night and then nods. "Fine. I'll survey the perimeter, and then meet you back here. Whatever you're going to tell Trevor, make sure it's believable. He has a way of knowing when people are lying." He steps closer to the front door, but before he reaches for the latch, he adds, "We'll make a decision about what to do with her then."

I won't burden Elijah with the poor girl's fate once we're done interrogating her. Taking a life isn't easy…or at least it isn't easy when you first do it. Looking to the pile of rocks, the Shade tucked away beneath the floorboards, I tell myself I'll have to come up with a new plan to get rid of the girl. Infiltrating her mind didn't go so well earlier. I'm still shaken by the dream-like encounter I'd had with whomever that woman was. I recall her words, *And now it seems you have something of mine. Bring her to me and all will be forgiven. For you… For Rune… And for your mother.*

My mother.

"I'll be back," Elijah says, snapping me from my reverie. He starts to open the front door when a muffled voice floats up from beneath the floorboards. Instinctively, we look at one another before shifting out gazes to the pile of rocks clustered on the rug. The Shade is awake.

I jump to my feet, still holding my boot in one hand.

Elijah shuts the door with a forceful push.

The girl mumbles something again.

"Be quiet down there." I stomp one foot against the hardwood. Silence follows. "Okay, let's be quick," I say to Elijah while donning my other boot.

But then, a bright light emerges from beneath the rug under the rocks, directly over the hidey-hole.

"What the…" I step back as the light expands outward into a perfect circle, about an arm's-length wide.

When the white light fades, the rocks, the rug, and floorboards disappear. In their place is a glassy surface, and we can see the Shade girl lying in the hole below. It isn't until she sits up, the top half of her body passing through the window-like surface, that I drop the boot and hurry to remove my gloves.

I hold both hands out in front of me, ready to defend myself.

"I don't want to return to the Under Realm," the Shade says, staring up at us. "I want to stay here…with you."

CHAPTER 15

There's a giant hole in the cottage floor. The edge of the round hole cuts perfectly into the surrounding rocks piled over the rug. The Shade sits there in the hidey-hole, the top half of her body sticking out above the floorboards. It's hard to ignore the pleading look in her eyes.

I point to the mystical "escape hole" and demand, "How did you do that?"

She climbs out, and the surface ripples as if she's just climbed out of a pool of water. Elijah and I take a few steps back. His back presses to the door while I bump into the ladder leading up to the loft. She then kneels beside the edge and lays one flat palm to the glassy surface, and it wavers before disappearing. The pile of muddy rocks over the worn rug returns as if never disturbed.

"H-how…? What…?" Elijah stutters.

Her abilities are nothing like those of the man who subdued and controlled Kit's will. This is an entirely new ability. "Well, that explains how they're getting into the village." I lower my hands and slip my gloves back on.

"Don't send me back or kill me," she begs. "I don't want *my will* to be her will. I wish to stay with the stars."

I recall hearing that phrase: *My will is her will, and she is all that matters.*

But before I can respond, Elijah asks, "You want to stay with the stars? What does that mean?" Slowly, he inches away from the door, closer to the girl. "Do you not have stars where you're from?"

He didn't see the pitch-black world through the doorway at the back of the cave like I did. There was no plant life, no moon or stars in the sky, and the ground was covered in fiery cracks. I couldn't imagine any living thing surviving in those conditions.

The girl shakes her head, pale lips pursed. "The Under Realm is not like your world. It's a realm beyond."

"Beyond?" I ask.

She opens her mouth to answer, but then slowly closes it. Her attention drifts to the fireplace, where wood crackles as the flames of the dying fire burn through what's left of the logs.

After a long moment, Elijah knocks on the wood table. "Hey! Answer her. What do you mean when you say 'a realm beyond'?"

"I'm having trouble remembering," she answers, then quickly adds with surprising eagerness, "I may not recollect how I know we're from different realms, but I know it's something I sense within. When I create a doorway, my energy drains depending on the distance, especially when opening a portal to where humans live. That toll is much greater than when I open a passage through objects or walls." She gestures toward the rocks on the floor.

I'm struggling to wrap my mind around the idea of there being other realms, but I've seen her world firsthand. So, for now, I'll give her the benefit of believing she's speaking the truth.

"Okay," I tell her.

"Okay, what?" Elijah asks, coming around to face me. He searches my expression for an explanation. I'm not sure what he sees, but his eyes go wide as realization dawns on him. Shaking his head, he blurts, "Oh, no! No, no, no. She can't stay here! No way!" He then tells the Shade girl, "Look, I feel bad you're wanting to escape this Under Realm place, but you can't stay here. Your kind hunt and kill our people."

She says nothing. Her gaze searches over him, from head to feet. "You are a strong one."

"See! Once a Shade, always a Shade," he says, shuffling away. "They only take the strong. She's too much of a risk, Adele. She's got to go!"

A crow caws from the tree in the front yard, and I quickly move to stand in front of the window, hoping to block the pesky bird from seeing inside the cottage. We need to hurry the interrogation along before Trevor shows up. Wanting to get back on topic, I ask, "What do you do with those you take?"

The black smudges I'd seen beneath her eyes yesterday, during the attack, are completely blended in with the thin layer of dirt covering her cheeks. "Her will has always been about building numbers," the Shade girl says. "We're sent to collect the strong as offerings to her allies, the demon spirits. When one of the dark spirits inhabits a living creature, they become a Reborn. And the Under Realm queen prefers her Reborns to be strong soldiers rather than skittering insects or useless rodents."

I try to imagine the villagers of Bricen being sacrificed—their bodies being occupied by these demon spirits. All these years. All those people, including Kit, Alya, and everyone else they've kidnapped…my mum. Every single one of them is over in that realm, walking around possessed by a demon.

My insides flare with rage. How can she stand there telling us with such calmness—with such indifference—about her role in all this?

"My will is her will." The Shade girl repeats the mantra I'd heard while falling through that strange, endless dark sky. I wanted to let those words sink in—to feel the happiness that came with them.

Then I remember that's how she gets you. Whoever *she* is? The moment I separated myself from the warm happiness, I regained self-control. Those who embrace her lure must become her mindless servants, seeking out the strong to grow her numbers.

The thought makes my stomach turn.

Staring at the girl, I can't help but wonder if the Shades are prisoners as well. Their wills are forced to carry out the wishes of whoever is controlling them.

"My sister," Elijah cuts into my thoughts. He moves closer—closer than he's ever been to the girl. "You took her yesterday. You're telling me they're putting a demon inside her?" His hands are shaking.

She nods.

He paces the small space, raking his fingers through his short curls. Then he drags his hands down his face and mutters, "This can't be real. They're putting a demon inside Kit." When his hands are at his sides again, he lurches toward me. "Adele, we have to do something!"

"There might be nothing we can do." I hate being so blunt but giving him any kind of hope will only make matters worse. He opens his mouth to argue, but I raise my hand to stop him. "Hold on. Let's hear what else… Sorry, do you have a name?"

"Rune."

Rune. The woman's words resurface in my mind. *And now it seems you have something of mine. Bring her to me and all will be forgiven. For you… For Rune… And for your mother.* Rune is what the woman wants. Information I may be able to use later, but for now I return my attention to the question at hand. "Okay, Rune. Can you explain how they put one of these demons inside a person?"

"I don't know. The offerings we bring go into the mountain fortress where Queen Merigoth rules. Then, when they come out, they're Reborn."

"Merigoth? Is that whose 'will is your will'? This Under Realm queen?"

Rune nods. "Please don't send me back. I want to help. I want to stay." She stares at us, her skin glistening beneath the layer of dirt covering her body. Her whole appearance looks as if she's been living in the wild. The black strips of fabric wrapping her body are dingy and worn.

Ignoring the crow cawing outside the cottage, I inhale a deep breath and reel in the fury boiling through my veins. There's no point in taking out my anger on this girl. That's something General Onica would do to whatever poor sap stood too close when relaying bad news. Instead, I focus on what I need from her—answers.

"I'd like to know more about you and your people…the Shades. Have you always lived in the Under Realm?"

Rune looks to the ceiling. "I don't think so. All I remember is waking up in a dirt pit surrounded by a dark world, unsure of how I got there. But I knew something wasn't right—something was missing. Then, shortly after I woke, I heard the most alluring voice floating into my mind. From that day forth, my thoughts faded, and her will became my will."

"The stars," Elijah says. When the girl gives him a puzzled look, he repeats, "The stars. It's what was missing."

"I believe you're right," Rune agrees. "I'd forgotten about the stars until that day when I first opened a doorway into your realm. As soon as I stepped through, something felt off. I searched the trees, clouds, and sky for answers. Over time, I came to realize it was the stars that called to me, although I didn't understand why, and still don't. And to make matters worse, I forget everything the moment I return to the Under Realm. It's only when my head is clear that I can recall these things." Picking at the dirt beneath her fingernails, she looks to me and asks, "Do the stars call to you?"

I wish they did. "No. I feel nothing when the stars come out at night."

Elijah opens the wood panel covering the back window set between the two oversized cupboards. Sunlight stretches across the open space, over the table and along the rocks piled on the floor. Rune walks closer, moving past Elijah to the open window. I can't see her face, but her head is tilted up, hands clutching the wood frame of the window.

"It sounds like you were taken too?" I suggest, glancing over my shoulder and looking out the front window. That pesky crow is still out there. It releases a string of *caw*s, as if it knows I'm hiding something from it. Though, I highly doubt it could fly off and tell Trevor about Rune being here, which is why I don't protest the back window being open. But there's something strange about Trevor and his crows that has me holding my position and blocking the window.

Continuing, I add, "Do you think it's possible you were taken from somewhere, brought to the Under Realm, and turned into something else…like the villagers?"

She scratches her wrist and shrugs, still admiring the outdoors behind the cottage. "You mean like a Reborn?"

"No," I say, then clarify, "Not Reborn, but maybe you and the others were turned *into* Shades."

Rune glances over her shoulder, away from the open window. "I believe we were. All the Shades were. The only true Shade is Marcellus. He's one of the original three Shades born in the Under Realm, created to serve Merigoth." She returns to basking in the sunlight, holding a hand in a sunbeam and studying the effect on her skin. "The rest of us might not have been born Shades, but we became Shades—servants to Queen Merigoth—the moment we woke up in those dirt holes—the moment *she* claimed our minds."

Elijah moves to my side. He's a bit too close, but since he's not touching me, I let his proximity slide. With one hand cupped over his mouth, he whispers, "Now I'm torn; I almost feel bad for her!"

Nodding, I understand his predicament. Though, in the end, she's not really our concern. We've got bigger problems. "I would try to help," I say, turning my hands over, "but looking into your mind didn't work out so well."

The girl abandons the open window and approaches me. Her gaze fixes on my hands. "I'm curious to know how one of the three original Shades ended up living among the humans."

Her words hit me hard, like a blow to the gut.

It's not possible. I mean…I know I'm different…but…no. It's not possible.

To come from that place…a place consumed by darkness and evil. A place where humans don't live, and monsters are born.

"What are you saying?" Elijah asks Rune while staring at me. "I've known Adele practically my whole life. She's not a monster."

I gasp, the air catching in my throat. I can barely spit out my words. "Y-you're lying! I am not like you!" I shuffle backward, bumping into the small table beneath the window. The pillar candle wobbles but doesn't fall. "Never call me that again! Do you hear me? I've never set foot in your world, or, or—"

"Hurt people," she finishes, her voice calm and emotionless. It feels as though my heart has stopped.

Rune goes on, "From what I understand, Merigoth created the three original Shades for vengeance." Her gaze falters again, drifting to the floor, and she stumbles on her next words. "But for what? I cannot recall." Then, in a more confident tone, she explains, "She doesn't share her plans with anyone but Marcellus."

Every word twists my gut tighter and tighter. My fists ball at my sides and I want to punch her in the face—to silence her from telling these lies before the entire world thinks I'm a monster from a nightmare realm. I covertly glance at Elijah, who quickly looks away. His gaze focuses on the floor.

It can't be true. I mean, I know there's some kind of evil coursing through my veins, but...to be born in another realm—to be created for vengeance—that can't be right.

I've always thought I was cursed.

But it's not a curse.

I was born this way.

I was born a monster.

Pressing the heels of my gloved hands to my forehead, I force myself to get it together. This is what I came to Bricen for—the truth. I just wasn't expecting to hear that I'm not even human—that I come from another world. It does explain why I feel so different inside. And why I can do horrible and invasive things to anyone I touch. But still…this is not what I was expecting to discover.

"These original Shades…" Elijah moves alongside the wood table, closer to Rune. "They're not human, are they?"

I face the window, unable to look at Rune as she answers. Outside, Trevor's crow has flown away. Good. Pesky bird is nothing but trouble. From behind, Rune answers, "I don't know. There are stories, about a human woman living in the Under Realm under Merigoth's protection. The queen of the Under Realm blessed the woman with her blood, which ultimately turned her into something other than human. The woman eventually gave birth to triplets."

"The original three Shades," Elijah says.

"Yes. I can't say how much of you is human and how much is demon, but I can sense you are one of the three. You are strong, like Marcellus."

It was only three moons ago that I lay in my bed at Castle Forge, planning my escape to Bricen and hoping to find out the truth about who…or what…I am. I'd never heard of Shades, Reborns, or the Under Realm, and as far as I know, no one outside of Harvesgrove has either. General Onica would've brought such information to the attention of her council if she'd discovered a formidable force comparable to her own. Yet, the Shades have been terrorizing the eastern lands of Harvesgrove all these years. How long before they expand into other territories, collecting more offerings for their queen? I don't want to believe Rune, but I can't dismiss the seriousness of what could cross over into our world—a horde of Reborns.

A sudden scrape of wood against wood, followed by a string of curses, cuts through my thoughts. Spinning away from the front window, Elijah's scrambling to clean up the burlap sack of flour he spilled at the end of the table. While scooping up the grainy powder, he says, "Okay, well, that definitely brings up more questions." When he's done cleaning the mess, he leans against the table again, careful not to knock over the flour, and asks, "Is there anything we should know about Marcellus—besides him being one of the first three of his kind?"

Elijah glances my way. It's a quick look, but his gaze lingers long enough for me to see something in his eyes. Fear? Shock? No. It's sadness.

Well, I don't want his pity, because it's not true. I'm not a Shade—the original kind or whatever version Rune is. There's no way that I share the same blood as those that took my mum from me.

"Marcellus has the ability to command others with a single touch," Rune explains.

That must be the Shade who compelled Kit.

"What happened to the other two original Shades?" I demand, unable to help the anger rolling off my tongue.

"I don't know what happened. We're not to speak of the past. Merigoth forbids it."

I cross the room in two wide strides and stand inches from her face. The muscles in my jaw clench, and my breaths come fast. I want to scream, but instead I say in a low, demanding tone, "You must know something. Rumors. Anything?"

This close to her, I can see a faint ring of gold circling the outer part of her pupils. She barely reacts to my advances, but she does look to Elijah for a long moment before turning her attention back on me. Eventually she nods. "Okay. So, there might have been rumors that the woman who birthed the original three betrayed Merigoth, escaping the Under Realm with two of the Shade babies."

Elijah turns his attention to me. "Do you think she's talking about Sara—your mum?"

I back away from Rune. I wish we were outside or somewhere with more space where I can walk around and think. This cottage feels as if it's growing smaller by the minute.

While Elijah and Rune quietly talk about the Under Realm, I try and rationalize the rumor of a woman stealing two Shade babies. Was I one of those babies? I don't want to believe that my mum was the woman and that she has demon blood running through her veins. Mum was one of the kindest souls in all of Harvesgrove. She helped people with her healing sessions… Not hurt them.

"Adele?" Elijah shifts his position against the table so he's facing me.

Shaking my head, I tell him, "I don't know. I don't know anything anymore."

Elijah makes a *hmm* sound, then asks, "Anything else?"

"I only remember waking up in a dirt hole," Rune says. "Where we came from is a mystery. Marcellus constantly reminds us that our lives before were meaningless, and that we should embrace the bliss Merigoth offers. She's given us purpose—to make a difference in the Under Realm as well as other worlds. But now that my head is clear, and my thoughts are my own, I want to stay here and discover the truth about where I came from. I want to know why the stars call to me."

Elijah crosses his arms over his chest, chin tucking beneath his red scarf. "This is not what I was expecting to hear."

"Nor I," I say, weighing our options with the abundance of information Rune has given us. Suddenly, it all sinks into place. Everything Rune has told us. About the Under Realm. About Merigoth, Marcellus, and the Shades. About my mum. And about me.

There's no more denying it.

I'm a Shade—a monster.

My heart pounds against my chest, and the room spins. Swaying, I slam my hand on the table to catch myself from falling. Elijah tries to steady me, but I push him away. "Don't touch me!"

My muscles hum with rage and my head throbs, as I realize I was created to do exactly what General Onica had me doing. But then Selene's face appears in my mind. The way she laughs, and how she rolls her eyes at almost everything I say. Her kindness and generosity are qualities monsters don't possess.

But picturing her face eases my anger, so I hold on to that. My one true friend who never cared about the pain I caused others. I can't bear to think of Selene's reaction when she learns the truth about what I really am.

Elijah closes the wood panel to the back window, taking the last of the sunlight from the room. Surprisingly, he tells Rune, "We'll try to help you, but you'll have to stay out of sight." I glance at him curiously; what changed?

"Are you sure," I ask Rune, voice trembling, "that I'm a Shade? One of these original three?" Uncertainty roils in my gut.

"I have no reason to lie to you."

A hole of despair forms in my core. I can feel it spreading, weighing on my existence.

"Adele," Elijah calls to me, careful not to get too close. "What do we do now?"

I have no answer for him. I only want to run far from here. To live in solitude away from everyone, never to hurt anyone ever again.

"I need a minute," I tell him.

A loud knock drums at the front door.

Elijah frowns. "I don't think we have a minute."

CHAPTER 16

ADELE

Elijah's talking to someone outside the front door, but I can't see who. It doesn't matter—nothing matters anymore. I came to Bricen to find out why I am the way I am. And now I know.

Sinking onto the edge of the bed, I stare at my hands. These hands will only ever know torture. To cause others to suffer.

I am a monster. An actual creature of evil. There is no curse. I was born—created—for vengeance.

But how did I come to be in the Human Realm? And was the woman who stole the two Shade babies my mum or some other woman?

It's all too much. I drop my head into my hands and squeeze my temples until an ache throbs inside my skull, taking precedence over my thoughts and senses. I keep pressing until the pain is too much.

The second I lift my head from my hands, everything Elijah and I learned…about the Under Realm, what's happening to those taken from the village, and the truth about me…all comes flooding back.

My gaze is drawn to my bag sitting on top of the table and how easy it would be to escape the moment by downing a giant swig of my tonic. To let the others handle the situation while I just lie in my mum's bed and sleep the minutes away.

Out of the corner of my eye, I catch the Shade girl staring at me. We hold each other's gaze for several heartbeats until she breaks the silence. "You might have been born Shade, but that doesn't mean you are Shade. You were not brought up as Marcellus was. You were raised around humans."

Tears well under my eyes, and I quickly wipe them away with my sleeve before they make their escape. The last thing I need right now is anyone's pity or grief. With a sniffle, I straighten my shoulders and tell her, "That may be true, but it doesn't change who I am or the pain I inflict on others."

Giving her words more thought, I realize she's right. Even if the last eight years of my upbringing were around humans just as evil as the Shades, I've escaped that life. And I refuse to be controlled by anyone in any realm ever again. My only option, after helping Bricen, is to strike out on my own. I'll have my freedom, and those I care about will be safe from my touch.

Still sitting on the end of my mum's bed, I reach up and graze the edges of the rubies set in the borrowed hairpin. It pains me to know I'm breaking my promise to return, but it's better this way. Selene deserves to be in the company of those who can protect her from monsters like me.

The iron latch on the front door closes, and Elijah faces me. Rune has returned to the back window where the panel is open again. She stands in the sunlight, looking out at the trees behind Lauren's cottage.

Wood scrapes along the floor. Elijah sets a chair in front of me and sits down. "That was Magdala. I don't know if you remember her, but her—"

"I remember her. And her parents," I explain, pressing the heel of my palm to the center of my forehead. The soft, worn leather of my glove rubs against my skin. It wasn't until my abilities manifested over in Fayatin that I started wearing gloves. And now I rarely take them off.

I look at the door and think of Magdala. The last memory I have of her is when Kit and I were out on the grassy common area of the Green, watching Magdala learn how to walk. From the glimpses I saw walking up to the cottage last night, the Green has lost its lushness. Now, it's more dirt than grass. But back then it was the perfect place to train a young tot to walk.

My mind still lingering on the memory, I tell Elijah, "Her mum worked the gardens, while her dad was Bricen's carpenter, if I remember correctly."

He nods, then sits straighter. The wood chair creaks from the shift of his weight. "Yeah, they were."

"Were?"

"Her mum still tends to the gardens, but her pa… Well, he was taken a few months after you disappeared."

Rune casually glances over her shoulder at us before returning her attention to the trees. Outside, the birds are singing and the sun is shining, but inside, my rage is brewing. Magdala's father, taken too? I remind myself not to lash out at Rune. It's not her fault, especially if she was taken from her home and enchanted to serve this Merigoth queen. A person…or some other creature…that we still know little about.

"Magdala's a good kid," Elijah continues. He adjusts the scarf around his neck, then fidgets with the frayed ends.

"Where did you get that scarf?" I ask.

"My mum, before she was…" His words trail off, and he quickly reverts to our previous conversation. "Anyway, Magdala's braver than she looks for her age. She's saved many villagers on more than one occasion. And she's fast. Never been caught or seen by the Shades."

"Merigoth has no use for children," Rune interrupts without turning away from the open window.

"Why's that?" Elijah asks. His fingers stop fiddling with his scarf.

From outside, a warm sunbeam shines in, outlining the girl's gloomy body. She raises a hand and slowly passes it through the sunlight as she explains, "We've strict orders to ignore the children. Not until they've grown stronger."

Elijah abruptly stands, the legs of the chair scraping along the wood floor. For a second, I assume he's had enough and is about to march right out of the cottage, but he doesn't. He stands there, rubbing his hand over his short hair, grumbling words I can't decipher. After a long moment, he spins and faces me with a pained expression. "I'm not sure what to do with that knowledge. She's basically telling us it's only a matter of time before they come for the children."

I forgot how emotional Elijah gets. When we were younger, he'd take everything so seriously, believing anything Kit and I would tell him. Well, more Kit than me. After a while, it wasn't fun watching him cry at every jest we played on him.

"Take it for what it is," I tell him. "That for the time being, the young ones of Bricen are safe."

He doesn't break eye contact with me, but his shoulders sag in defeat. Part of me still wants to run away and let them deal with the problem of the Shades. But it's the other half—the better half—of me that's insisting I stay and help. I adjust my seat. The blue quilt beneath me twists under my legs.

"What now?" Elijah asks, nodding toward the back of the room. "Do you still want me to walk the barrier wall? I don't think we should leave her here alone. That's if you're planning to go and talk to Trevor."

"I am, and no. You should probably stay here with her. We can't have her wandering off." Narrowing my eyes, I add, "And I don't trust you to talk to Trevor."

"That's probably a good plan. Lying isn't one of my strengths." His gaze flicks over to Rune. "Adele, we have to help her." My silence has him shifting his weight from one hip to the other. Then he leans closer, a hand cupping his mouth, and whispers, "You weren't thinking of sending her back to that place, where you? Because—"

"I didn't say I was," I cut him off, not caring if she hears. "We've got bigger things to worry about than what to do with her. The good thing is, if Trevor discovers her here, at least we can explain she's not a threat."

Elijah straightens and nods in agreement.

Chewing the inside of my cheek, I think about what to do next. My first thought is to run. To grab my bag, bow, and quiver and leave. I mean, I'm doomed to live in solitude, anyway. Why not get a head start while I can?

But then I think of Aunt Lauren lying on the floor in Goslings. If there's any way we can help her, make her more comfortable until the inevitable happens, then that'll be my parting gift before leaving. What I witnessed up in Noviska, Aunt Lauren healing that boy with a drop of her blood, still confounds me. But the second her consciousness slipped, I knew I lost all hope of discovering what she was doing up north and how she could heal that boy with her blood. I came to Bricen seeking the truth about who…or what…I am, and Rune has enlightened me with those answers. Now, it's about tying up loose ends and accepting my future fate has laid out for me.

Elijah leans against the wood table and says, "You're doing that thing you used to do whenever you were trying to come up with an excuse not to do whatever wild idea my sister was trying to talk you into." Crossing his arms over his white tunic, he continues, "But you know Kit. She always got her way, and we always got roped into some mischievous plan."

I think back to those days, he's right. I often tried to come up with a reason or two for why we couldn't go or do whatever it was Kit wanted us to do. She never bought into any of my excuses.

"Change of plans," I say, standing from the bed. "You go and find Trevor. Tell him I'll come and see him soon. I want to check in on my aunt first." What I don't add is that I want to say my goodbyes.

"What? No, we can't leave her here alone."

We both look to Rune, who is still gawking at the trees outside. "I highly doubt she'll cause any problems."

Rune slowly turns to face us. If she hadn't blinked, I would've thought the girl was frozen in time. She stands like one of General Onica's soldiers. The closer I look at her garb, I can't help but wonder how uncomfortable she must be wrapped up in those worn linens.

I'm about to repeat my instructions to Elijah, for him to go and talk with Trevor, when Rune says, "I can help with the wounded."

"No!" Elijah and I say in unison.

"I can be helpful."

Elijah steps closer to Rune and asks, "How?" I'm still in awe at how fast Elijah has become comfortable around Rune. It was only thirty minutes ago he was flush against the wall, ready to defend himself with a rolling pin. I can't imagine any Fayatin warming up to a stranger, or enemy for that matter, like Elijah has with the Shade girl. "How?" he repeats.

"Your villagers were attacked by demon spirits, yes? Merigoth sent them as a distraction, reducing the time needed for your people to hide."

How did we not think of asking her about a way to help Aunt Lauren and the others earlier? Ugh. I'd make a horrible healer. I don't know how Mum did it all those years.

He exhales an exasperated breath, grumbling out, "I don't like it." Then turns to me. "What do you think?"

"I'm still deciding," I say with a subtle tilt of my head, searching for a sign that she's toying with us. But there's nothing. No hint of trickery or deception. And something in my gut tells me she's not lying. "We'll take her to see the injured. If there's a chance she can heal them, then we have to let her try."

Elijah scratches the side of his face and sighs. "I don't know, Adele. That sounds like a bad idea, letting her walk around."

"I want to help," Rune repeats.

"Yeah, I heard you the first time," he says in a defeated tone. Then he walks over to the front window and checks outside. "How are you planning to sneak a Shade around the village?"

Moving closer to Rune, I inspect her face. The prominent features of her jawline and cheekbones only appear sharp because of the layers of dirt and grime hiding her face. I imagine beneath all that dirt Rune looks no older than Elijah or me. But her looks may be misleading because when I touched her earlier, the bombardment of memories was far too much for someone so young. Whatever she is, I suspect her kind ages differently than humans.

I also notice the black smudges below her eyes have faded. "When was the last time you bathed?" I sniff the surrounding air. She smells like an old campfire.

Rune narrows her eyes, then mimics the sniffing gesture at me. "What's a bathed?"

"You've never washed? With water?" I ask, one brow raised. That almost sounds impossible. Everyone—even animals—bathe.

"There is no water in the Under Realm. Only fire and rock and thunder and dirt and…"

"Okay, we get your point. No one bathes in your world," I cut her off. "Sounds like a lovely place to live."

Elijah stops looking out the window and turns to me. "You're seriously going to let her parade around the village?"

With a not-so-subtle eye roll, I ignore him and walk past Rune to open the linen cupboard. Even though I'm eager to be on my way, cleaning up Rune and getting her into Goslings to see if there's anything she can do for the fallen is worth a few extra hours. After that, I'll decide what to do with her. Maybe I'll take her north until she finds her own way or something. But I can't leave her here in Bricen.

"If I recall, there's a creek behind the village?" I ask, picking out some clean clothes.

"Yes, but it's a ways back, and we've got the barrier wall blocking our path. We'd have to go out the front gate or sneak through my secret hatch. Either option is a bad idea since it's daytime."

Looking at Rune, I say, "Oh, I think we can manage. Isn't that right, Rune?"

She nods. "I can be helpful. I can get us through the barrier wall."

Finishing up, I close the cupboard doors and tell Elijah, "See! Everything will be fine."

"I highly doubt that," he says with a groan as we make our way outside.

CHAPTER 17

ADELE

After Rune makes a temporary passageway through the barrier wall, we head east, away from Bricen. The forest is dense with trees, much more than the stretch of forest we walked to the cave. It isn't long until we reach a large clearing. A gentle breeze tickling the tops of the tall grass.

Creating the passage through the barrier took a toll on the girl, but she insists it's not as bad as when she creates doorways between realms or across great distances.

Down the clearing's center, the grass has been sheared, creating a path for us to walk. I linger behind, letting Rune walk with Elijah. He hasn't stopped asking questions. Her answers are short and vague, as if she's unsure or unable to remember. When we reach the creek, it's bigger than I recall. There's a sizable pool that wasn't there when we were kids.

I'm taking in the creek's size while Elijah helps Rune climb down a shallow rock side. He holds out a hand to me, but I ignore him and jump down on my own.

"Almost there," I tell Rune, taking the lead and walking toward the creek.

Rune's admiring a flock of birds passing by above, chin to the sky. "They fly like the demon spirits."

"They're called birds," Elijah explains. "Why don't the demon spirits attack you or change the Shades into the Reborns?"

I slow my pace so I can hear her answer.

"I'm not sure. They've never tried to inhibit any Shade I know of. Though, the Reborns do—as we all do—whatever Merigoth wishes."

Trailing the side of the creek is a mixture of coarse sand and patchy grass, sprinkled with gray rocks of various sizes. The creek's current gurgles steadily downstream. The pool that's formed along the creek is a considerable size. I would've loved to swim and play in this as a kid. Following the stream, I see how it's formed. Pointing, I tell Elijah, "There's your problem. You've got beavers."

"Trevor's given strict instructions to leave the beavers alone." Elijah gestures across the glistening pool to a giant pile of logs and sticks spackled with mud. Then, with one pointed finger, he directs our attention to the right of the dam, where there's a handmade rivulet. "I created this alternative route for the flow of water to continue downstream. That way, the beavers keep their dam, and we don't get stale water." He then says to Rune, "You can wash up here. The water's clean and not too deep."

Searching the horizon, I don't see any threats or reason to be on guard. There's an oversized flat rock off to the left. The perfect spot for me to sit and wait while she cleans up. "Rune." When her eyes find me, I continue, "When you're done washing and there's no dirt left, come and find me on that rock over there."

Rune takes a few steps into the water before we both shout for her to stop. "You're going to have to take off…" I wave a finger to the black strips of fabric wrapping her body. "…whatever that is."

Elijah walks away, toward the forest we came from. "I'll try and see what I can forage from the forest for us to eat, giving you ladies some privacy."

"Such a gentleman," I say under my breath.

After climbing the rocky embankment, he disappears behind the line of trees, and when I turn back to Rune, she's stripped free of her garb and is shoulder-deep in the water. While she's wading in the pool, I walk over to the flat rock. It's twice the size of my double bed back at Castle Forge. Lying back, I soak up the warm sun. It feels nice, comforting and soothing my restless nerves.

Since this morning, the overcast has cleared up, leaving only a few lingering stray clouds in a blue sky. Yesterday's rain clouds have moved west, toward Fayatin. Thinking about Fayatin has me wondering if Barclay made it to Castle Forge. That bird better have delivered my message. Storm or no storm, I need Selene to know I'm all right and to send word back letting me know she's well.

Lifting my shoulders and propping myself up on my elbows, I check downstream. Rune is neck-deep, her shaved head tilting down as she stares into the clear water. Satisfied she's not causing any mischief—or drowning—I return to basking in the sun.

With my eyes closed, I listen to the sounds of the forest. The birds chirp from above, the creek gurgles to my side, and a gentle breeze rustles the leaves in the trees from somewhere behind me. I wish the serene sounds of nature were enough to keep the onslaught of noisy questions about my past from surfacing in my mind, but they aren't. I've circled back to the one person I'm hoping can give me answers—Aunt Lauren. If Rune can heal her, then I'll get some clear answers.

That's *if* Rune can heal her.

How exactly is Rune planning on healing the villagers? She can create holes in floors and walls, but what's she going to do to help my aunt and the others? A mosquito lands on my arm and I smack it. I wipe the smears of blood and remnants of the tiny insect off my glove and onto the rock.

Blood.

Aunt Lauren healed that boy in Noviska with her blood.

Will Rune's blood do the same?

Resting my hands on my stomach, I close my eyes and think about who else might know more about my mum.

Trevor.

That old man is definitely hiding something. I mean, how has he aged so much in less than a period of ten years?

He wasn't a young man back then, but he wasn't such an old man, either. Yet now he is *older than old*. And he knows things—about me and my mum—that make me wonder what other secrets he's hiding.

"I'm done." Rune's voice cuts into my thoughts, and I quickly sit up on the rock. The sun shines from behind, outlining her now-clothed body with golden beams. When she kneels by my side, my mouth gapes. She's wearing one of Aunt Lauren's white tunics, the bottom tucked into a knee-length brown skirt. Her skin is flawless, completely free of the layers of dirt that were hiding her soft, round features. No more hard edges to her cheeks or jawline. It's as if she's a whole new person. The gray cloud fogging her eyes has cleared up, revealing vibrant brown eyes. There's a soft ring of gold circling each pupil. It's barely noticeable, but since I'm so close and staring right into her eyes, I can see it. My gaze drifts up to the top of her head and I gawk at her full head of brown hair.

"You have hair!" How did she grow her hair so fast?

She sits on the rock and rubs a hand through the short dark-brown locks that are sticking out in layers. "I do."

I slide my knees under me and use them to push myself up. Standing over her, I say, "We shouldn't have a problem getting you into Goslings now." She admires her skirt, dragging her hands over the woolen fabric. "Do you like the clothes?"

"Different" is all she says as she continues to fuss with the details of her simple, borrowed garments.

When she lifts the bottom of her skirt, I yell, "Whoa!" grabbing the hem before quickly bringing it down over her legs. "No need to show the world what you've got under there."

"Right." Her eyes light up and a friendly smile appears. I turn to see what's caught her attention. It's Elijah walking out of the forest.

"Hey, there!" he says, carrying a handful of berries. Getting comfortable on the oversized flat stone next to Rune, he drops the blackberries between them. I crouch to one knee, scoop up three of the largest berries, and pop them into my mouth. They're sweet and tart, bringing back memories of me, Kit, and Elijah playing out here for hours, eating blackberries whenever we got hungry.

Elijah is fixated on Rune's new hair. He's not short of questions. The girl shrugs and tells him, "I saw Adele's hair and thought about how I'd like hair too. Then, somehow, I had hair!"

"That's impossible," I say through a mouthful of berries. "You can't magically wish for something and *poof*, it happens." I stand and step off the rock. We're going to have to get back to Bricen soon.

"The Shades must possess magic," Elijah says, leaning forward and lightly touching her hair. She doesn't seem to mind him touching her. If anything, her smile grows.

He withdraws his hand and looks over at me and asks, "Do you have any magic?" There's a short pause before he adds, "Besides trapping people inside their own mind."

Rune gets to her feet, following me off the rock. "You can control the minds of others?"

Shaking my head, I clarify, "I can see into a person's mind, and…" I look at Elijah, then Rune. "And I can force them to believe they're reliving one of their memories—usually something they fear. Those are the easiest to manipulate."

"You *are* like Marcellus. You can command a person's will."

"But I'm not like Marcellus." I snap. "I can't command people or brainwash them to follow my orders." Which makes me realize Marcellus is much stronger than me. I'd surely lose if I were ever to face him.

Rune holds a blackberry to her mouth and before she eats it, she says, "If you can control their minds, then you can control their actions."

Rubbing the back of his neck, Elijah says, "That's scary. No one should have that kind of power."

I say nothing because he's right. If what Rune is saying is true, and I do have the ability to control people's actions, then that is information I don't ever want the general discovering. Even if I never return to Fayatin, if the general ever discovered this new ability, she'd send out search parties to find me and drag me back, regardless of the peace treaties in place.

Wanting to change the subject, I hand Rune the pair of leather boots I brought. "You should put these on too."

She takes them and holds them up at eye level with pinched fingers.

Elijah reaches for one and says, "They go on your feet." He lifts his foot and shows her his boot. Then he gestures for her foot, and she obliges, slipping her foot inside.

As he's lacing the second boot up, Rune presses her hand to his face. Her smile falters, and she lets her hand drop from his cheek. "You lost your sister."

Elijah's fingers freeze over Rune's boot. "Yes. She was taken yesterday."

"There's no coming back once a Reborn takes possession."

I watch his Adam's apple bob as he swallows. He finishes tying the knot, stands, and walks away toward the forest.

Rune also stands, then looks at me. "I have no reason to lie."

"I know. But not everything needs to be said out loud, especially if it's obvious. And heartbreaking."

She watches Elijah getting farther from us. Then, after a moment, I say, "Come on. Let's get back and check in on the injured. It should be easier now that you don't look so much like a Shade."

Once we're in the woods again, Rune jogs to catch up to Elijah. I can't hear what they're saying, but he seems to accept whatever apology the Shade is offering. Five minutes into our trek, and they're smiling and talking as if they are old friends catching up.

I trail behind in solitude. This is the future that awaits me. To travel the path alone while staying on the outskirts of everyone else's happiness.

But my happiness isn't what concerns me at the moment. Whatever enchantment Merigoth cast over Rune might be wearing off, but that doesn't mean she isn't a threat. I know—like General Onica, who would search all of Fayatin for my whereabouts—that the queen of the Under Realm will eventually come for Rune. And possibly me, too.

CHAPTER 18

Once we're back inside the village, I let Elijah lead our small procession across the Green, which is nothing more than an open ground filled with sad patches of dry grass surrounded by dirt. Now that Rune's grown some magical hair, I'm not as worried about anyone seeing her. Any questions that arise can be answered with a simple 'she's a traveler looking for shelter for the night' or something like that.

Rune stops at Goslings' porch steps, staring up at the front door. I continue up, leaving her and Elijah at the base of the stairs. "Come on, what are you waiting for?"

Elijah moves to Rune's side. "Are you feeling all right?"

There's a long moment before she looks to the sky, then to him. "I feel like I've woken from a long sleep. I know I was here yesterday, but everything looks different now. More colorful." She dips her gaze, a slight scowl forming. "Though, I'm still unable to remember my life before the Under Realm."

Bricen is anything but colorful. If only she could have seen the village before her kind attacked.

"Give it time," Elijah says, comforting her with a palm pressed to her back. He waves his free hand toward the steps. "How about we go inside?"

She nods and follows him up into the tavern. Before I head inside, I look out from the porch and scan the surrounding area to see who's around, but the village is silent. There aren't even guards watching the front gate. A loud *caw* startles me. I go for my dagger tucked inside my waistband but don't follow through because I realize it's one of Trevor's pets. The silky black bird swoops low and flies behind the tavern.

Well, if Trevor didn't know where we were, he soon would.

I hurry into Goslings. Elijah is behind the bar, setting a large metal pitcher on the counter while Rune kneels by one of the villagers.

"We have to hurry. I'm pretty sure Trevor will be here soon."

"You saw him?" Elijah asks me while ladling water into the pitcher from a large barrel by the back door.

"Not exactly," I say, then look at the injured. All six lie as if sleeping, including Aunt Lauren. Three of the unconscious people are elderly women with gray hair, another one is a delicate-looking young woman with barely any muscle on her, and the last one is a man who's missing a foot. I can see why the Shades haven't already taken any of these people. However, my aunt, who is someone I'd consider "strong," defied being captured. What hidden talent does she harbor to evade detection? Or maybe there's an altogether different explanation safeguarding her well-being.

Rune pivots from the frail young woman to my aunt. While tracing a hovering finger over the dark red veins sprouting out from the deep gashes, Rune tells us, "She's been afflicted by the demon spirits."

"They all have." I move closer. "Do you know how to heal them?"

She nods. "But this one's different. She admires the stars. They speak to her."

Aunt Lauren did love the stars. She loved everything about the sky—birds, clouds, even the wind that swept through the cottage on breezy days. But maybe there was something more specific—something that has to do with her healing that boy up in Noviska.

"Did you fill the pitcher with water like I asked?" Rune looks to Elijah, who's putting the lid back on the barrel of water. He nods, then moves behind the bar counter.

I crouch on the other side of my aunt and ask Rune, "You said she's different. What did you mean by that?"

Lifting my aunt's arm, Rune gently twists it to get a better look at the deep scratches. "I don't know exactly, but I recognize these markings." She points to the red veins visible beneath my aunt's skin. "There was this one time when one of the Shades got caught up in a flock of demon spirits. He had the same afflictions." Rune gestures to the others lying about the tavern and explains, "The contact from the demon spirits isn't visible on humans, but..." Her voice trails off as she looks at my aunt again. "Very visible on nonhumans."

So, Aunt Lauren isn't human.

Maybe she's the woman who stole me away from the Under Realm. No. That's not likely since the woman from Rune's story who stole the Shade babies was supposedly once human. If my aunt isn't the woman who brought me to the Human Realm, then maybe she's like Rune—whatever Rune was before her enslavement as one of Merigoth's Shades. But since Rune can't remember her life before the Under Realm and Aunt Lauren is unconscious, I'm not sure how I'm going to confirm my suspicions that they come from the same place.

Elijah hands Rune the metal pitcher full of water and asks, "Is this how they healed the Shade man who got attacked by the flock of demon spirits? With water?" He kneels on the floor by Aunt Lauren's feet. He's holding a tall wooden cup in his hand.

With the pitcher on the floor next to her, Rune looks to me and asks, "May I borrow your blade?"

Hesitantly, I withdraw my knife from my waistband, grasp the steel blade with my gloved hand, and hand it over. Rune takes the knife by the hilt and quickly swipes the sharp edge across the tip of her finger. Instantly, red blood seeps out. She moves her finger over the pitcher, letting several drops fall into the water. The fourth drop of blood struggles to fall from her finger, and with a shake, it finally breaks away. "I think that's all I'm able to get." She wipes her finger on her skirt. The blood blends in with the brown woolen fabric. And when she brings her finger back up, her skin has healed.

"We bleed, but not for long," she tells us, lifting the pitcher and giving it a gentle swirl. "There," she says, handing it to Elijah. "Give everyone some of that water and they'll recover from the demon spirit's infliction."

This is exactly what Aunt Lauren did in Noviska.

I'm certain Rune and my aunt are from the same place. They have to be. Because there's no way Aunt Lauren is an evil being from that nightmare realm. Her heart is full of kindness and empathy, and she bakes the best breads and desserts.

Elijah has finished with the others and is tending to my aunt. When he's done, he asks, "How long will it take?"

I let Rune answer, but from what I witnessed up north, the results were practically instant. Though the small child remained resting in bed, I saw him open his eyes. The blood-tainted water revived him.

"I don't know," she responds. "I've never actually healed a human before. But I've heard rumors that our blood has healing powers."

"Elijah? Adele? Is that you in here?" Trevor shuffles into the tavern. His walking stick bangs on the floor with each small step. "And..." He abruptly stops. His clouded gaze drifts from the ceiling to Rune.

There's no way he can see her. Yet, he continues to stare at her.

"Well, now. What do we have here?"

Before anyone can say anything, the man with only one foot coughs. Everyone except Trevor turns to him. The man's eyes are open, but he's wincing from the sunlight shining in from the front windows. Elijah rushes to the man's side, blocking the bright light with his body before offering him some more water.

The others slowly stir into consciousness. A few of the old women who were tending the injured last night scurry inside the tavern, making their way to help those lying on the floor.

"It's a miracle!" one of them shouts.

"The stars have answered our prayers!" another exclaims.

"It's no miracle," Trevor whispers under his breath. I probably wouldn't have heard him speak, but in the commotion, he stalked closer to Rune and me. With a winded breath, he asks, "What's your name, girl?"

She looks at me, and I nod. *Might as well*, I think.

"Rune. I'm visiting from the south."

His gaze lifts from her face to over her shoulder. Leaning on his walking stick, he asks, "And how long do you plan on staying in Bricen?" She opens her mouth to answer, but he cuts in. "I only ask because guests usually check in with me before getting comfortable."

"Sorry about that," Elijah says from across the room where he's crouched down, squeezed between the edge of one of the tables and the recovering frail woman. Her bony arms are trying to carry her weight as she struggles to sit up. Elijah's arm supports her, helping her to sit upright. She coughs before taking the cup of water Elijah's offering. "That's my fault."

"Our fault," I correct. "I suggested we wait at Goslings for you, that's all. Elijah was on his way to find you so you could officially greet Rune."

Trevor makes an *mm-hmm* sound. I don't care if he believes me or not. Rune carried through. She helped heal the villagers. All but one—Aunt Lauren.

I'm expecting a lengthy address about village safety from Trevor, but instead he cries out a painful yelp as his walking stick drops to the floor with a loud *bang!*

The old man stumbles backward, mumbling while trying to regain his balance. Elijah lets one of the caretakers take his place next to the recovering woman and hurries over to Trevor. En route, he grabs a chair and drags it across the room. Then, he takes a hold of Trevor's arm before guiding the old man to sit.

"What's wrong?" Elijah asks. Rune and I give the old man some space.

"Oh, no! No, no, no!" He presses his hands to his forehead.

Rune picks up the walking stick and sets it against the wall before asking, "Is he injured?"

"I'm not sure," I answer while watching Elijah try and ease whatever episode Trevor's caught up in.

Tears stream down Trevor's cheeks. His pale skin is covered in sunspots and deep lines from old age. Whatever troubles him consumes his attention and for the moment, he's nonresponsive to Elijah's efforts. Eventually, the whimpering subsides, and his body relaxes. Both knobby hands are patting his face, arms, and body.

"Are you okay?" Elijah asks.

Shaking his head, thin strands of white hair sway over his shoulders, he explains. "It's Barclay!" His words tremble. "Oh, my dear, poor friend."

I jerk my head to attention. "What's wrong with the messenger bird?" If something is wrong with Barclay…something might be wrong with Selene.

"He won't survive!" Trevor sobs.

"Trevor!" I yell. "What happened?!"

He lifts his head and waves for me to come closer. Sniffling, he pulls at my sleeve when I'm within reach. For once, I don't shove his hands away. I'm too worried about Selene. His gaze is focused up, head swaying with nervous energy. With a shaky voice, he tells me, "He was attacked. The whole castle…" He stops to catch his breath.

I'm hunched over in front of him now. Both hands gripping the arms of the chair. My face inches from his. "The whole castle, what? Tell me!"

Between shallow breaths, he says, "The whole castle is under attack."

Straightening, I try and imagine Castle Forge under attack. There's no way it's true. What enemy would be foolish enough to try and take on General Onica?

Regardless, I have to get to Selene. She's the only thing in this entire world that means anything to me. Our friendship was the only thing that kept me sane—gave me hope that there's something better in this world than being the Interrogator for a power-hungry general.

"Are you sure?" I demand, and Trevor nods.

Clenching my fists, I say, "Then I need to go to her."

"Her? Who's her?" Elijah asks, blocking me from leaving Goslings. "And there's no way you'll get there in time."

"I have to try. Now let me pass." Heat fumes beneath my skin. My blood feels as if it's boiling through my veins. I can only hope Elijah has learned not to test my patience.

"He's right, Adele," Trevor says weakly, still trying to catch his breath. "The time it would take you to reach and cross Bowmans Straight, then travel west to Castle Forge is too great. Everyone will have perished by then."

Elijah hesitantly takes a step closer, but then retreats. His red scarf has unwound and is barely hanging around his neck. I want to take that scarf and strangle someone. But I'm glad he's come to realize I don't need consoling or comfort, and he's keeping his distance. Because what I need is to *do* something.

Rune, on the other hand, has yet to realize I don't like my personal space to be infringed upon and stands so close our shoulders are touching. Sidestepping, I put some space between us while she says, "I can get you there fast."

Everyone looks at her, even Trevor. Though he's not looking directly at her, but in the general direction.

"You're talking about opening a doorway?" The words spill from my lips before I realize what I've done. My gaze shoots to Trevor, who only inhales a deep breath and releases it with a shake of his head. I don't have time to explain who…or what…Rune is, so I press on. "Can you make one here?"

She looks about the room, then shakes her head. "The doorways I make out here to pass through the wall don't require a lot of energy. But ones between worlds or over great distances require me to draw energy from another source to create the passage. Like in the cave. It goes deep into the earth, providing a direct connection to your world's natural energy."

I tell Rune, "Wait for me by the front gate. I need to run and get my bow."

Elijah's still blocking the tavern's front door. "I can help. Let me come with you."

Shaking my head, I tell him, "It's too dangerous. The Fayatin soldiers are ruthless, like nothing you've ever faced. You won't be able to fight them. And I can't get distracted."

"But…"

"No."

"I won't be able to go with you, either," Rune explains. "I can create the doorway, but these kinds of portals take a toll on me. I'd be useless after." Her gaze flicks to Elijah, and he seems to pick up on whatever silent message she's hinting at.

"I can watch over Rune! Keep her safe and guard the doorway."

It's risky, and I don't like it. But if something goes wrong and Rune is compromised, I don't want to be stuck in Fayatin, especially if I find Selene. I'll want to get her out of danger as quickly as possible.

"Fine," I agree. "You've got two minutes to grab any weapons you can."

"Got it!" Elijah shouts, running out the front door. "I'll grab your bow and quiver for you!" His voice fades the farther he gets from the tavern. I'm about to shout no, but he's already halfway up the hill to Aunt Lauren's cottage.

From behind, Trevor calls for me. "Take Valor!" Both Rune and I turn to the old man, who's found his walking stick and is shuffling toward us. "She'll be helpful."

"Who is Valor?" I'm kind of hoping Valor is some secret, super-strong warrior Trevor's been keeping stashed away somewhere, hidden from the Shades.

He raises his hand and whistles. A few seconds later, a *caw* rings through the air as something black swooshes by my head and into the tavern. There on the back bar counter is one of Trevor's crows.

"Oh, no. Keep your pets here!"

"No!" He slams the end of his staff onto the floor; a loud *bang* echoes through the room. The old women tending to the injured pause in their efforts, all looking to their village leader. He staggers closer, using the stick to carry his weight. Then, when he's right before Rune and me, he holds out one arm. Valor launches herself from the bar counter and lands on it. The bird's dark talons curl over the sleeve of his arm.

"Listen here. I'm not sending Valor with you to watch you, but to watch *for* you. She'll be your eyes in the sky. If she flies, then all is safe. If she remains perched, then it's best to wait because danger lurks. She is fast and observant and will listen to your commands. Please, take her with you. Rescue your friend and bring Barclay home."

"Dead or alive?" I need to be sure.

"Yes. Dead or alive."

I don't know why I agree, but I nod, and the bird instantly takes flight out the door. "I'm probably going to regret this," I grumble while jogging down the porch steps of Goslings. Rune is by my side as we hurry toward Bricen's front gates, where Elijah is waiting with my bow and quiver full of arrows.

Our group of three, now four, heads out with Valor flying high above.

Chapter 19

Rune

The moment we step off the dirt road and into the woods, the lure that would bind me to Merigoth floats into my mind. Though, it's not her voice carrying the enchantment and floating through my mind. It's my voice. A conniving trick to get me to listen to her lure.

Your will is her will.

The phrase repeats over and over, growing louder with each turn. I try to listen to the leaves rustling or seek out the sounds of the river's current, but it's like she knows I'm nearby.

Ahead, Adele leads the way while Elijah stays close to me. I want to answer all his questions, but I have trouble remembering anything from my life before the Under Realm. That life…if there was any at all…is like trying to remember a dream but you can't recall any of the details. I know I had a life before waking up in my dirt hole, or at least I hope I did. I don't want to believe that my life had no meaning. Marcellus is lying to the Shades, saying that we were brought to the Under Realm to serve Merigoth—to bring purpose to our lives.

Your will is her will.

No! I trip over a root and stumble into a tree. Squeezing my eyes shut, I hug the tree until Elijah's arms are clutching my shoulders.

"What is it?" he asks.

I shake my head, trying to clear it.

"It's that bad, huh?"

I nod.

"What can I do?"

His kindness gives me hope I can turn my life around and be more than one of Merigoth's mindless Shades.

"Walk with me," I suggest. He does, and it makes it a little better. The voice in my head grows dimmer the longer I focus on Elijah's footsteps next to mine.

"Almost there!" Adele shouts from ahead. The arrows in her quiver rock with each step. As we make our way deeper into the forest, she puts more distance between us, checking our surroundings and making sure it's safe. She is nothing like Marcellus. They both might be original Shades, but Adele has a strong will that she uses to protect others, and I admire her for that. I also like her long braid, and how she decorates her hair with red stones that glint in the sun whenever she passes beneath a break in the treetops. I hope to one day decorate my hair with shiny stones.

For a moment, my mind goes quiet, and I listen to the sounds of the forest. But the silence gives room for the lure to beckon me.

Your will is her will.

No.

Trying to ignore the voice growing louder in my mind, I silently list off the things I see around me: rocks, trees, leaves, sticks, Elijah. His smile. His brown eyes.

Your will is her will.

"No!"

A black bird flies over my head, crying out a piercing *caw!* I realize it's Valor and not one of the demons. The bird lands in a nearby tree, where it keeps cawing.

"Insufferable bird! Be quiet!" Adele shouts.

"No, it's fine!" I call, making sure she hears me. "I think Valor's trying to help me block out the lure."

"Well, we're almost there. You good?" she asks me, and I nod. Without another word, she turns and continues toward the cave.

I look up at the blue sky in a gap between the trees. I know they're up there—the stars, waiting for nightfall so they can be seen.

"You sure you're okay?" Elijah asks in an oddly muffled voice. When he speaks again, I don't hear any sounds. My eyes momentarily blur, and I know Merigoth's enchantment is working hard to take hold of my mind.

I can feel myself teetering into the darkness.

"My will is her will," I whisper.

Elijah steps in front of me, blocking my path. "Oh, no! Don't start that! Listen to my voice. Stay with us, Rune!"

I want to listen to him, but the warmth and comfort that comes with those words grows stronger. Each word taking root, blooming, and spreading its hold over my awareness.

Then, the lure suddenly retreats. The sounds of the forest return, and my will and thoughts are my own again. Blinking, I press a hand to my cheek. "Ow," I say. The surface of my skin is tender. "Did you hit me?"

Adele now stands in front of me, Elijah watching from behind. The girl nods. "Are you good?"

Stretching my jaw, I can hear the lure slowly creeping its way closer. "I don't know." If we're going to do this, then I need to be honest with her. If I slip away…lose control…then that makes me a risk. And I don't want to hurt them.

"What can we do?" Adele asks. From above, Valor claws and flaps its wings. The creature then takes flight, the tree branch bouncing in her wake, and flies down a narrow path behind the large oak tree.

I can't be here, I'm about to say when Elijah starts singing. At least, I think it's singing. It's a sound I vaguely remember from another life. His voice carries a beautiful melody that filters through my thoughts.

> *Home is where we build our fire.*
> *Home is where we build a life.*
> *Home is shared with those we love.*
> *That's the home for me.*

The sun will rise and set each day.
The moon and stars own the night.
No coin or trade compares to time.
So best to cherish the days.

Home is where we lay our heads.
Home is where we take our rest.
Home is respite from the storm.
That's the home for me.

The leaves will turn, and snow will fall,
Til flowers bloom again.
No coin or trade compares to time.
So best to cherish the days.

His eyes meet mine, and he continues to sing. Adele says, over his song, "Focus on his words. Listen to his voice."

And I do. I focus on each word and its meaning. Soon enough, all I hear is Elijah singing. Reassuring Adele, I give her a nod.

"Good, now let's keep moving. We're almost there." Elijah keeps up the tune as we walk. Adele goes first down the narrow trail behind the giant oak tree while Elijah and I follow. When he starts the song over for the third time, I join in, softly singing the words I remember. I'll have to ask him later more about the song's origin and what it means. For now, I'll sing along and try not to get distracted.

The sounds of the river muffle Elijah's singing, but I can still hear him. I hold onto the tune while following Adele into the cave. Inside, I move past her and stand in front of the tall black rock embedded in the cave wall. I've created this doorway so many times that a permanent impression of obsidian has formed.

"Can you use that?" Adele asked, pointing to the smooth surface.

"No. That one goes to the Under Realm." A passage I never want to walk through again. Sidestepping a few feet closer to the mouth of the cave, I tell her, "I'll make it here. A new doorway."

Elijah stands at the narrow entrance, sunlight outlining his body. His singing has turned to humming, and I'm grateful for his efforts. The tune fills my mind, blocking out the lure that's no doubt trying to weasel its way into my thoughts.

"I can create the doorway, but you'll have to show me the destination." Although the surface of the cave wall isn't completely flat, the energy emanating from within the stone is abundant. Despite not being ideal, this location will have to do.

Adele rests her bow against the wall, next to Elijah. Then she looks at my hands and asks, "And how exactly am I supposed to *show you* where to open a magical door to?"

"Use your hands—"

"Uh, no," she cuts me off before I can finish explaining. "There's got to be another way. I can describe the castle or draw you a map in the sand by the river, but removing my gloves is not an option."

Lowering my hands from the wall, I turn and face Adele. She's not much taller than me, and doesn't appear to be any older than me—though I can't recall how long I've been whatever age I am. But this consistent need to keep everyone at arm's length is unusual. She shouldn't fear her abilities. Unless she's unable to control them. It is said that the original three Shades are powerful beings. And I never doubted it. I've seen what Marcellus can do.

"I want to help you," I say.

"Yes, yes. You already said that. And you are helping." Adele slaps the rocky surface of the cave. "By opening this magical door! Now, let's get to it."

She's right. The door first, rescue those at the castle, and then afterward I'll help Adele learn how to control her abilities.

But I can't make a doorway until I've seen the destination. Usually, Evander shows me the destination, and since he's not here… Adele will have to.

Elijah hums in the background while I explain to Adele, "I cannot open a doorway to a place I've never seen. You must show me the destination through your memories."

She tips her head back and releases a protesting groan that echoes throughout the small cave. "This isn't going to end well."

"I promise you, I'm ready for your touch this time."

Rubbing a gloved hand over her face, she asks, "Are you sure that's the only way?"

I face the cave wall and press my hands to its cold, rough surface. "Yes. I am sure. Now, when you press your hands to the sides of my face, be sure to focus on the destination. Picture it in your mind and I will see it. It's that simple."

Elijah briefly breaks away from his tune. "You got this, Adele." Then he quickly resumes his melody, returning to singing. The words are comforting to hear, working their own kind of magic to keep the lure at bay.

"Oh, and you may hear Merigoth's enchantment," I remind her. "If you do, you too will have to focus on Elijah's song, because if the lure entraps you, then you won't be able to rescue your friend."

Adele purses her lips, understanding what's at stake. She removes her gloves, then tucks them into her leather vest. "You ready out there?" Adele shouts, her head facing the entrance to the cave. From outside, a loud *caw* answers. She then moves to stand behind me. "And you… Are you ready?"

I inhale a deep breath, steady my palms against the rock, and tell her, "Yes."

The moment her warm skin presses to my temples, a flood of images flashes behind my eyes. I try to decipher them, but they're random, and they don't seem to focus on a place but rather a single person. A woman with long, wavy blonde hair and fair skin. The shape of her eyes and the warm brown color within are identical to Adele's…and Marcellus's.

So many memories flash behind my eyes. One shows the same woman walking down a road, holding hands with a young girl, the bright forest surrounding them. Then another memory, again, with the same woman, sitting in a small grassy clearing…in the village…with the little girl skipping in circles around her.

"Come here, Adele," the woman says, laughter in her voice.

From behind me, Adele cries, "Rune! There's too many! I-I can't concentrate or focus!"

Whatever bombardment of images she's receiving from me is preventing her from showing me the destination. "Listen to Elijah!" I shout. "You're used to invading a mind and not sharing your thoughts. But you need to relax. You need to listen to Elijah's song!"

Elijah's voice grows louder. He's singing as loud as he can, and I hope that's enough.

Slowly, Adele's memories fade from my mind. Whoever that woman was, she's important to Adele.

"I think I got it." Adele adjusts her hands on my head. "I've pushed aside your memories so I can focus. Okay, here I go."

I am curious to know what memories of mine she saw. Were they from my life before or my life as a Shade? A question for later, after she's returned.

"Great. Now, think about the castle. Picture it in your mind and I will see it too."

A familiar landscape emerges behind my closed lids, and I can see what Adele is remembering. "I've seen this place before!" I shout. It's the same stone castle with red flags pitched on the roofs of all four high towers. Behind the castle is a series of tall mountain peaks, spanning a great distance.

"You can let go!" I tell her, then focus on the energy building in my core. The second I tap into that power, an intense pain rakes along my spine. There's some connection between the power deep within me to the reoccurring pain, like something scratching to be released from beneath my skin. I push through the pain and focus on Elijah's song.

Once I've gathered enough energy from within my core and from the rock beneath my hands, I focus on the destination while redirecting the energy out of my body through my palms. The cave wall around my hands glows a bright white and continues to expand outward until the shape of a doorway forms. When the shape is complete and filled with light, I stagger away, knees weak. The light fades, leaving a smooth surface and a new doorway in its place. The glass-like surface wavers with a gentle ripple before settling flat.

On the other side is the castle. Except this time there's smoke and fire, and people screaming and running in all directions. Looming over the castle are heavy gray clouds, blocking out the sun. I step aside and let Adele get a closer look.

Her head snaps to me, and with her bow gripped tight in her hand, she asks, "I can go?" The second I nod, she leaps through the doorway and takes off running toward the castle. Valor swoops in from outside the cave and dives through the passage, following Adele toward the chaos of whatever's happening inside that castle.

I collapse onto the cave floor. Elijah hurries to my side. I lean against his arm and tell him, "Don't stop singing. It's all I have to keep the lure away."

He sings, "Are you okay?" in between lyrics.

"Yes. I just need to rest. Making doorways drains me. I'll be fine. Just keep singing."

He does. And I lie there, Elijah's arms wrapped around me, hoping Adele will find her friend before Merigoth's lure gets to me.

CHAPTER 20

Castle Forge is under attack. Smoke rises from open windows and behind the battlements of the castle walls. What lunatic would be crazy enough to bring the fight to General Onica's front door? Maybe the miners finally organized a revolt? Or one of the Fayatin lords is trying to take control of the country? Whoever it is, they don't know what they've gotten themselves into. The general doesn't back down from a fight or let others make a fool of her. She'll burn villages and maim innocent people just to make a point. And those messages are usually read loud and clear—don't ever cross her.

My heart races, my lungs burning as I swiftly weave around large rocks and leap over smaller ones strewn about the rocky meadow. Above, Valor flies low. Her wings spread wide as she soars through the thin veil of smoke filling the air. She stays in the lead, and I'm a bit surprised she knows where to go. The black crow veers away from the main gates of the castle and heads to the east entrance. She lands in a nearby tree and waits for me to catch up.

Breathing heavily, I search the grounds, looking for anything to tell me who has attacked the castle. Yet there are no guild flags, crested shields, or fallen soldiers anywhere. Nothing but screams coming from inside the castle.

Did Rune say she knew this place? I should've paid more attention to what she was saying. There I go again, rushing before thinking. But surely it can't be the Shades. Why would the Shades attack Castle Forge?

The air carries an eerie weight, as if something is amiss. And the sky above, blanketed by a thick layer of overcast clouds, casts a gloomy shroud over the castle grounds, enveloping the land in perpetual twilight.

I make my way toward the side entrance. The gate doors are partially open. I'm almost there when one of the wood doors slowly swings back. Its rusty hinges creak loudly as men shout from behind it. Valor releases a loud *caw*, and my boots slide along the gravel.

Valor flaps her wings but doesn't leave her perch on the stone wall. I take cover behind an old tree, my bow pressing to my side. A few seconds later, a group of Fayatin guards riding horses comes racing out. They're hollering to one another to hurry…to head for the forest. When the last horse sprints out from beneath the stone archway, it's followed by an arrow—which strikes the rider in the shoulder. He falls from the horse and lands on his side in a patch of dry grass.

With a groan, he scrambles to his feet, pulling the arrow from his flesh.

I remain in the tree's shadow as another Fayatin soldier charges out the side entrance. He's got a sword raised over his head, ready to strike the fallen rider. And he does. Though, the injured man withdraws his sword just in time to block the attacker's blade from slicing into his neck.

"Gregor, stop!" the man pleads.

Gregor doesn't flinch and continues to swing his broadsword with wide sweeps. Their blades collide with harsh metal clanking. Above, dark clouds roll in, banishing the moonlight so only the fire burning the castle grounds illuminates the night sky.

"Please, Gregor! What's gotten into you?" the man shouts, trying his best to block his supposed friend's blows. "It was that man! He did something to you when he touched you, didn't he? Gregor…stop!" Again, Gregor doesn't falter. He pushes on, and only stops when his sword connects with flesh. The man falls to his knees.

Valor cries, releasing a *caw*. Gregor looks to the sky, searching for the bird. The bleeding man seizes the opportunity and stabs the distracted man in the gut. Gregor stumbles backward, then falls onto the gravel. The injured man wastes no time and hobbles over to his horse, gets on, and rides away.

Ignoring Valor's chirps, I run over to Gregor. He's grasping at his shirt just below the bottom of his leather vest. I know I can't get information from a dead man, so I drop my bow to the ground and rip off one of my gloves. His distant gaze is focused over my shoulder, and I can tell his final moments are upon him. I need to hurry. Pressing my palm to his blood-spattered cheek, I search for an explanation of what's going on. Recent memories flash through my mind, and I almost lose my balance at what I see.

It's Marcellus. The same Shade who subdued Kit.

In the vision, I can see Marcellus is reaching for this guard. The second the Shade man withdraws his hand, Gregor turns and starts attacking the other Fayatin soldiers.

Marcellus took control of his free will—commanded him to turn on his fellow guards.

Looking up to Valor, I say, "The Shades are here." Standing, I slip my hand into my glove, and then I grab my bow and jog over to the side entrance. "We need to be careful. I don't know how many are here."

Valor caws, then takes off and flies into the bailey. Inside the enclosed courtyard, she doesn't continue into the castle but soars over the roof of the stables. I duck inside, squeezing between two large steeds just as more guards flee the castle. They don't go for the horses, but head straight out the side entrance. I wait to see if there's anyone chasing them, but no one comes. I'm about to run toward the stone archway that leads into the castle when a low neigh catches my attention. Turning around, careful not to slip on the wet hay scattered over the ground, I see Bessie tied to a post in the far back of the stables.

When I reach her, she nudges her nose into my face and whinnies.

"I'm happy to see you too, girl." I rub my gloved hand along her neck, giving her a gentle scratch before withdrawing. "Come on. I'm not leaving you behind this time." I untie her reins and lead her toward the front of the stable. Looping the leather rein over another post, I tell her, "Stay here. I'll be right back."

She neighs, but then turns her attention to the nearby heaping pile of hay.

"Valor!" I call out. When the bird comes into view, she sweeps low along the packed dirt of the bailey before darting inside the castle. More screams erupt, and I think back to the night I made my escape. How I left men crying and screaming in my wake to free myself.

When we reach the Great Hall of Castle Forge, Valor flies high and perches on one of the wood beam rafters crossing the cathedral ceiling. Long red banners adorn the gaps between window slits of the stone walls, adding a splash of color to the otherwise somber hall. The only furnishing is a long wood table at the rear of the hall. The only chair, a high-backed wood chair with a red upholstered seat, has been knocked over onto its side. I sneak over, then crouch to hide behind it. The ornate carvings have been rubbed smooth from handling over the years.

The stark absence of any other furnishings accentuates the space, as if it were purposely designed to intimidate those who seek an audience with the general. The only focal point visitors have is her, seated behind the expansive table, which seems almost like an overcompensating desk, reflecting her towering ego.

But the general isn't here, and her Great Hall is anything but absent of things to look at. Peeking out from behind the chair, there are fallen guards everywhere. I look at Valor, but she remains still on the beam.

If she's perched, then stay put, I remind myself.

Voices come from the main stairwell at the front of the hall. My muscles tense the second I hear her. "Where are the intruders now?" General Onica demands.

Every muscle in my body tenses at the sound of that woman's voice. I duck lower behind the fallen chair, not wanting to be seen. I use one of the fallen guards to hide my bow. Then, carefully I peek over the chair. I can only see Alister and a small group of guards behind him, but not the general.

"They've taken out the south-side guards. Whatever magic these assailants possess forces our own soldiers to turn against us!" Alister's leather vest is stained dark across his chest. Presumably not his blood.

"They're after the demon creature," General Onica says with a seething tone. "Take whatever guards you can find and blockade the south cellar—that's where it's locked up."

Alister grabs the closest guard behind him by the collar of his vest. "You. Go to the front gates and tell the guards there to meet me by the south cellar." He pushes the young man, who almost stumbles over a fallen body. The young soldier regains his balance and rushes out of the Great Hall. Alister then reassures General Onica, "I won't let them escape."

"Good," she answers. "I need to find Lord Caldridge. Once I know he's safe, I'll meet you at the south cellar."

Valor caws from her perched position above.

Both the general and Alister look up at the ceiling.

"Go," General Onica commands.

Alister turns his attention from the bird to the few men lingering behind. They've been staring at their fallen friends sprawled out on the stone floor.

"Let's go!" He leads them toward the archway in the back corner of the hall.

General Onica marches up the grand stairwell, broadsword gripped in her hands.

Valor releases another *caw*, but this time it's mid-flight. She circles the hall before diving and flying down the corridor closest to me. I move, and race along the back of the hall, then make a sharp turn down the corridor, following Valor. With my bow over my shoulder and my dagger in my hand, I follow Valor up the east tower stairwell, two steps at a time.

"You better know where you're going!" I say with a low enthusiastic tone. Being locked up means never getting to explore the castle grounds. I only know Selene resides in the eastern tower because she's mentioned it a few times during our courtyard conversations.

At the top of the landing are two dead guards. My bow slips from my shoulder and hits the stone floor with a clatter as I rush forward. Ignoring the blood splattered across the dark wood and decorative iron hinges of Selene's bedchamber door, I knock while shouting, "Selene! Are you in there?" No one answers, so I pound my fist harder. "Anyone? Please, I'm here to help!"

Glancing down at the two fallen guards, I fear I'm too late.

I stumble away from the door. My head spins and I'm struggling to breathe, and when my back hits the stone wall, I slide down until I'm seated on the cold floor. Valor lands on a nearby wooden table beneath a tall, narrow window. On the ground is a broken vase. The wilted flowers lie among the broken ceramic pieces. I pray to the stars that my dear friend hasn't fallen like these poor flowers, because I'm not sure I'll be able to handle losing the one person who has kept my humanity afloat all these years.

CHAPTER 21

ADELE

Ignoring the screams echoing up the stone stairwell, I stare at the moon peeking in through the narrow window of the tower. I don't even flinch when Valor flies from the side table to the shoulder of the dead guard slumped against the bedchamber door. It seems she's not ready to give up and pecks her dark beak against the thick oak wood of the door.

"There's no use. I can't pass through doors or walls like Rune. We can't get inside."

"Who goes there?" a muffled voice shouts from within Selene's room.

A sudden alertness shocks my senses into action. Rushing to the door, I call out, "I'm here for Selene! Is she in there? Is she all right?"

"You're not one of them?" she asks, her voice shaky and cautious. "One of the possessed guards?"

"No! Now, please let me in!"

Valor returns to the small table beneath the window and caws.

The thick oak door of the bedchamber creaks open, but only enough for the old woman wearing a linen coif to see out. Her complexion is pale, and her mouth trembles as she asks, "And who might you be?"

"My name is Adele. I'm a friend of Selene's."

The woman looks me up and down. "Adele, you say. The girl from the secret garden?"

My lips curl into a smile, and I'm elated to hear Selene has spoken of me. "Yes! That's me. I'm here to help you escape."

The door slams shut, and for a second, I think it won't open again. That she doesn't believe me. I raise my fist to the door, ready to protest, but then something heavy on the other side is being dragged across the floor. While I wait, I tell Valor, "Stay here and keep watch." The crow chirps and rustles her silky feathers but obliges and remains at her post on the small side table.

Once the scraping sound is done, the door opens. A few candles in a nearby candelabra are lit, giving off a soft glow that illuminates the front half of the bedchamber. The rosy-cheeked woman stands before me, hands clutching her dirty apron. Gray hair, damp from sweat, sticks to the sides of her face.

"We did all we could for her," she tells me, stepping aside so I can see the four-post bed set in the center of the room. Lying on top of the red satin quilt is Selene. I rush to the bedside, taking in her condition.

Blood seeps through her white nightgown over her abdomen. An older woman, much older than the one who'd answered the door, kneels on the bed beside Selene, holding a stained towel to Selene's stomach.

"We're not healers. We don't know what to do for such an attack," the elder woman whimpers. The swollen knuckles of her bony hands are covered in dried blood.

Caw! Caw! Valor flies into the room. She circles over the bed before landing on the rug over by a writing desk near an open window. Glancing at the floor, I notice a small creature covered in black feathers. It's Barclay, and he's not moving. His wings are tucked close to his body, and I can't tell if the creature's eyes are open or closed.

"I'll help him in a minute," I promise.

Valor sits low on the faded red rug, next to her fallen friend.

"What can we do for the lady?" the woman who answered the door asks.

Looking about the room, I tell her, "She needs her cloak. And a spare nightgown."

"Agnes," the elder woman, kneeling on the bed next to Selene, calls, "everything's in the chest!"

The woman's voice is hoarse and weak, so I repeat the instructions to Agnes just to be sure she heard. "The chest… Over there against the wall! That's where…" I turn to the other woman, her hands still pressed to Selene's midsection.

"Edith. My name is Edith," she tells me with ragged breaths. Her face is almost as pale as Selene's.

Agnes is bent over, rummaging through the oversized trunk embellished with gold corners.

"Is there anything we can do for her here?" Edith asks.

I brush aside strands of damp hair from Selene's resting face. Beads of sweat frame her face along her hairline. Her lips are drained of color, and I fear the worst. But then I catch her chest slightly rising, and my insides hum with hope. "She's still breathing, so I'm not giving up. But I can't help her here. We need to leave, and fast."

"Here!" Agnes hands me the spare nightgown. Draped over her other arm is a navy velvet cloak.

I take the nightgown and flip it over so I'm holding the bottom. Then, with my knife, I cut a slit into the hem. After a few hard tugs, tearing up the nightgown, I've got four long strips of fabric. "Help me sit her up," I tell them. "We need to wrap these around her body, tight over the wound. It doesn't have to be perfect. They just have to hold until we're safe from the castle." Both women hurry to help me secure the torn strips of fabric around Selene's waist.

"Adele?" Selene's voice croaks. My friend's eyes crack open. The corners of her eyes are tinged red.

"I'm here," I tell her, holding the side of her head with my gloved hand. But she doesn't respond. Her eyes close and her head slumps off to the side. "Selene, stay with me!"

"Ma'am, we need to hurry," Agnes says with haste.

We can all hear the screaming, but no one knows where it's coming from. Agreeing with Agnes, I tell her, "We're going to have to carry her—you and me." I don't trust Edith's frail state and age to carry Selene.

Valor caws, and I ask Edith, "Can you bring the injured crow? He's an important messenger, and his owner wants him returned." Edith carefully withdraws her red-stained hands from supporting Selene's side to fetch the injured bird.

Locking eyes with Agnes, I nod, and she nods back. With a big heave, we slide Selene's arms over our shoulders before lifting her legs and carrying her off the bed. Agnes struggles, so I shift Selene's weight to lean more on me. Edith follows us out of the bedchamber, Barclay cradled in her arms. Valor flies over our heads, her body and wings tilting to soar with the curve of the spiral stairwell.

We take our time but keep a steady pace. I can't recall the last time I've touched anyone for this long. Selene's limp body presses into my arm and shoulder, while her head slumps against the side of my head. Silently, I remind myself that it's only my bare hands that can hurt her. Carrying her out of here is saving her life. A risk I'm willing to take.

Both women gasp, stumbling to a stop when we reach the Great Hall. Agnes almost loses her grip on Selene. I imagine the sight before them is hard to bear, the ground covered with fallen guards. Some could be mistaken for sleeping while others are more obviously gruesome. One body off against the far wall is in three pieces.

"Keep moving!" I say with haste. "And try not to look around the room." Edith is behind me, muttering soft prayers.

We exit the Great Hall and Agnes readjusts her grip as we hurry down the east corridor toward the stables, where

Bessie is waiting. The pounding of our feet echoes inside the stone hallway. A refreshing breeze greets us as we enter the bailey. I search the courtyard for Fayatin guards, and when there are none around, I yell to Edith, "It's clear! Head to the white mare out front and put the bird in the satchel."

The old woman speeds up, a limp in her gait, while Agnes and I follow behind. She's breathing hard, and I want to yell at her to push through the exhaustion, but I refrain, knowing the poor old woman is doing the best she can. One step at a time, we make our way across the dirt yard over to the stables.

Once we've got Selene's body draped over the saddle, I turn to the two women, about to tell them to unhitch another horse and get ready to ride, when a familiar voice calls to me.

"Adele!" Alister roars.

Our luck has run out.

Quickly, I tell Agnes, "Help Edith onto another horse, then you ride Bessie with Selene. Head to the stony field. You'll see an old tree with a doorway in it—"

"A door? In a tree?" Agnes cuts me off.

"Well, something like a door. Just go! And don't wait for me!"

The old woman drags over a tall wooden stool and says, "We'll get her to safety. Don't you worry."

"Adele!" Alister calls me again. "You pain-in-my-ass witch!"

Witch, huh? That's a new one. I walk out from beneath the stables and stand face-to-face with the man who took part in making my captivity hell.

The overcast of gray clouds has grown darker…angrier…rumbling with thunder. It's bad enough we have to deal with Alister, but add rain into the mix? That's going to make escaping with two elderly women and an unconscious Selene even harder.

Alister steps out into the bailey from the castle's eastern entrance. Blood streams down the left side of his long face, glistening in his thick black beard. The light from the torch in his hand reveals a deep gash above his left ear. When his gaze lands on me, his dark brows pinch, and he points his sword at me. "I knew it! It was you who brought this madness to Castle Forge!"

Drops of rain begin to dot the dirt of the courtyard. I need to keep Alister's attention on me so the others can make their escape. "I don't know what you're talking about!" I shout, inching to the center of the yard. Then, as I take off my gloves and stuff them into the front opening of my vest, I tell him, "You'll let us go if you know what's best for you." It's then that I realize I left my bow outside of Selene's bedchamber.

Damn it. I loved that bow.

Alister stops and bellows a laugh. "Oh, I've been waiting for this day to come. And now I'm going to enjoy killing you!"

"And what will General Onica say about that?"

A mischievous smile spreads on his face, and he throws the torch to the ground between us. "Ah, she's got something much better than you now. An actual dark spirit." He lunges, taking a swing, but I duck and roll beneath his blade, coming out behind him. He spins, ready to strike.

There's no way he can mean one of Merigoth's demon spirits. But then again, Marcellus is here somewhere inside the castle.

A piercing shriek fills the air. It's coming from inside the castle. My body tenses and my gaze darts from the general's lapdog to the castle corridor behind him. The shrieks are getting louder. I don't want to be here when—

A whizzing sound cuts into my thoughts, and I catch the glint of steel flying through the air toward me. Seconds before it connects with my skull, I jump out of the way, rolling onto my side in the hard, wet dirt. Getting to my feet, I hear someone scream. Not wanting to face away from Alister, I stumble backward, then glance over at the stables. Agnes is hunched over something lying on the ground.

The rain picks up, and I yell to Agnes, "Is that Selene?"

Using a nearby wood post as support to help her to her feet, Agnes hurries over to Bessie where Selene's unconscious body is draped over the saddle. It's Edith lying on the ground with a steel blade sticking out of her stomach.

That blow was meant for me. Not that poor old woman.

"You monster!" I scream, moving to stand between Alister and Bessie.

A sinister grin perks up from within his beard. He takes a step closer, still a good distance from us. Over my shoulder, I shout to Agnes, "Get on the horse and go! I'll handle this oaf!"

"I can't just leave her," Agnes whimpers, holding the wood stool in her hands. Her gaze focused on her dead friend.

"You can and you will! Unless you want to end up lying next to her, you'd best get up on that horse and go! Head to the stony field and find the doorway in the tree!" There's a brief moment of silence before Bessie releases a loud neigh. Agnes is using the stool to climb up on Bessie.

Alister comes closer, but at a leisurely pace, as if he's got all the time in the world to kill me. His eyes are locked onto mine, paying no attention to the mare as she trots from the castle grounds. I imagine he wants to remember this moment—to savor it as though it's some sort of monumental achievement. Killing the mighty Fayatin Interrogator.

Well, I refuse to let him have his glorious moment.

Valor swoops down from the stable rafters, flies by with a *caw*, then follows Bessie out the eastern gate. I can only hope Edith put Barclay in the saddlebag before her demise.

The light rain has washed away the blood trailing the side of Alister's face, and any resemblance of humor has left his expression. Behind me, all the horses tied up in the stables become anxious, moving around, and bumping into one another. It's as if something has spooked them. Then I see it. A large black-winged creature soars out from the open corridor of the castle. Its screeches are so deafening I swear the people at Port Helve could hear it.

It's without a doubt one of Merigoth's demon spirits. But how did it get here in Fayatin?

Then I recall the unmarked freight from the other night. The one that arrived at the docks the night I escaped from Castle Forge. They must've gone to Harvesgrove to restock the general's miner numbers and caught a demon spirit instead.

Hands balling into fists at his sides, Alister watches the creature fly above us. He straightens his broad shoulders, then dips his gaze to me. "I don't know how you did it, but it's your fault that insidious thing is free!"

"I did no such thing!" I retort. "You should've left the creature where you found it! It's your fault—yours and General Onica's—that Castle Forge has fallen!"

The creature screeches again, circling one of the castle towers behind a tattered red flag waving against the wind and rain. It's coming around straight for us. I creep into the shadows of the stable stalls, while Alister stands his ground. He unsheathes a dagger from his side and holds it tight in one hand. For the moment, he's not concerned about me, and I don't waste the opportunity. I keep to the shadows along the stone wall surrounding the bailey, and only stop when the demon spirit swoops down, clawing at Alister.

"Wretched creature!" Alister shouts while swinging the dagger at his attacker.

The dark-winged spirit continues to circle his head. It's moving at an incredible speed, dodging the steel of Alister's blade. Black smoke wafts off its body. Its unnatural, beady red eyes are focused on its target—Alister. If I had my bow, I could've tried to save him, but I don't. This one is much faster than the ones I encountered at Goslings. It's bigger too. And this thing is pissed off.

It takes off, flying high into the sky before disappearing into the dark clouds. Alister stares up, as do I. With another piercing shriek, it reappears, high over the castle. "Alister, run!" I yell, but it's too late. As it gets closer to us, it transforms from its bird shape to something you'd see coming out of a chimney. Then the slender, evil black smoke dives...straight for Alister.

"I'm not afraid of a little smo—" His words are cut off as he unwillingly consumes the demon spirit. Instantly, his arms go rigid and his fingers curl unnaturally. When his eyes roll back into his head, I stumble along the wall, not wanting to stick around and meet a Reborn firsthand. I'm almost at the gate entrance when I hear the sounds of bones cracking.

I reach the exit and I'm about to step through when Alister hollers, "Child of the Under Realm! You do not have to fear me. But you will come with me." The voice coming from Alister's mouth is his but at the same time not his. It's deep and reverberates through my ears.

Gripping the stone archway to the gates leading out of the bailey, I look at him. His eyes are black and there are thin red veins bulging from beneath his skin along his face and arms.

I'm not going to toy with whatever this is, so I take off running. Terror pushes my legs faster. I have no idea if the Reborn is following me, and I'm not going to turn around and check. I need to get to the doorway—get back to Harvesgrove Country.

Racing through the rocky meadow, I search for Rune's doorway. At the edge of the woods, I spot Elijah waving for me to hurry. When I reach him, I don't stop to talk, and run straight through, back to Harvesgrove. Elijah follows, leaving Rune to close the doorway.

"Where…" I struggle to breathe. "Where's Selene?"

"She's outside the cave," he reassures me. "We got the horse, the old woman, and Selene through."

"And…" I inhale a deep breath before finishing my question. "…the crows. Valor and Barclay? Did they—"

He nods. "The old woman has Barclay, and Valor flew through right after we got the horse to safety." Then he tells me, "Go. Check on your friend. I'll stay and help Rune."

"Thank you," I say, using the rocky wall for assistance. With shaky legs, I walk toward the cave's exit.

I'm almost out when Elijah shouts, "No! Adele! Run!"

Spinning to him, I gasp. There are two Shades, Marcellus and another man, standing on the other side of the doorway—over on Fayatin soil. One of the Shades has Elijah, while the other—Marcellus—stands behind Rune, holding her by the neck. He's got his hand pressed to her forehead and is whispering words I can't hear.

When he notices me stalking closer, he holds up his free hand and says with a threatening tone, "Continue, and the boy dies right here, right now."

My boots slide to a stop along the pebbles of the cave floor. Rune raises her hands to the doorway and the edges start to draw inward. The girl's eyes are distant and clouded. As the view closes in, I tell Marcellus, "I will come for them, and end you."

The last thing I see before the doorway closes is the panic in Elijah's eyes.

CHAPTER 22

The trip back to Bricen is steady and somber. The moon's hidden behind the treetops as we walk down the road to the village. Agnes sits atop Bessie, keeping Selene secure while I walk beside them, holding Barclay. The bird's chest is barely rising. If he survives, I may have to be nicer to him.

Valor glides over us, beating her wings every so often. If she gets too far ahead, she lands on a branch and waits for us to catch up.

It's nighttime here whereas only a few moments ago, while in Fayatin, it was late afternoon. Though the sun was shrouded by storm clouds, the sudden change of time surprisingly didn't faze me. My mind is too busy replaying what happened and what I could've done differently.

I know there was nothing I could've done to save Alister. The general's lapdog might've been a thorn in my side, but he didn't deserve to be transformed into one of those things—one of the Reborns. And I thought we were safe when he didn't pursue me from the castle grounds.

How wrong I was.

I'd lead the Shades straight to the doorway…straight to Rune. Damnit! This was all my fault. I should've had Rune close the door the moment I crossed through, but no. I'd been so concerned for one friend that I failed two others. Maybe if I'd seen the Shades sooner, I could've fought them off…but deep down inside I know I'm not strong enough to take on Marcellus. One touch from him and I'd be brainwashed and under his control.

I can't stop thinking about the look on Elijah's face before the portal closed. Maybe Selene isn't the only one in this messed-up world I care for. I've just been away for so long that I forgot how much the people of Bricen meant to me.

And now I have to return and face Trevor. To tell him the unforgiveable news about Rune and Elijah.

With Rune in Marcellus's custody, I'm sure they're on their way back to the Under Realm.

If I am truly one of the three original Shades, then there must be a way for me to travel into the Under Realm, right? I mean, I could see the realm through the doorway, but that was it. I'm not able to travel over to that realm. There's got to be a way. Rune and Elijah wouldn't give up on me, so I have to at least try to save them.

But first, I need to get Selene somewhere safe and talk to Trevor.

"Don't fall behind, love," Agnes calls out. Strands of gray hair have fallen loose from her linen coif, which is now stained with smears of blood and dirt.

With Barclay cradled in one arm, I speed up and walk alongside Bessie. She greets me with a nudge to my arm with her muzzle. We're almost at the village when a familiar voice calls my name. It's Magdala.

"What are you doing outside the barrier wall?" I ask as she runs up to us.

The young girl stands clear of Bessie, her eyes focused on the old mare. And when I wave to catch her attention, she sidesteps off the road, away from the horse. I don't ask, and she doesn't offer any reasoning. "Trevor asked me to watch for you and Elijah." Her gaze breaks away from the horse to comb over the group. "Where is he?"

"Not here. Now, why did Trevor ask you to watch for us?"

When Bessie neighs, Magdala stumbles farther back into the edge of the forest. "Uh, he wants you to go straight to Goslings."

"Thank you," I say. The second the words leave my mouth she spins and bolts off, running toward Bricen. Elijah wasn't kidding when he said she was fast.

As we approach the front gates to Bricen, the villagers standing guard open the doors for us. Once we're inside, they secure the gates. I catch Magdala talking with someone off in the distance, and I'm glad she's safe inside the village barrier.

The two torches posted at the gate entrance provide little light. And since thick clouds have rolled in, blocking out the moonlight, it's hard to see anything but the silhouettes of the homes and buildings.

"Come on. Just a little farther," I say, rubbing Bessie's neck. The old mare trudges forward, clopping her hooves along the packed dirt of the village road.

As we approach Goslings, I notice the torch staked into the ground outside isn't lit. However, the warm glow coming from the building's windows guides us to our destination. The light spills out onto the porch through the open front door. As we get closer, two villagers, a young woman and an older man, descend the steps toward us.

"We can bring her inside," the man tells me. The girl helps me slide Selene off Bessie. I let them carry my friend inside, then turn to help Agnes climb down.

"You'll be safe here," I tell her, even though I don't know how safe any of us are. The Shades could come at any given moment. Agnes climbs the porch steps before me, and I follow her into the tavern. She finds a seat near the door while her attention roams over the room, specifically the people lying on the floor.

"What happened here?" she asks, concern lacing her voice.

"They were attacked, but we've healed them. Or at least most of them." Aunt Lauren still lies unconscious on the floor. I leave Agnes to rest and make my way over to Trevor by the fireplace. There's a fire burning, but not a strong one.

"Magdala says you return without Elijah or Rune. What happened?" he asks, leaning on his staff.

I don't have the heart to tell him right away, so instead I offer him his messenger. "I have Barclay. He's badly injured, but alive."

Trevor lets his staff fall to the crook of his arm and reaches for the fragile bird. I pass Barclay over, and he cradles his injured friend close to his wool sweater. "Thank you," he whispers, cupping one hand over the bird, his bony knuckles covered in age spots.

I'm about to ask how the villagers are doing when Barclay rustles his feathers beneath Trevor's hand. When Trevor slowly draws his hand away, the crow's eyes are open and alert. He lets out a few soft chirps.

"How did you do that?" I ask, glancing over the bird from head to tail feathers.

"Thank you for returning Barclay to me" is all Trevor says. He turns and hands the crow to a woman standing by. She makes her way to the back door, where she disappears outside.

"Elijah? Rune?" Trevor repeats.

There's no escaping this conversation. Before I answer, I accept a cup of water from an old woman. She then takes the pitcher over to Agnes and offers her a drink.

"They didn't make it." I set the wooden cup on the underside of a table that's been flipped over and placed on top of another table. More than half of the tables are turned upside down and pushed out of the way to make room for the injured. "Castle Forge was under attack by two Shades. We'd made our escape, but they caught us off guard, grabbing Elijah and Rune before I could do anything." I wasn't sure that was the entire truth, thinking there might've been something I could've done—or should've done—but didn't react fast enough. It was the first time in a long time that I felt helpless, unhinged, and afraid.

I don't know if it's possible for me to save them unless I figure out a way to cross over into the Under Realm.

For the time being, I can only worry about what's in front of me. Kneeling next to Aunt Lauren, I rest a gloved hand over her hands clasped at her waist. A wool blanket pulled up over her chest keeps her warm. Shifting my weight to my other knee, I turn and face Selene, who is now lying next to my aunt. A woman drapes another thick wool blanket over my injured friend. It's not as luxurious as her satin quilt, but it will keep her warm.

"I've sent someone to gather fresh supplies," one of the caretakers says. "We'll clean her up and tend to the wound."

I thank the woman, then ask, "Do you think she'll survive?"

"Only the stars know when it's time to leave this world. But we'll do our best."

"Much obliged." It's all I can hope for at the moment. Getting to my feet, I turn to Trevor. "I'm sorry about Elijah."

He grabs hold of his smooth walking stick and hits it hard against the aged floor planks. "And what do you plan on doing about it?"

"What can I do?" I say, throwing my arms up in frustration. "I can see the other world, but I can't get through."

He stares off into the distance, as if waiting for me to come up with a better answer. But I can't. Looking at Selene, I know I would cross impossible seas or trek over desolate lands to save my friend. And I want to do the same for Rune and Elijah; I just don't know how.

"Adele," Trevor says softly, as if trying to reassure me I did my best. I don't have the heart to tell him I didn't do my best. That I froze in the moment.

He lowers his blind gaze, and his cloudy eyes somehow find mine. This is the second time I've seen him acting as though he can see. Then he steps closer and takes my hands before I can pull away. "What if there was a way to open the doorway to the Under Realm? Would you go? Would you save our people?"

I search his face for some explanation about whatever secret he's been keeping. But instead of asking, I simply say, "Yes, I would."

CHAPTER 23

ADELE

It feels good to ride Bessie again, and I'm sure the old mare appreciates the casual late-night stroll. Maybe not the midnight part, but at least we're not rushing from any danger. Next to me, Trevor rides a gray steed that makes Bessie look like a young mare.

Once Bricen is out of sight, I ask, "And how are you planning to open a doorway to the Under Realm?"

Trevor's crows are following us. Occasionally, I'll hear the beat of wings overhead or the subtle chirps from within a nearby tree. I glance off to my right and hear a loud *caw*, as if the bird is protesting our late-night journey.

"Will your friends be joining me this time?"

"No. They cannot enter the Under Realm."

"And why's that?"

Instead of answering my question, he asks, "What do you know of the Under Realm?"

Our horses stroll on. We're about five minutes from the spot along the forest where we'll need to dismount. It's going to be a long five minutes.

"I only know what Rune has told me, and what I saw when it appeared to me through the obsidian stone."

He makes a *hmmm* sound. The shadows of the treetops stretch over the dirt road, moonlight peeking through every so often. Trevor's got his walking stick resting across his lap, one hand holding it in place while the other hand grips the reins. "And?"

"And," I tell him, "Rune explained that there's this Merigoth being—their queen—that rules over the realm. She can control their minds."

"Ah, I suspected Merigoth might be the reason the Shades are here."

I glare at the old man. I'm sure of it now—he knows more about what's going on than he's led others to believe. But why hasn't he done more to stop the Shades? Whatever game he's playing has cost the village innocent lives.

Pulling on Bessie's reins, I slow to a stop. "You're not really some huntsman from the southern lands of Harvesgrove, are you? That's just the story you told everyone back when you were trading pelts and dried meats."

Trevor's horse also comes to a standstill. The old man's gaze travels up to the night sky. "My life has had many acts. Though, the years I spent as a huntsman were by far my favorite. The solitude and freedom to reflect on my existence while engaging with local villagers whenever I felt due for some friendly interaction or intimate companionship couldn't have been more perfect. And believe me when I say it's been a long time since I've been content with my life."

I give Bessie a gentle nudge with the heels of my boots, urging her to move up next to Trevor.

Trevor continues, "After I heard the rumors of some strange attackers invading villages along the eastern side of Harvesgrove, I knew change was coming."

"You knew about the Shades?"

Shaking his head, his white hair rustling over his shoulders, he explains, "Not exactly. Merigoth is a story as old as time. She comes from a realm with angels, a world—"

"There's an Angel Realm?" I cut in.

"Yes, but it's called the Starlight Realm. Now, let me finish." Both horses are moving slower than a tortoise down the road. But I don't press him to pick up the pace, because if I can't beat Marcellus with strength, I might be able to outwit him. And to do so, I'll need Trevor to tell me everything he knows.

He clears his throat and continues, "There are many realms."

"How do you know this?"

"Child, if you keep interrupting me…"

"Sorry. Go on."

"As I was saying, there are many realms. How I know this isn't important right now. What you need to know is that Merigoth comes from the Starlight Realm. A world filled with magical creatures and enchanting lands. The angels living there aren't eternal beings, but their life spans stretch much longer than any human's. They are the keepers and caretakers of their realm, and of other realms as well. Many of them are sent out to other worlds to observe and spread hope by doing good."

"Is this some story you tell children before bed? My mum used to tell stories like this."

"Yes, well, your mother was a special woman. A wise woman with many gifts."

"Did you love her?" The question leaves my lips unbidden. But there is something meaningful in his tone whenever he speaks of her.

There is a long pause of silence before he says, "I did, at one time."

"Are—are you my father?"

He bursts out laughing, and a heat flushes beneath my cheeks. "Oh, for the love of all the stars in the sky. I'm not your father. But that doesn't mean I didn't care for your mum. We understood one another. Actually, the first time we met, she and I loathed one another. Couldn't stand to be in the same room!"

I find it hard to hear that Mum hated anyone.

We've reached the spot of forest where we need to dismount and go the rest on foot. And after I get to my feet, I assist Trevor off his horse. "It took years for us to warm up to each other becoming friends, then…well, more than friends."

It's hard for me to imagine Mum being with this frail old man. But back in the day, before the Shade attacks, he was a strong, handsome fellow. One that all the single ladies of every village admired. How did time claim so much of his life over the years?

With both horses' reins in hand, I lead the way through the forest, Trevor walking by my side. It's too dangerous to leave the horses on the road. And it'll be easier for Trevor to find his horse by the enormous oak tree after I've gone.

"Merigoth was once known as Loralai Songwielder," Trevor tells me. "It's said that she was banished from the Angel Realm, but for what reason, I don't know. Not only was she banished, but so was her name. It was proclaimed all throughout the lands that she was to be forgotten—never to be spoken of again."

"That's a cruel punishment," I say. "She must've done an incredible act of misconduct to have such a punishment bestowed upon her."

He nods and hums in agreement. "The North Star ruler, the most powerful angel of all four ruling Stars, banished Loralai to live in the Under Realm. A dark and isolated realm. Who knows what kind of evil infiltrated her soul. You must be careful and mindful of your surroundings while there."

"Tell me more about Loralai," I say, leading Trevor into the woods.

"She was an angel with great power." He pauses and asks, "Did you know that angels have abilities, depending on their family lineage? Most angels only have one ability, but occasionally there are some that possess multiple. Some can heal with a single touch, some can nourish the soil with their fingers, and some can even speak to any living thing—no language barrier."

Moonlight shines over us whenever we pass beneath a break in the trees. "Even talk to animals?"

"Even talk to animals," he attests before continuing, "Loralai's gift was to ease the afflicted or injured with bliss. To numb their mind while the healers tended to their inflictions."

I say, "So, her ability is to numb not control."

"Yes, I believe you are right."

"How do you know all of this?" I ask, stepping over a root sticking up from the ground. I go to help Trevor avoid tripping over the same root, but he steps right over it. As if he somehow sees the obstacles of the forest in his path. I wave a gloved hand in front of his face, and he gives no reaction. How is he walking through the forest without falling on his face?

"Like I said, I've lived a long life and traveled across far lands. I've heard stories and I've met people."

I don't believe him. He's not telling me the entire truth.

When we reach the oak tree, he lifts his chin and looks to the stars through a gap in the branches. Then, whispering, he says, "I don't have much more to give. This will be my last act of hope. I pray to the stars it's enough to welcome my spirit home."

"Are you going to make it?" I ask. "Should we stop and rest?"

"I'll be fine," he says, but I'm not so sure I believe him. The exhaustion in his hoarse voice weighs heavy in the night air, as does his aging posture and weary mood.

With one arm looped through mine, I carefully lead him along the steep path trailing toward the river. In his other hand, he uses his walking staff for support.

He gently pats my arm and says, "Your stubbornness for allowing others to get close to you has lessened."

"Do you want to fall on your ass?"

A weak chuckle escapes. "I see your candidness hasn't faltered over the years. Good. Honesty is a trait to be appreciated. Never lose that."

"Now isn't exactly the time…" I say and almost slip on some pebbles along the trail. "To be lecturing me about civility," I finish, making sure the old man isn't about to fall from my misstep.

At the bottom of the path, the forceful river currents crash against unseen jutting rocks from within the darkness. The downpour from yesterday's storm must've swelled the river because it sounds much louder.

"Not much farther," I tell him and continue leading him toward the cave. "You sure you know what you're doing?"

"I hope so. Because if it doesn't work, then Elijah and Rune are forever lost to us."

And Kit, too, I think.

Well, then we better hope for a miracle. Because I have no idea what this old man can possibly do to open a doorway between realms.

CHAPTER 24

RUNE

The rough surface beneath me grows warm, waking me from whatever forced slumber Marcellus compelled me into. In the far distance of my mind, the phrase continues in a loop, *My will is her will.* Yet my thoughts remain my own—Merigoth's lure hasn't claimed me.

I sit up when the heat within the rocky surface beneath me subsides, my hands pressing into the pebbles that have fallen off the walls. It's then that I realize where I am. I've been brought to the Idle Tombs.

Merigoth's personal prison for those she deems guilty.

A soft reddish-orange glow flickers outside the round opening of the cave pocket I'm in. Lifting my hand to the ceiling, I can tell there's room to move around, but not enough to stand. I think of Adele and Elijah and where they must be. Hopefully safe and far from the Under Realm.

I never expected to wake up here—where the punished are sent and forgotten.

The Idle Tombs, built deep beneath Merigoth's throne room in her black mountain castle, are forbidden to any Shades, unless they're sent for punishment. Only the Reborns and demon spirits are permitted inside the prison area. Day after day, it's the Reborns' responsibility to carve out new cells and expand the prison's domain while the demon spirits guard the tombs and dole out cruel punishments to those condemned by the queen.

If you're a mortal, the darkness will claim you eventually, and you'll die peacefully in your cell. Death doesn't come so easy for those of us who have lives that extend over centuries. The poor souls who do slowly unravel, causing them to descend into madness while their bodies petrify into a living statue within the tomb.

I refuse to be one of those living statues. I crawl toward the cave opening, but the second I reach the hole, a demon spirit shrieks, flying and blocking me from exiting. The dark creature continues its shrieking until I've backed away. No need for locked doors when there are demon spirits guarding the cells.

Pressing my hands to the back end of the cavern pocket, I think of the cave by the river. The energy in me stirs, but something's blocking me from opening a doorway. Dropping my hands, I wince at the stabbing pain poking the bones of my spine. It seems pointless to hold on to this pent-up energy if I can't use it to escape. With a deep exhale, I release the force, causing a ripple of air to surge throughout the cave and sending powerful shock waves into the surrounding mountain.

Bits of dust trickle down from the ceiling. Once they've cleared, Evander's voice floats into my prison. "Where did you go?"

Sitting up, I look at the opening. When he speaks again, he's standing in front of the round doorway, though the opening only shows him from the waist up. The tomb's torchlight flicks behind him. There's no sign of the demon spirit. When I don't answer, he says, "You were supposed to return to your sleeping hole."

His presence surprises me. The queen must've granted him permission to venture into the depths of the Idle Tombs for this visit. This is my opportunity to convince him we do not belong in this world. "Do you trust me?"

"There's no reason to trust anyone but Merigoth. Her will is our will." He looks like every other Shade—black strips of fabric wrapping his body, his head shaved, and a thin layer of dirt coating his skin. Adele would make him bathe in the water.

Crawling closer, my long brown skirt catching and ripping on a jagged rock, I tell him, "We don't belong here, Evander. The Under Realm is not our home."

"How did you grow your hair?" he asks with the same flat tone he's had ever since I've known him.

"That's what I'm trying to tell you. This," I say, gesturing to his shaved head and ragged clothes, "is not who we are."

"Then tell me, who are we supposed to be?"

I spread my arms, but they don't quite reach the sides of the cave pocket. I miss the open sky of the Human Realm, where I can see the stars as they call to me in the night. I miss the warm, bright rays of sunlight during the day. Most of all, I miss Elijah and his kind heart.

If I can convince Evander to help me escape, then maybe there's hope of returning to the village. "I don't know," I tell him. "But I know we don't belong here. Something happened—"

"What happened?" he snaps, impatience lacing his tone. Evander has never been one to ask questions. He follows Merigoth's orders like the rest of the Shades—regardless of the task and without hesitation.

"The humans have one of the original Shades living among them. She's helped me see the truth. And I'm sure she can help you, too."

His silence tells me he's trying to understand the words I've spoken, but I know from experience that trying to form a thought is almost impossible when Merigoth's enchantment has ahold of your mind.

I press on, hoping to get through to him. "When she came in contact with me, it was like she reached deep inside my mind and unlocked a hidden door."

"There's a door inside your mind?" His dust-covered brows pinch.

"No, not an actual door. A part of me that's blocked off, and I realized that I had a life before I was a Shade."

"And what of this previous life?" The torchlight behind him outlines his body. The dark strips of fabric wrapping his torso, shoulders, and arms make him look more like the shadow of Evander than Evander himself.

"I'm not sure," I say. "I still cannot access those memories. The point is, something is keeping us from remembering our pasts. And while I was gone, I had a glimpse of what freedom felt like—away from Merigoth and this evil place. She's got the Shades under some trance, and I need your help to free them."

His shoulders relax. "You really met one of the original Shades? You think she can help us?"

Finally. I'm getting through to him. "Yes, I believe she can. She's nothing like Marcellus. Her power is strong, possibly stronger than Marcellus, except she doesn't know how to fully use it. The poor girl didn't even know who she was or where she came from."

A long silence follows, and when he steps away from the opening, I think he's moving so I can climb out. But the second I inch closer to the exit, a stream of demon spirits darts by. When they're gone, so is his relaxed posture. Chin raised and shoulders straight, he says in an informative tone, "I've got what you asked for."

He isn't speaking to me.

"Don't listen to her!" I lean forward, reaching for him as he walks away. "Evander!" But the demon spirits swarm the exit again, blocking me from leaving. Their shrieking is alarming. A warning to stay put. I've nowhere to go, and there's no one to help me. The grim possibility of turning into one of those living statues seems more and more like the future that awaits me.

After multiple attempts to leave the cell, all met with more shrieks, I finally take a break and rest against the warm, rough wall. Defeated, I start singing Elijah's song, hoping to find some joy in the words.

"Are you a Shade?" a distant voice calls to me from somewhere outside the cell's opening. Are they in another cell?

Leaning closer, but not so close as to draw the attention of the demon spirits, I answer, "I am. Or at least I think I am. Who are you?"

"You spoke of a girl—a Shade—living among the humans. Did you not?"

The voice is getting slightly louder somehow, but I'm still not able to identify or place them. Is she in a nearby cell or has she discovered a way to walk the Idle Tombs freely? "I did," I answer. "Her name is Adele. Now, I insist you tell me: who are you?"

There's no answer.

Worrying I've frightened off the stranger, I try another approach. "My apologies. It's nice to hear another voice. Have you been locked away in the Idle Tombs for long?"

There's another stretch of silence before the stranger speaks again. "I've lost count of the years." Demon spirits cry out in the distance, as if another prisoner tried to escape. The torchlight flickers and a flock of dark spirits whooshes by, almost causing the torch outside my cell to extinguish. When the silence returns and the warm glow resumes its post outside the cells, she says, "Is the girl all right?"

Unsure of what *all right* means, I offer the best answer I know. "She's unharmed, or at least she was when I last saw her."

"No. I mean…is she happy?"

I consider her words. "Adele does not smile. She's withdrawn and cautious, but she has a good heart. It appears she's still trying to find her place in the human world."

Soft sobs fill the Idle Tombs beyond my cell. "I tried to protect her. To keep her from this dark world."

I realize that this woman is somehow acquainted with Adele. "What's your name? And what are you doing locked up here?"

"My name is Sara, and I helped Merigoth with her plan for vengeance. But I couldn't follow through. So I ran, taking what was rightfully mine from her. Or at least, I took what I could carry. I'll never forgive myself for not being able to take all my children from this place."

Leaning against the warm wall of my cell, I say through the opening, "You escaped, yet here you are. Locked up in the Idle Tombs."

"It was only a matter of time before she found me—found us. I was naïve to think we'd found our freedom."

Her words make no sense to me. "Who's Merigoth seeking vengeance on? You?"

"No. The Starlight Realm. I've never been there, but it's where she comes from. Where you all come from."

I'm from the Starlight Realm? How is that possible?

Sara's voice floats into my cell as she continues to explain where I come from and who the Shades really are. "I had a hand in creating the three original Shades, although the term 'Shade' doesn't refer to a particular species or race. Instead, it's the name that Merigoth uses to identify the powerful force or group she commands."

Silence lingers while I process her words. After a long stretch, Sara calls to me, "I know it's a lot to take in."

"I am not 'Shade'?"

"No, you are not."

"I am from the Starlight Realm."

"Yes. You are an angel from the Starlight Realm."

I knew it. Evander, I, and the other Shades are not Shades at all—and we're not from this horrid place. Merigoth's enchantment has kept us from remembering who we really are. I need to find a way to undo that. To free them from her influence. Moving closer to the opening, I say, "I need to get out of here. Do you know how I can get by the demon spirits and the Reborns?"

"If I tell you how to escape, will you promise to find Adele and keep her from ever coming to the Under Realm—keep her away from Merigoth's lure and Marcellus's touch?"

Escaping the Idle Tombs wouldn't be an easy feat, yet this woman seems to know of a way. I have to take my chances and try. Even if it means risking drawing the attention of Merigoth, because it wouldn't be hard for her to reach into my mind and pull me back under her control.

"I will keep Adele safe," I say. "You have my word."

"Good. Then listen carefully. It's not the cell within the mountain that confines you. Nor is it the lure you constantly hear in the back of your mind. The real prison holding you back is the mental block Marcellus placed inside your mind. You need to break those binds to release your wings. Only then will you be able to save the others—and save my daughter."

Reaching one hand under my shirt, I feel the smooth skin of my back. "I don't have wings."

"Yes, you do. Now, listen. I need you to collect as much energy as you can in your core. It's going to hurt, but you must push through the pain. Keep drawing in more energy until you've broken the invisible binds concealing your wings."

The pain she's speaking of, I know exactly what she's referring to. I feel it every time I open a doorway. "Are you sure?"

"Yes!" she shouts.

With a deep inhale, I concentrate, drawing in energy from the power within me. The pain in my back aches, spiking from the top of my neck down to the middle of my spine. I don't let up as the energy swells in my core. The pain becomes almost unbearable, but then I think of Elijah, and Adele, who might need me.

I keep drawing in more energy…and then it happens. Something breaks free and I scream. Pain like I've never experienced rips through my entire body, and I fall to the floor, hands scraping the warm rock.

When the pain finally subsides, soft feathers brush against my sides.

I remember everything. I know exactly who I am and where I come from.

And it's time for retribution. Merigoth is going to pay for what she's done to my kind.

CHAPTER 25

ADELE

The inside of the cave is dark and empty. No Rune. No Elijah. The doorway to the Under Realm is nothing more than the smooth black obsidian slab. I don't have my flint with me, so Trevor and I make do with the sliver of moonlight illuminating the front half of the cave. Outside, I walk over to where Trevor waits by the river. He's holding his walking stick, sitting in silence.

"You sure you can do this?" I ask, helping him to his feet.

Taking hold of my forearm, then patting it with his bony hand, he says, "Trust me."

I don't flinch or pull away. I just help him carefully walk up the rocky dirt path to the cave. Less than twenty-four hours ago, I would've pushed him away, not wanting anyone to get too close to my hands. Silently, I remind myself, *As long as I've got my gloves on, then the old man is safe.* We approach the mouth of the cave, and I tell him, "It's dark in there, and the ground is uneven, so watch your step."

He presses a palm to the side of the entrance. Fibrous roots from the oak tree growing above rustle beneath his hand. "Adele, I'm blind. The dark doesn't affect me."

"Well, I don't know what you can and can't see," I say. "Seems to me that you're still keeping secrets too." We slowly make our way toward the rear of the cave, into the shallow nook area where the obsidian is hiding. The end of his walking stick hits the hard ground, banging against rock with each step forward. When we've reached the slab, I tell him, "Okay, we're here. Now what?"

He rests his trusty walking stick against the wall next to the obsidian slab before shuffling closer. He raises his hands but pauses mid-stretch. The moonlight doesn't reach this far back, but my eyes have adjusted enough to see his hesitation. I'm about to ask if there's a problem when he reaches behind his head and pulls off his wool tunic.

"Let me help," I say, grabbing the shirt and helping him get it over his head. His long white hair clings to the sides of his face. He brushes the wispy strands aside, then resumes his focus on the dark slab, pressing both palms flat to the smooth surface.

I roll up his tunic and rest it on the ground next to his walking stick.

"Listen, Adele." His voice is raspier than usual, choked up with emotion for some reason. "Don't linger. Find Rune and get out. If you can find Elijah, and he's still himself, then save him, too. But the only way you'll be able to return to the Human Realm is with Rune. Otherwise—"

"Yeah, I get it. I'll be stuck in the Under Realm forever."

"I wish you the best, dear child. And remember, the greatest power you possess isn't in your hands, but in your freedom to choose. Trust your instincts."

Before I can thank the old man for his encouragement, he begins spouting words in another language. A white light illuminates from in front of Trevor, reflecting on the black slab embedded in the cave wall. At first, I think he's opening a doorway like Rune, but then I see it isn't the rock that's glowing—it's Trevor.

My mouth drops open, and I can't believe what I'm seeing. Giant wings covered in white feathers gently unfurl between his shoulder blades. How has he managed to keep those things hidden? I briefly glance down at the tunic folded on the ground next to his walking stick. Has he been hiding wings beneath his clothes all this time?

"You're an…"

"There aren't many of us left," he says with a weak smile. "Now, let me focus." The light from his body travels through his arms and over to the obsidian slab, outlining the doorway. "The passage won't stay open for long. So, make haste when it's open." The doorway wavers like dark water rippling over the surface, and slowly the Under Realm appears. "Go!" he tells me, his voice booming through the cave and out into the night air. Trevor's crows fervently caw from outside.

With my knife in one hand, I give Trevor a nod of gratitude before passing through the doorway. The second I'm through, the cool autumn air of the Human Realm vanishes, quickly replaced with hot, dry air that envelops me. It takes me a second to adjust my breathing.

It's then that Merigoth's enchantment hits me. I stagger, gripping the wall for support. The lure punches the sides of my temples, persistent in trying to break into my mind.

"Fight it!" Trevor shouts from the other side. "Distract your mind from her lure!"

Remembering Elijah's song, I start humming the tune. The enchantment subsides a little but doesn't completely disappear. Standing tall, I turn and face Trevor, still on the other side of the doorway. But something strange is happening to him. It's as if he's fading at the edges. He stretches his wings open, but the space inside the cave prevents him from spreading them too wide. The energy he used to open the portal surrounds him. A bright white light. The forest outside the cave entrance becomes visible through his fading body.

"What's happening to you?" I shout.

With a proud, nearly translucent smile, he says, "That was my final act of hope." The edges of his body break away into specks of light, like sparkling dust.

"No!" I cry and reach for him, but my fingers jab hard against solid rock. The doorway is closed. All I can do is watch as he continues to disappear, pieces of him floating toward the open sky.

Find them and save them. His last words echo in my mind as the remaining specks of light float away, leaving behind the darkness of the cave.

I slam my palm hard against the solid rock. No one asked him to sacrifice himself like that. We could've found another way. My heart wrenches as I slide my hand down the rock. How am I going to explain this to the others?

That's if I make it out of here alive.

My boots scuff along the rock floor of the cave, away from the doorway. The dark world outside the mouth of this cave is my only option. There's no way to return to the Human Realm without Rune's help. Stretching my fingers and rolling my neck, I inhale a deep breath, taking in the warm, dry air. Leaving the cave, I make my way out into the Under Realm.

CHAPTER 26

ADELE

A path covered in dark gray gravel leads me away from the cave entrance. A shriek echoes from somewhere high above, and I spin, holding out my knife while checking my surroundings. I gaze up at the jagged rocks lining the black mountainside until the peak disappears into the pitch-black sky. It seems to be a lone mountain, but I can't be certain if there are more highlands in the distance since the horizon is veiled in darkness. Short, spiky rocks protrude randomly from the base of the mountain, surrounding the mouth of the cave. A faint red glow emanates from behind the rocks, creating an eerie and infernal impression on the mountainside. When I feel it's safe to continue, I resume walking along the path.

Ignoring the persistent chant lingering at the rear of my mind, I quietly hum Elijah's song. I'd hate to make it all this way, only to fall under Merigoth's lure.

It doesn't take long for beads of sweat to form along my forehead, under my shirt, and inside my gloves. To the left of the gravel path, the expansive barren land is covered in oversized cracks, creating plate-like pavers. Bright molten lava bubbles between the crevasses, lighting the land with a soft red hue. On the other side of the path there are thousands of graves, identical in size, row after row.

But they're open graves.

Many of the holes are occupied by Shades, but some are empty. And they're just lying there. It looks as if they're sleeping, but it's hard to tell. Every one of them looks identical to the next, with shaved heads, and the same faded black strips of fabric wrapping their bodies.

I need to be furtive in my search for Rune and Elijah. With each crunching step along the gravel path, I keep a watchful eye on the resting Shades. My heart pounds inside my chest, and I can't help but feel as if they could come alive and grab me at any second.

I continue along the path, quietly humming Elijah's tune. Suddenly, I hear whimpering. Picking up my pace, I press on through the hot air that consumes this realm, until I discover a grave with someone tossing about inside it.

It's Kit.

Gauging the depth of the hole, I crouch by the edge, then lower myself in, careful not to land on her. A chunk of dry dirt breaks away and crumbles to the floor of the pit. The top of the hole comes up to my waist, and before checking on her, I scan the path in both directions for movement. After tucking my blade into my waistband, I kneel beside Kit and shake her shoulders. "Hey! Wake up!"

With her eyes closed, she moans, twisting from side to side as if trying to escape some horrid nightmare. Not sure if it'll do more harm than good, I pull off one of my gloves, tuck it into the front of my vest, then press my palm to her cheek. Kit's muscles instantly tense up.

Closing my eyes, I reach into her mind. Her memories are there but blocked off by some kind of ghost wall. I can see them back there, images of her past, but I'm unable to reach them. There's only one memory not locked away—it's a moment from our past that I remember from when I was a child. But something is off... I reach farther into her mind, entering the memory.

In her memory, I open my eyes. Kit and I are young children. Except Kit—who's sitting next to me out on the Green behind Goslings—isn't a child, but as she is today. Everything feels real. The sun's shining down on us, the grass is lush, and the scent of bread baking from Aunt Lauren's cottage fills the afternoon air.

Normally, I avoid entering anyone's memories to this degree because it's never anything joyful. The memories that come easiest for me to see are always a person's greatest fear or a traumatic experience from their past. Those moments from a person's life rarely subside in a person's mind. Time helps, but it doesn't erase. So, I try not to enter the memories of those I'm interrogating. They often return to haunt me if I don't take my sleeping tonic.

But this memory is nice. A moment in time that I long to go back to. Older Kit and younger me sit in the green grass, making bouquets for our mums from wildflowers we picked from a neighbor's garden. Villagers bustle about in the distant parts of Bricen while Kit and I watch a young Elijah. He's busy trying to catch grasshoppers.

I step around to the other side to get a better look at myself. The sun highlights my wheat-colored hair and rosy complexion. Thank the stars I outgrew those plump chipmunk cheeks. Tato keeps me company by my side, watching me arrange the small purple flowers in my fist. I have to remind myself that this Adele—the one with no problems, no fears, and plenty of people who loved her—doesn't exist anymore.

"Let's go make some mud pies by the creek," full-grown Kit says to my younger self.

"Last time we made muddy-pies your mum wasn't too happy," little me says, squinting from the bright sunlight. "She kept you inside for three moons! Besides, we're supposed to watch Elijah."

Older Kit looks over her shoulder at her little brother. "Well, let's leave him here then. He can't get into any trouble out here on the Green."

"I don't know." Little me scrunches her tiny button nose while picking up Tato and squeezing him tight around the middle.

"Come on, Adele. Elijah will be fine." Kit stands and starts skipping for the forest, leaving her bouquet sprawled out on the grass. Back then, of course, there wasn't a giant barrier surrounding the village. Just an open forest.

I look at the little girl—me—and for a second, I think about how I'd do anything to go back in time to be this little girl again, but then I shake that thought from my head. Going back means no Selene. And I can't imagine a world without her friendship. She's my confidante and anchor to the person I want to be. Well, wanted to be. Now, I'm not so sure. I'm one of the three original Shades, created to wreak havoc on this realm and others.

"You coming?" Kit calls from between two cottages at the edge of the woods. Returning my focus to Kit's memory, I watch as young me gets up, brushes off her blue skirt, and runs after Kit.

I don't understand why Kit is trapped in this memory. Did she choose it, or did Marcellus pick a random memory to trap Kit's consciousness in?

Next to me, little boy Elijah, brown curls covering the top of his head, gets to his feet. A green grasshopper is captured between his dirt-smeared hands. He circles in his spot and calls for Kit but can't find her. Wanting to show her his prize, he heads toward the forest, but in the opposite direction of where Kit ran off.

"Wait!" I call out, but he doesn't hear me. He keeps running with those stocky, short legs straight into the forest. Now, I really remember this day. It was the day Elijah got lost. The entire village searched the surrounding woods for him. It wasn't until two moons later that the huntsman strolled into Bricen with the missing child. Kit cried the entire time her brother was gone.

Pulling myself out of the memory and back into the open grave, I slip my glove back on and try to wake Kit again. Whatever mental trap Marcellus forced Kit into is too strong for me to break. I'll need Rune's help.

Tight brown curls have escaped the ribbon tying Kit's hair back from her face. I clench my jaw and awkwardly press my hand to the side of her head, whispering a promise that I'll return with help.

Climbing out of the hole isn't a challenge. I stay low while lying on the packed dirt. I'm about to get to my feet when the *crunch* of gravel suggests someone's coming. Quickly, I roll into the adjacent hole. Thank the stars that it's empty, but I curse from the pain spiking along my side from landing hard on my back. I suppress my groan and lie perfectly still, pretending to sleep but keeping my eyes open just enough to see through my eyelashes. It sounds like two sets of footsteps. When whoever it is approaching walks by, I try and estimate how close they are to me. Their feet shuffle off the path, followed by a soft *thud*. I'm guessing one has jumped into a nearby grave. I can only hope they're not in Kit's.

It isn't long before they're walking along the gravel path again, dragging something...or someone. I wait a long moment before slowly peering over the edge of the pit. The two Shades and whomever they're dragging fade into the darkness. I pick up my knife, which has fallen out of my waistband, and crawl out of the hole. I glance into Kit's grave and curse. It's empty.

Staying low, I hurry along the path, following the direction of the Shades. The path curves slightly to the right and seems to go on forever, the graves on one side and the expansive, barren, cracked world on my left. The black sky above rumbles as if a storm is coming, but there aren't any clouds or moon. There's absolutely nothing. It's just a void of nothingness.

How does anything survive in this place?

And how can I be from this realm?

Ahead, fading in from the darkness, are flames floating in the air alongside the path. As I get closer, I see they're not actually floating, but coming from tall iron torches staked in the ground. As I creep closer, the end of the trail comes into view. There are at least twenty Shades standing like statues, spaced out in front of another cave, except the mouth of this cave is a hundred times grander than the one I passed through to get to the Under Realm. It's also perfectly carved into the mountainside like one of the graves.

Without hesitation, I dash to the right, nimbly running between rows of dirt holes, until I reach a sizable boulder that tapers toward the top. From there, I'm mere steps away from the entrance to the cave, hidden from plain view. Even the flickering torchlight fails to reach this far into the shadows. Taking a quick peek, I survey the area. The Shades remain motionless, their piercing gazes fixed straight ahead on the gravel path.

Kit's in there. I know it. And I need to get in there before they turn her into one of those Reborn creatures. After the recent encounter at Castle Forge, I cringe just thinking about the pain Alister must've endured while that demon spirit entered his body.

With my heart racing and my senses on high alert, I scan the area. I wish I had my bow so I could cause a simple distraction. Not ready to part ways with my knife, I pick up a rock and throw it off into the distance.

Just my luck. The Shades don't react.

"There's no need to hide, child." A woman's soothing voice floats into my mind.

I quickly duck behind the stone, kneeling on one knee.

She calls to me again, *"Come. No one will harm you. We're all family—we're all monsters here."*

At the word *monsters*, the Shades standing at attention in front of the cave entrance turn their heads and look my way.

"Come," she repeats. Her alluring voice draws me out from my hiding spot, and I don't resist. The group of Shade men and women parts, making a wide path for me to pass through. With each foot forward, I can feel my mind fading, and oddly, I'm okay with that. A sense of acceptance and love envelops me, reaching into my core.

"Welcome home, Adele."

CHAPTER 27

ADELE

My feet are moving, but I'm not controlling them. The tunnel into the mountain has no torches or cracks of magma to light the way. I have to trust the enchantment to guide me. One step after another, I continue walking deeper into the darkness. It's not fear or anger humming beneath my skin, but hope and eagerness to finally find a place I can call home. Rune was wrong, I am sure of it. The Under Realm isn't a prison. It's where I come from… Where I belong… My true home.

The bliss caressing my mind reassures me not to be afraid or ashamed of who I am. In the human world, I am a monster. But here, I'm a *Shade*.

As I continue along the dark tunnel, memories of my past resurface in my mind. The many faces of the men and women General Onica had me interrogate. The fear in their eyes and the way their bodies writhed in agony once I left them prisoner to their own traumas. Night after night, I fell asleep in my bed alone, thinking about how everyone in Fayatin feared me. Even if they didn't know the identity of the Interrogator, I knew it was me. And because of that, I would forever be alone.

Except for Selene. Her face appears in my mind, dark hair framing her pale skin and rosy cheeks.

My feet shuffle to a stop, tiny rocks scuffing beneath my boots. I can't remember what I was doing.

Then, two more faces appear in my mind—Elijah and Rune.

My friends. Those who didn't shy away after learning certain truths about what I am. Selene was a friend to me even though I tortured all those souls at Castle Forge. And Elijah's persistence to rekindle our friendship even after seeing what I did to Heathrow. Then there's Rune. She knew my true nature and still wanted to stay in Bricen and help. How did I forget about—

"You're almost here. Come, Adele. I want to show you something." Another wave of bliss accompanies Merigoth's words, clouding my focus. I can't recall my last thoughts. It must not have been that important. Strolling on, the momentary distraction is gone from my priorities, replaced with an elated sense of homecoming. Like a soldier returning to loved ones after battle.

"If you give yourself to me, then I will reunite you with your mother."

Merigoth would reunite me with…my mum. A memory pushes through the fog and surfaces in my mind. There's a woman who shares the same long wheat-colored hair as me, and she's hugging me while sitting on the grass, sunbeams outlining her body. It's my mum. And I remember this day as if it were yesterday. Warmth floods my entire body at the recollection.

"You can have that happiness again." Merigoth's voice floats into the scene of my mum and me, like a cool breeze passing by. *"Isn't that what you've always wanted? To be with your mother again?"*

When I don't answer, the bliss withdraws, and I stop in my path, hands pressing to the rocky wall of the tunnel for support. A sharp coldness fills the empty spot left by the retreating memory. My heart pounds beneath my chest, and panic sets in. "No! Wait! You're right! Please, don't take it away! I belong here. My family is here!"

Slowly, the warmth of her bliss returns, washing over me like a sudden downpour of rain. I sigh, all anxiety dissipating as if it had never existed. A doorway comes into view, and I make for the bright white light waiting for me beyond. I don't care what is inside. All that matters is holding on to this embracing feeling of love and acceptance. To finally find a home where I can feel comfortable in my own skin.

When I finally reach the threshold, I leave the dark tunnel behind and enter a brightly lit throne room. I've seen throne rooms before. General Onica has one adjacent to the Great Hall at Castle Forge, though it's not as elaborate as the throne room in the Verglas Palace in Noviska. The king and queen of the northern country have several ice sculptures adorning the grounds, inside and out. There're also thick icy-blue winter vines, sprouting blue and white flowers, trailing up the walls and stained-glass windows of the throne room. It's a magical place but doesn't compare to the beauty here.

How can there be so much beauty in a place that's said to be filled with darkness and hate?

Thick white fog coats the throne-room floor, and I feel as if I'm walking in the clouds. My gaze soaks in the grandeur of the space. Her bliss hugs my thoughts, making me smile, and I brush a gloved hand through the cool mist rolling up my legs. The polished white walls of the room show the reflections of all the pristine furniture in the room—a few side tables and upholstered armchairs, and one long chaise lounge. I only know what a chaise is because the general gifted me one a few years ago, thinking material things would counter the guilt I accumulated from my line of work.

The general.

Her face appears in my mind through the cloudy haze. The stern look she often wears, demanding obedience. Dark sable hair frames her face as the ends graze the tops of her shoulders. One side of her pale red lips curls up into a wicked grin.

"No!" I shout, squeezing my eyes closed, hoping that's enough to not see her face.

The blissful haze reacts, pushing the general's face from my mind. Another round of bliss releases, easing my nerves. The warm, comforting heat fills my mind and body, and I don't care to remember what had upset me anymore. It's gone, and I'm happy again.

Moving farther into the throne room, my legs walking through the clouds, I look up and take in the expansive domed ceiling that's decorated with ornate gold filigree. And in the center hangs a massive chandelier full of crystals and candles. Dropping my gaze, I notice more pieces of gold in the torches lining the cavern walls. They appear more for decoration than functionality as the bright light filling the throne room seems to come from within the lustrous walls.

Still in awe, I make my way toward the rear of the throne room where a beautiful—no, not beautiful, breathtaking—stone chair rests on a platform. The seat is made of white marble with gold veins running through it. Sprouting out from the back side are giant stone wings. They're stretched out wide, each feather carved perfectly. The brilliance of the overall design radiates a sense of power and supremacy.

From behind the throne, a woman strides out toward me. She's beyond stunning. The silky, white, floor-length dress she's wearing hugs her slender body. I've never seen a gown without sleeves, or at least I don't think I have. My memories of anything before are evading me at the moment. But her pale skin is so unbelievably flawless. Not a single scar, freckle, or blemish.

She tilts her head, and her soft blue eyes look me over. Part of her long, wavy hair sweeps forward, over her bare shoulder, and I think how the color resembles my own blonde hair. A color Selene would often describe as "when warm sunlight hits a field of wheat."

Selene, I silently say her name, trying to remember.

But the second my dear friend enters my mind, another rush of external bliss hits me, forcing my thoughts back into submission. I refocus my attention on the queen of the Under Realm standing before me.

"You must be Queen Merigoth?"

Her full, red lips part into a smile, the whitest teeth I've ever seen peeking through. "You are family, my dear. You can call me by my birth name, Loralai Songwielder." Her voice is musical and warm, carrying more bliss for my body to absorb. "Loralai will be fine." Her feet move as if she's floating. "We must celebrate your return!" She clasps her hands together, intertwining her gold-covered fingertips.

She descends the steps, coming within arms-reach of me. The white dress she wears shows off her bare shoulders and trails along her slender body, the bottom disappearing into the pillow of clouds at our feet.

Narrowing my eyes, I study our similarities. "Why do we look so alike?"

She reaches her hand to me and touches my cheek. It's at that moment everything changes. "We share the same blood—you, me, and your mother."

The room around us flickers from existence, showing something dark and gruesome in its place. The beautiful woman standing before me momentarily shifts, revealing pasty, cracked skin with frail, thinning hair—no longer the color of wheat but a sad gray. Her blue eyes disappear, replaced with a blackness that consumes her irises. But as quickly as it happened, the room flickers and returns to its pristine whiteness, and I blink. What is happening?

Unfazed by the brief lapse, Loralai continues talking as she strides by me. "This is your throne room—" She opens her arm to the expansive cavern. Again, the brilliance of her white dress falters, revealing worn dark garments wrapping her pasty body. Flat spikes the size of my hand and resembling black bones protrude from both collarbones and the sides of her neck. From within the wild strands of her thinning hair are two short black horns, each one sticking out the side of her head just above her pointed ears. But then, the nightmarish moment is gone, and all is beautiful again, and she continues her sentence: "—as much as it is mine."

Narrowing my eyes and scanning the room over again, I can't make sense of what's going on. The lure tightens its hold on my mind, applying pressure inside my skull and spreading more warmth and bliss into my veins. Yet, something has unhinged between us. The room continues to shift between what's real and what's not—yet I can't tell which is which.

"Don't listen to her!" a familiar voice shouts in the distance. It's Elijah, yet he sounds worlds away. "Adele! Stay with us!"

Loralai's smile grows. Her brilliant white teeth gleam, but for a split second they disappear, and her smile is filled with serrated teeth, like broken glass jutting from her black gums. I flinch, and Loralai's smile flattens.

"What's wrong, child?"

Wincing, I dip my head and try to think. Where are my thoughts? I silently list off things I know to be true and real, hoping to sever whatever hold Loralai has over me.

Elijah and Kit.

Bricen and Trevor.

Aunt Lauren and Mum.

Castle Forge, the general, and Alister.

And Selene.

Forcing myself to remember each one gives me enough self-awareness to realize where I am and who I'm with.

It was all a glamour.

"Adele, come. Let's make this official." Loralai—no, not Loralai but Merigoth—beckons and walks toward the throne, a discreet limp in her left leg.

While she's facing away from me, I take in the ominous ambience of the cavern. The real throne room. Obsidian walls with jagged rocks stippling the surface. Along the ground, the white fog no longer resembles fluffy clouds, but an inky black fog that's thick and rolling with life.

"Yes, Loralai," I answer, using the name she asked me to use, hoping she doesn't realize I've broken free from her ruse. To keep up appearances, I don't smile, nor do I express the anger building inside me. Because that's all I have going for me right now—the element of surprise. Merigoth's lure pecks at my thoughts, but I'm able to hold the mental shield I've constructed to protect myself.

The queen of the Under Realm continues up the platform steps. The stone tread is cracked and deteriorating all the way up to the landing where her throne sits. But this time I see it for what it really is. The seat I saw earlier—the smooth marble stone with beautiful angel wings carved into the sides—is gone. And her so-called throne isn't a throne at all, but a pile of bones held together with mud, poorly made to resemble a chair for a creature that's desperate for power and control.

I almost want to laugh at the pathetic attempt to look like royalty but refrain. I still don't know the extent of power this Merigoth creature can unleash.

Playing on her hopes to make a connection with me, I ask in a curious voice, "What do you mean, we share the same blood? Are we really family?"

She continues as if nothing's changed, and gracefully sits upon her pile of bones. From beneath her, a long slender bone cracks at the center, releasing gray dust into the air. When I look at her, her expression remains loving and welcoming, but within her soulless eyes, I sense hunger and deception.

"How much do you know about where you come from?" she asks.

"Rune told me I come from the Under Realm," I answer honestly.

"Ah, yes. Rune. She's quite the handful, you know, always straying from her responsibilities." Wrinkles line her cracking gray skin and have me thinking she must be centuries old.

Merigoth continues, indulging my curiosity. She even tries to appear happy to explain, though all I see is a dreadfully terrifying smile. "I'll tell you a story about a young couple I met a long time ago. They were in love and happy but living in poverty. So, I offered them an opportunity to help make a better world where everyone was equal."

I'm not sure I like where this is going, but I stay quiet and let her finish her tale.

"I brought them here, to the Under Realm." She feigned a hand over her eyes, as if the memory was hard to relive. "We were happy here. Then, one day I asked them to bear children. The woman said she could not, so I shared my blood with them to boost their chances—and it worked! Three precious babies were born."

"What happened to them?"

"Well, I don't know. Two were taken from me. They were barely a year old. You were one of those babies."

"Well, I'm here now," I say, continuing to play along. "And the parents. What happened to them?"

"Let's not discuss your mother quite yet. And you should know that the man—your father—well, he left." I'm about to ask where the man went, but she cuts me off. "No, no. Don't worry about the details."

So, it's true. The woman from Trevor's story—the one who stole two of the Shade babies—is my mum. She was brought to this malevolent world and turned into something dark and evil. But—but how is she that woman? Mum barely ever cursed or raised her voice. She was the kindest, most empathetic woman I ever knew, always giving to others and never asking for anything in return.

I need to keep Merigoth talking. So, beating down the anger rising inside, I ask with the calmest voice I can muster, "You said I could see my mum again? That we can be a family again?"

Merigoth's soulless eyes glare at me. A wry grin curling at the corners of her pale lips. "So, you want to stay in this glorious place I've built? Pure with beauty and power." She waves a hand through the air. The cracks running along her ghastly arm look as if they are going to peel right off her skin. "I created it in the image of our true home—the Starlight Realm—a place I plan to return to one day." Her voice is the only thing that hasn't changed. It remains soothing and calm, with an invisible tug to it.

That tug is the lure. Poking the back of my mind, it continues its efforts to wiggle its way into my thoughts again. *My will is her will*, it repeats. As tempting as it is to feel the blissful warmth again, I maintain the mental shield protecting my mind.

"In due time, you'll see your mother again. But first, you'll have to prove your loyalty." With a long, decrepit-looking finger, she brushes a strand of hair from my face. "Tell me what it is you want."

To find those you've taken is what I want to say, but then I recall the phrase of her enchantment. It's those words she wants to hear—to know I'm hers to command. "My will is your will."

Her colorless lips stretch into a wide smile, showing off the vile teeth lining her dark gums. "Yes, well," she says, then shifts her attention to somewhere behind me. "Bring her here!"

Stepping down off the platform, she gestures for me to follow. I obey, and the second I'm facing the other way a tall man comes into view. His chafed skin sags from his bones. My body flinches—an internal survival instinct of some sort—but I quickly recompose my posture. Merigoth's attention is on the man. Thank the stars she didn't see me falter.

The man's mouth hangs open, his breathing heavy. His clouded eyes are focused on his queen as she hobbles toward him. She holds a hand up and he tips his head lower so she can reach him, anxious for her attention. When she pats his cheek, the skin jiggles as if barely attached to the bones and muscles beneath.

What happened to this man? And then he opens his mouth and releases a piercing shriek into the cavern. The black fog around my legs responds, rippling with an intense ferocity. Understanding washes over me. When he closes his mouth and the deafening noise ceases, I realize this man has succumbed to one of the demon spirits—just as Alister did—and is now a Reborn.

Merigoth steps aside, allowing me to see the Reborn's grimy hand on Kit's shoulder. A layer of dirt coats not only his skin and clothes, but also the spaces beneath and around his fingernails. I have to reel in the urge to whip out my blade and sever his hand from his arm.

"That'll be all," she commands and the creature leaves. He disappears behind a large pillar chiseled out from the mountain, revealing a second entrance into the throne room. Something I might need later. Come to think of it, Rune might be down there, too.

Metal chains rustle from behind me, and I hear Elijah struggling, but I don't look because compelled me wouldn't care about him, and that's who I need to be right now.

"Child, come here." The queen beckons me with a wave of her bony hand in the air. Her fingers curling in and out like legs of a spider. "I want you to witness how we're preparing to overrun the human world. A world undeserved by those worthless mortals."

Kit's eyes are open, but they aren't looking at me. They're focused over my shoulder, off into the distance.

"Adele! Don't let them hurt my sister!" Elijah yells, metal chains clanking against the stone floor. His voice is much louder and closer than before.

Merigoth swirls her hand into the dark fog rising around her legs. Her short black demon nails caressing the lively fog as if it were a pet. Then, when a winged creature, more black smoke than beast, with blood-colored eyes, bursts out into the open, I realize it's not just a murky fog covering the cavern ground. The demon spirit circles high above us, releasing a menacing shriek that causes a spike of pain deep within my ears. Trying to hold onto the ruse, to appear obedient, I resist the urge to muffle the sound. When the creature finally silences, I know what's coming next. The same thing happened moments before Alister's body was overtaken. Alister died in that moment, and in his place was a Reborn.

I can't let the same thing happen to Kit.

Head tilted up, Merigoth's attention is on the demon spirit. Dark smoke trailing as it flies about the domed cavern. Her pasty-gray hands are clasped at her chest, a look of exuberance beaming on her face as she waits for another Reborn to enter this world.

Well, I'm not going to let that happen. This ends now.

CHAPTER 28

ᴀDELE

Slowly, reaching behind my back, I slip off my gloves, letting them drop into the dark, billowing swarm of demon spirits covering the cavern floor. While Merigoth is still distracted, watching her pet fly about the throne room, I rush forward, closing the space between us. Reaching up, I clasp my palms against the sides of her face.

Instantly, she falls to her knees. Her mouth stretches unnaturally as if her jawline has detached from her face. Flaky skin tears along her skin, causing dark oily blood to ooze out. A strangled cry wheezes its way out, and I know she feels my reach crossing over into her mind. Her eyes are open to their fullest. The soulless black circles consuming her irises and pupils roll toward her upper eyelid.

Above, the demon spirit goes wild, flapping its dark wings and shrieking that deafening squawk. Heavy wafts of black smoke trail its chaotic flight path.

"What are you doing?" Merigoth finally gasps. I don't let the surprise of her being able to speak affect my hold on her. If anything, I reach farther into her mind, forcing her into submission.

"You will not...break me," she forces out. "You...obey...me!" Her eyes tremble, refusing to roll completely back into her skull. She's trying to look at me. I thought she'd be more powerful—harder to trap—but she, like everyone else, is begging for her life.

A sense of satisfaction washes through me and amplifies the invasion. Merigoth screams. The demon queen of the Under Realm is mine now. Exploding past the last barrier of resistance the pathetic queen has, I reach her mind. Instead of her memories playing out behind my eyes, the glamour used to disguise the room flickers to life again, showcasing her memories on the cavern walls.

I've never seen anything like it before. One memory after the next displays all around us. Eventually, the carousel of memories stops, and one in particular plays out.

We're in a warm, well-lit forest, similar to the woods of Harvesgrove, but the trees are taller and thicker. The tips of the leaves on the trees sparkle with specks of light. The glamour has somehow manifested, making it seem like I'm actually standing in whatever forest this is.

Three people...no, not people...angels, stroll into the wooded area. They could easily be mistaken for common villagers by the look of their casual clothing, but no villager I know has beautiful feathery wings coming out of their back. Craning my neck, hands still pressed to Merigoth's leathery skin, I see their wings are tucked close to their bodies like feathered cloaks.

"Are…are those angels?" Elijah asks from somewhere behind me.

Glancing over my shoulder and seeing him for the first time, I notice he's chained to the rocky wall. "You can see this?"

"I can." His wide eyes soaking in the magical view. "Everything feels so real. The warm sunlight, the fresh air. What exactly am I seeing?"

Turning my attention to the angels again, I explain, "It's one of Merigoth's memories."

The tallest of the three angels steps forward. Her soft gray hair draped over one shoulder matches the color of her wings. With a pale hand, she waves for someone hiding in the woods to come forth. "We need to see you. Come out and show yourself, Loralai, of the Songwielder family." The other two angels, one with black wings and the other with brown, stare intently, awaiting Loralai to come forth.

A young woman, wearing a beige dress tattered at the ends and smeared with dry dirt, cautiously peeks out from behind an oversized tree. She holds the trunk as if she were clinging to her mother for security.

"Come," the gray-winged angel calls again.

When she breaks away from the tree, I see she's got white wings trailing from her back. Except they don't look so good. With each step forward, more of her feathers break off, falling to the forest ground. Lining the edge of her neck and forehead are dark sores, and her pale arms are covered with swollen veins.

Brushing aside her disheveled blonde hair from her dirt-covered face, she pleads, "I was attacked, ambushed by a demon horde, and now I can't fly. I can barely walk. I need help!" Soft sobs follow as Loralai tries to step away from the tree. Her weak body doesn't allow her legs to work, and she quickly hugs the trunk again.

"That is not possible, Loralai," the gray-winged angel says sadly. "You've come in contact with demon blood. Sadly, there is no cure for that. Your fate is no longer here with us."

"But… You are the North Star. And as one of the four rulers of the Starlight Realm, you have the power to rid me of this infliction. Please, Nataria. Don't let me die out here."

Pursing her lips, Nataria shakes her head. "I cannot make that allowance. Not even for one of the ruling Stars."

The angel with brown wings steps forward, her glossy eyes trembling. "Oh, Loralai. We're so sorry for this unfortunate day. We'll have one of your kin step up and rule in your place as South Star." Nataria and the other leading Star angel nod in agreement.

Slipping from the support of the tree trunk, Loralai crawls forward, poisoned white feathers falling from her wings. She reaches for the three Star rulers, wincing with each movement forward. "Please, I beg you. Don't force me to leave. This is my home."

Young Loralai collapses to the forest ground, and the few feathers remaining dissipate into black smoke. The three angels take several steps away, covering their noses and mouths as if afraid they, too, might catch whatever demon poison has infected Loralai.

As the last of her feathers and flesh vanish from her wings, she spits with furious, weak breaths, "I fought for you, and this is how you repay me? By abandoning me?" A sob rips through her, but they say nothing.

"You'll regret that choice." With energy she doesn't appear to have, she stands, spreading her bone wings wide for them to see—to remember her—before running off into the woods.

The glamour flickers, and for a second, I think another memory will begin, but the same one starts again. The three angels enter the forest, calling forth the angel in hiding. Calling forth Loralai.

Staring down at the queen kneeling in front of me, I ask, "Is it here you wish to stay?" She doesn't answer—she can't—but tears stream from the corners of her black eyes.

Just as I begin building my entrapment within Merigoth's mind, the room erupts in deafening shrieks. The memory glamour flickers from existence, and the shiny obsidian walls of the cavern return. The dark fog covering the cavern's floor churns aggressively. One by one, demon spirits fill the room.

"Adele!" Elijah shouts.

"Yeah, I know. I'm hurrying!"

Ignoring the evil spirits, I focus on the memory. There is no need to alter or amend it to make Merigoth suffer any more. This memory is the absolute low point of her existence. It was the moment she was turned away from this Starlight Realm. The sorrow and heartbreak were physical, and I could feel her pain as she knelt on the forest ground, sobbing tears of forgiveness—but forgiveness for what? She was the one who got struck and infected with demon blood, right? She was the one who paid with her life for whatever conflict she was sent to fight for. The angels standing before her showed no sympathy or sorrow for the afflicted angel before them.

And for a second, I feel sorry for Merigoth.

The second passes and my pity for her vanishes. She chose vengeance and domination in the wake of her banishment. The things she's done since then are unforgivable. She needs to answer for her crimes, and in the meantime, until I know what justice means for her, she needs to stay here—in this moment.

Concentrating, I add an extra layer of security to her mental prison. I've done this hundreds of times, but she's an all-powerful demon with the ability to enchant others with her mind. Best not to take any risks. When the final thread of containment is locked into place, I observe my handiwork. The scene plays out again, except this time it isn't a sickly-looking young woman with decaying angel wings that steps out from behind the wide tree trunk. This time, it's Merigoth—the creature she is now, stepping out to face the ruling angels. Merigoth's gaze avoids the angels, her hands wrapping her waist, shoulders hunched as she staggers closer. She cowers before them, the pasty-gray skin along her shoulders, neck, and face cracked like a desert that hasn't seen water in ages. And her long pale hair has gone thin and brittle. But she doesn't see herself this way. Not at this point. Right now, she believes she's still that angel who has returned home from the battle, facing rejection. After she's been denied any help, she turns to flee and sees the one thing I've added to this memory. An ornate mirror hanging from the front of the tree. This is when she sees what she's become.

Merigoth screams, pulling at her face and scraping at the cracked skin of her arms as if to shed her appearance like a dirty frock. Her cries bellow up into the treetops of the Starlight Realm, shaking the roots and the memory so vigorously until it abruptly stops. Then, the scene plays out all over again.

Satisfied, I release my hands from her face. The all-powerful queen of the Under Realm topples over onto her side. The cluster of demon spirits clears away, forming a thick smoke ring around the base of the throne room. I brush my hands off on my pants.

Then, something happens that's never happened before. My prisoner moves. Merigoth's hands twitch, and her body curls in. I step away, worried that she might break free and launch herself at me, but she doesn't. Instead, her eyelids lower and her gaping mouth slowly closes.

I listen for the voice in the back of my mind. There's nothing but silence. The lure is gone. Hopefully, it's gone for everyone else, too. Exhaling, I finally have a moment to relax. The air in here is disgusting and dry but that doesn't stop me from sucking in deep breaths. I've never felt this drained before after interrogating anyone.

I straighten my back and go to help Elijah, but I'm met with a stabbing pain straight through my collarbone. I stumble backward, screaming and falling to the ground. Elijah cries out, but the pain overpowers his voice, inhibiting my ears from working. My hands clasp the iron spear sticking out of my shoulder. My vision blurs and all I see is a shadow of a person standing over me. Then more pain, as the spear is wrenched from my body, slicing the palms of my hands in its extraction.

There's a bloody hole in its place. Blood soaks my white linen shirt and stains the leather vest. Everything is spinning. My head, the room, my bloody hands. I can't see straight.

How did I let someone sneak up on me like this? I got so far…defeated Merigoth…and for what? To be struck down at the end. Never to witness the outcome of the one good thing I did in my life.

My eyelids flutter as the pain increases. The warm floor of the cavern fades and my body starts to go numb. It's at this moment I realize: I don't want to die alone.

Someone kicks my foot, and I force my eyes open. It takes a moment for my vision to focus, and I'm able to see the monster standing over me. Marcellus. My blood drips from the tip of his spear.

"I told her you couldn't be trusted!" he sneers, then kicks me again, but this time the sharp pain shoots through my rib cage. I curl inward and roll onto my side. Dropping the spear to the ground, he crouches next to Merigoth. He shakes one shoulder, but the sleeping queen doesn't react. He then presses one palm to her face, holds it there for a few seconds before releasing an exasperated breath. He groans out in frustration and reapplies his hand to her face again, trying again.

"What did you do? I should be able to revive her!" He retrieves the spear and points it at me. "You're no different from me. If anything," he says, standing and towering over me, "I'm stronger and more powerful than you. Now, tell me… Why can't I wake her?"

I won't argue with him about that. I know I'm no match for him.

My voice barely above a whisper, I say, "I don't know." It's getting harder to breathe. The burning ache in my shoulder spreads like wildfire down into my chest.

"You lie!"

There's nothing I can do or say to make him believe me, because I don't know why he can't break her free. He is by far more powerful than me. And it never crossed my mind that he might free Merigoth from her mental prison.

It takes everything in me to slide along the rocky ground, away from him. He returns his attention to Merigoth, pressing one hand in vain to Merigoth's skin. His touch isn't affecting or waking her.

What seems like forever and a great distance is actually only a few steps. When I can't move anymore, I give in to defeat.

Elijah shouts in the background, but it's too muffled for me to make out what he's saying.

Marcellus demands, "You will free her, or I will force you to."

"I will not," I grumble, pressing a bloody hand to my shoulder.

The Shade stands over me, holding the bloody spear at his side. His shaved head glistens with sweat and his expression twists into a snarl. "Then you shall die a horrible death *after* I've forced you to free our queen!"

I don't know what'll happen if his hand touches me, and I don't have the fight in me to fend him off. He reaches toward me. A layer of grime coats the underside of his hand, caking in the grooves of his knuckles. This is it. Whether he takes control of my mind or kills me… This is the end.

"Wait," I say with a heavy breath. He pauses, his hand halfway toward me.

"Before you kill me, I need to know if our mum is here. Is she alive or one of those Reborn creatures?"

I hate saying "our," but it's my last attempt to save myself. To maybe get him to sympathize with our situation.

But he doesn't.

"She is not my mother. Queen Merigoth is the only one who cares for me. And you will release her!"

The room fades into darkness. But then something smacks me hard on my bicep, close to the spear wound. A sharp pain shoots through my body, reviving me from blacking out.

"Ow!" I shout, then spit blood onto the stone floor.

"Do you hear me? Your mother was a traitor! She feared Merigoth's power and fled, leaving me behind!"

He was left here in the Under Realm. My mum took me and…and the third child. But where is this child now? Something to think about later—if I survive.

He tosses the spear. It clangs to the rocky ground. Then, slowly, he crouches close, one corner of his lip curling up into a smile. "You cannot win against me. And after you wake Queen Merigoth, we will both make sure she gets her vengeance on those who banished her." He's about to take hold of my chin when something descends from above and lifts him straight into the air. The black fog viciously swirls as if its intangible tendrils could save him. Between the fog blocking my view and my vision waning, I'm unable to see what's taken hold of Marcellus.

The agony in my shoulder throbs, each pulse of pain synced with the cadence of my slowing heartbeats. My eyelids become too heavy to keep open. I may not be ready to leave this world, but at least I'm leaving with the comfort of knowing the world will go on without the threat of Merigoth in it.

CHAPTER 29

Rune

My wings spread wide, brown feathers catching the air, lifting me up as I circle the cavernous throne room. I remember everything, and fury hums within the quills of my feathers. That sharp pain stabbing my spine each time I used my power to open a doorway finally makes sense. A part of me was always trying to break free.

Escaping the Idle Tombs was easy after my wings were unbound. I'd opened a small doorway with a flick of my fingers in front of the incoming flock of demon spirits sending them miles from the mountain fortress. After I helped Sara from her cell, she led the way to the throne room through the labyrinth of underground tunnels.

But what we saw when we arrived—Marcellus standing over a fallen Adele—was not what we'd expected.

Now, with my hands clutching the dingy strips of Marcellus's black fabric at the nape of his neck, I dangle him high over the cavern floor. It wasn't only my wings and memories that returned—my strength did too. My strengthened muscles make carrying Marcellus through the air almost effortless.

Soaring across the cavern, still deciding what to do with him, I focus in on my revived senses. I can see the tiniest details in every object, hear the softest whispers, and smell the faintest scents of the cavern. The moisture in the air carries an unpleasant, pungent stench that stings my nose. My body hums with freed energy, and I feel alive—ready to punish those who shackled me and my kind.

Below, Sara tends to Adele while Marcellus lashes out, his arms and legs swinging in the air. Each time he reaches for my arm, I take a sharp swerve to the left and then to the right. The air catching between my brown feathers is invigorating.

Tilting his head up, Marcellus shouts, "Drop me, you treacherous creature!"

Instead of releasing him to plummet to his death, I spot a shallow ledge along the domed ceiling. With a hard jerk, I throw him forward. He slams hard against the rocky surface before falling and landing on the narrow overhang. When he takes notice of how high he is, he scrambles away from the edge, pressing his back to the cavern wall. My wings flap so that I hover at eye level with him. Slowly, he stands, holding his gaze on me. There's rage burning inside him. I can tell by his stern glare. Good.

"Rune!" Elijah shouts from the front of the throne room. As my attention turns to him, I catch Marcellus leaping off the ledge out of the corner of my eye. What Marcellus doesn't realize is that my senses are heightened, and I pick up on what he's doing the second he gets to his feet, knocking pebbles off the ledge. With both his arms reaching out for me, I thrust my wings forward, throwing a powerful force of hot air toward him. With a *thud*, his body smacks into the wall before crumpling onto the ledge. Serves him right. I wait, watching for movement.

Once I'm sure he's out cold, I fly over to Elijah, who's calling for help. He's swinging his shackled hands through the thick black fog, which creeps up his legs, as if trying to claim his body. "Rune, do something!"

With another burst of air from my wings, the black fog withdraws, receding into the dark corners of the throne room. "Are you hurt?"

He shakes his head, and after I've broken him free from the chains, he closes the space between us, wrapping his arms around my neck. The weight of his arms, embracing me, has my insides humming with delight, and I'm so focused on the sensation that I forget to reciprocate.

Elijah releases me and rushes over to the young woman standing at the base of Merigoth's throne.

"Kit!" he shouts, grabbing both arms and gently shaking her.

I walk toward Elijah and Kit, while shouting over to Sara, "How bad is she?" My revived hyperawareness flicks between the two afflicted girls.

Sara, who's been trying to save her daughter, yells, "Not good! She's lost a lot of blood."

"Rune!" Elijah calls. "I can't wake up Kit!"

"I might be able to help with that," someone says, coming from the side entrance that's concealed by the carved pillar. I turn to see Evander.

The dreary dark strips of fabric wrapping his body are gone. Now, he's wearing a white linen shirt that hangs low over brown pants. He's still barefoot with a shaved head, but at least he looks like his old self.

Without hesitation, I wrap my arms around him. I've known Evander since childhood, and I trust him with my life. When we part, I ask with a wide smile, "Evander! How…?"

"I don't know. I was in the Idle Tombs when suddenly, my head became silent. I couldn't hear the lure or Merigoth's commands. Then, an intense stabbing spiked along my spine. It wasn't long until my wings sprouted free—and just like that, I remembered everything." Vibrant reddish-brown feathers trail his back side.

"That's wonderful!" I tell him, clutching his shoulder.

He moves past me to assess the human girl standing in a dormant state. After a short moment, he says, "We need a healer." His gaze shifts to Adele, who's unconscious on the floor, and he adds, "For both of them."

"Where are we going to find a healer?" I ask.

"Wait here," he says, then runs out the front entrance of the throne room with blurring speed. Seconds later, he returns with another angel, former Shade, by his side. "I remembered which one of us is a healer."

The healer and Evander walk up to us, and I look to the healer. "It's Gianna, right?"

The woman nods.

"She comes from a family of healers," Evander says. "One of the best lines in all of…" He pauses, letting the silence emphasize his anguish.

Resting a hand on his shoulder, I say, "We will return to our rightful home in the Starlight Realm. All will be as it was, I promise."

Gianna stands in front of Kit and sweeps one hand up to the young woman's face. She then presses her palm to Kit's cheek. Within seconds, the entranced girl blinks with a wild alertness as she gasps for air. Gianna lowers her hand and steps away, allowing the girl to reunite with Elijah.

Elijah thanks the woman, and Gianna nods in return.

The healer then turns her attention to Sara. "I know who and what you are. I will help you this one time."

Sara nods in understanding, and says, "I'm not a threat to you or any of the other angels. I swear to you on my daughter's life."

"You spawned this thing?" Gianna asks, pointing to Adele. Her expression is a mixture of hate and confusion.

"She isn't a thing, and she was not *spawned* but born. And yes, I gave birth to this girl. I love her…" Then, with a brief glance up to the ledge, she adds, "…I love all my children." Dipping her gaze, she locks eyes with the healer. "I tried to prevent any of this from happening. But I wasn't strong enough."

Gianna lays one hand to the wound in Adele's right shoulder. A bright light appears from beneath her palms. When she's done, she stands and moves to Evander's side. "The wound is healed, but she'll need time to rest in order to regain her strength. She's lost too much blood. That's something I cannot heal."

Sara thanks the healer before clasping her fingers with Adele's. I'm fairly sure Adele would be livid knowing someone was touching her right now, especially without her gloves on.

Elijah comes up next to us. "We need to get out of here. Before those things—those Reborn creatures—find us."

He's not wrong, yet I cannot leave this realm without saving the other angels.

As if reading my thoughts, Evander asks, "What can I do to help?" Gianna stands at his shoulder, also awaiting orders.

"Find the others," I tell them. "They're most likely confused and scared. Gather everyone you can to the cave at the other end of the path. It's the best place to hide from the Reborns until I return. This cavern is too exposed and connected to the Idle Tombs."

"We will wait for you there," Evander says, then gestures with a flick of his head for Gianna to follow.

When they're gone from the throne room, I turn my attention up to Marcellus, still knocked out on the high ledge. "Sara," I call. She looks up at me and I ask, "What about him?"

Sara glances up and exhales a solemn breath. "Marcellus is too far gone. We can't trust him. He has to stay."

"Are you sure? He's your—"

"I know who he is." Tears well beneath Sara's eyes. She chokes back her emotions and says, "Maybe if he lived a different life, I'd say bring him, but I can't risk putting the villagers of Bricen in danger with his unpredictability. Not yet. Look," she says, standing and brushing her bloodstained hands on her worn pants, "he's not going anywhere. Let's get Adele home, settle in, and then we can come back for him later."

"Okay," I say, knowing she's right. Marcellus's ability to control others is a risk. And Bricen can't contain him anywhere. "We know where to find him when it's time to help him."

Sara and Elijah lift Adele by her shoulders while Kit grabs her legs. Then, with barely any drain or exhaustion, I wave my hands across the space in front of us. The air ripples, and a large white light forms. When the light subsides, there's a round window-like doorway in its place. On the other side is the road to Bricen.

"Okay, let's get her home."

CHAPTER 30

ADELE

"**A**dele, you need to wake up."

I have no desire to "wake up."

My mind's groggy, my body's aching, and my shoulder's killing me. So, I lie still, bright sun shining behind closed lids. Whoever's bothering me can be on their way. Let me be.

Yet…that voice.

"Adele, please open your eyes."

I've only heard that woman's voice in my dreams. Someone from a previous life.

When I crack my eyes open, the world is bright and blurry. Shadowy figures stand over me. The woman isn't alone. I try to sit up, but my shoulder stings. I'm lying on a dirt road for some reason.

"Take it easy! Don't move too fast," the woman tells me.

"I'm fine," I grumble.

"She's awake!" This voice I recognize. It's Elijah. Then, I remember what happened. I was in the Under Realm, struck down by Marcellus with a spear to the shoulder. But how had I escaped? Why wasn't I under his control?

My hand goes to my shoulder, and I wince. My finger easily finds the gaping hole in my vest. It's hard to ignore the throb behind my temples too. Pressing a bare palm to my forehead, I jerk upright, panic shooting through me. Everyone around me starts shouting, "whoa" and "easy there" as I try and scramble away.

"Where are my gloves?" I yell, frantically searching the ground around me. I need to sheathe these dangerous weapons.

"It's all right, Adele. You won't hurt anyone here."

I blink, my vision coming into focus. "Where are we?"

"Here, drink," Elijah says, holding a waterskin up. I let him pour the water into my mouth, but the moment I clearly see the woman sitting by my feet I choke, coughing up the water. Pushing Elijah's hand away with my forearm, I narrow my eyes at the woman. "Mum?"

"Yes, pumpkin. It's me," Sara says, moving closer.

I don't know where she came from or how I got back to the Human Realm, but it doesn't matter. She's here and we're safe. My insides feel like bursting with every emotion I've bottled over the last eight years.

Mum smiles a weary grin, like she needs a good night's sleep too. Then, from behind her, Rune appears. I gawk at her because the girl has giant wings sprouting from her back.

"D-do you have wings?" I stagger to my feet, accepting help from Elijah and my mum for support, careful not to touch them with my hands.

Rune spreads her wings. They're quite a sight. The midday sun shines over the tops of them, highlighting the brown feathers with a warm glow. "Your mother helped me remember who I am and where I come from."

My eyes widen. "She did?"

Mum dips her head, locking gazes with me. "How do you feel?"

Narrowing my eyes at her and tucking my hands under my arms, I clear my throat and ask, "You're—you're really here?"

"I'm really here. Now, tell me. How do you feel?" Her face is exactly how I remember: smooth skin, deep brown eyes, and hair the same fair color as mine. After all these years, she barely looks a day older than when I last saw her. Dark smears of dirt frame her face and travel across the bridge of her nose. Her clothes are loose and ragged, making me wonder where she'd been locked away all these years.

"Mum!" I say with a breath, then pull her in for a hug.

"I'm so sorry, pumpkin. I should've prepared you better." Pulling away, but not letting go, she brushes the stray strands of hair that have escaped my braid from my face. "You were so young. I thought we had more time to wean you from the binds we placed on you—to teach you how to use your gifts."

"Gifts?" My face twists in disgust. Take a step back, I hold my hands out in front of me. I can't help the venom in my voice when I tell her, "The things I can do…the way I hurt people…it's not a 'gift.' It's a curse. Or, at least I thought I was cursed. Turns out," I grumble the next words because I loathe acknowledging this fact, "I'm a monster from a nightmare realm."

"You are not a monster!" she snaps, causing me to flinch. I've never heard her take that tone, except for that day when the Shades first invaded Bricen. Stepping closer, she takes hold of my shoulders. "You are not a monster," she repeats. "I am not *from* the Under Realm. I was born here, in this world."

"So, you are human?"

She nods. "As are you. But we're not normal humans. Not with Merigoth's blood running through our veins. I was originally born in Noviska, a long, long time ago, in a small fishing community, barely surviving the harsh conditions of the north. Back then, before there was a king and queen, Noviska was a divided and feuding country. Each village was loyal to its clan leaders, and it was dangerous to wander outside your home village. My husband and I were approached by Merigoth, who offered us a better life. And because I assumed life couldn't get any worse, we accepted her offer."

"I have demon blood coursing through my veins?"

"Yes, we both do. But it's important to know that just because Merigoth is a monster, doesn't mean we have to be too. It's your life, Adele. You have a choice to be better." She then hands me my gloves. "Here. Once day I hope you will be comfortable enough not to wear them, but I understand for now—"

"I must," I say, finishing her sentence. "Thank you."

The leather feels right against my skin as I slip each glove over my hands. While doing that, I silently repeat my mum's words, *You have a choice to be better*. A sliver of hope stems inside my heart because I want to be better—I choose to be better. I don't want to be cut off from those I care about. And that list of people is growing. First, I only had Selene. Now, I have Elijah, Kit...

"You have a wise mother," Rune says, cutting into my thoughts. "We'd all be lost if it weren't for her help in freeing my mind and wings." Her brown wings are tucked in, the tops peeking over her shoulders. Her gaze shifts up and she says, "I've got to return to the Under Realm now. To help the other angels return home. Without me, they're trapped there with the Reborns looming about."

"You're leaving?" Elijah comes over, leaving his sister's side. Kit's standing on the road, looking ahead at Bricen's open front gates.

"I'll return one day. Right now, my fellow angels need me. I'm the only one who can get them home to the Angel Realm."

Elijah removes his red scarf and hands it to Rune. "I want you to have this."

She stares at the long piece of fabric hanging from his hand before taking it and draping it over her neck. "Thank you. You're a good friend, Elijah. And I will return to see you." Then Rune looks at me. "And you, too."

Rune turns to Elijah once more before spreading her wings and flying up into the clear blue sky. With a wave of her hand, she opens a large round doorway out in front of her. The dark horizon of the Under Realm lies on the other side. She dives through and closes the passage behind her.

Lowering my gaze, I ask Elijah, "Can you believe she's an actual angel?"

He shakes his head, and then his eyes meet mine. "The stars—they must mean something in the Angel Realm."

I recall Merigoth's memory, and how their leaders were referred to as North Star, and so on. "Yes, I think you're right."

Sara says from behind us, "It's the Starlight Realm. And there are more than just angels there. It's a place full of magic." Elijah and I stare at her, and then she chuckles, and adds, "So I've heard. I've never been, if you're wondering."

"We should get back to Bricen," Kit says, cutting into our conversation. "I'm sure Trevor's going to want to know everything that's happened." She turns and strolls along the dirt road.

"Trevor's gone," I say while accepting my mum's help for support. Her body smells of sweat and smoke.

Both Kit and Elijah turn to me. But it's Elijah who asks, "What do you mean…gone?"

Hobbling along, my mum's arm wrapped around my waist, I explain, "He used the last of his angel powers to open the doorway, giving me a chance to save you and Rune. To bring you home."

Kit embraces Elijah. "Brother, you know we had our suspicions that there was something different about him. The way he would tend to the injured or find lost things, then mysteriously age before our eyes."

From the sky, two loud *caws* sound off as a pair of crows fly by and vanish into the forest.

"Speaking of Trevor," I say, pointing to the forest, "those are not normal crows."

"Well, now we'll never know because…he's gone." Elijah faces his sister and leans into her embrace.

Mum and I let them have their moment, shuffling by and slowly making our way down the road toward Bricen. When the sound of pebbles crunching beneath their boots hits my ears, I know they're close behind.

Bessie and Trevor's gray horse are standing outside the barrier wall when we arrive at the front gates. I'm not sure how they made their way home, or why they aren't inside the village. But nonetheless, it's good to see my old mare. Limping away from my mum's hold, I hug Bessie's neck. She whinnies with a shake of her head, then walks away from the front gates.

"No, whoa!" I say, grabbing her reins. "This way."

Kit, who'd gone inside the village, comes jogging out, shoving Elijah toward the forest. "Shhh!" She waves for us to follow. "Leave the horses!"

Mum doesn't hesitate and grabs Bessie's reins from my hand. She drops them, then loops my arm over her shoulder and leads me to where Kit stands.

"Hey, I can't leave—"

"You will. Now, let's go," Mum says, her voice curt.

After we've taken cover in the forest, the tall barrier wall still in view, I ask, "What's wrong?"

"Soldiers" is all Kit says.

"Soldiers?" I look again at the open gates just as two men stroll out. They're wearing leather vests with red jackets. "Fayatin soldiers."

Elijah moves to a nearby tree and climbs it. "I'll get a better look from my watch spot. Give me a few minutes."

We stay put. The two men standing guard ignore the two horses. While we wait, I reach up to my braid and curse.

"What's wrong?" Kit asks.

"I lost my hairpin!" It must've come loose while I was bleeding out on the cavern floor in the Under Realm. Great. I've lost my favorite bow and now Selene's hairpin. It pains me to think I'll never see the latter again. I was supposed to give the borrowed item back.

When Elijah climbs down the tree and hurries over to where we're hiding, he whispers, "The village looks empty. There are a few Fayatin soldiers walking the grounds, but…I don't know where the rest are. That's if there are others."

"For stars' sake," I say, then groan from the pain in my shoulder. "I guarantee you there are others." Balling my hands into fists, I have the urge to punch something. With an exasperated sigh, I tell them, "It's General Onica. I know it."

A pang of guilt swells in my gut. I brought this problem here, so I have to be the one to fix it. "Okay, I can handle this. You three sneak in through Elijah's secret passage and get as many villagers out as you can."

"Adele," my mum pleads. "You don't have to do this alone. You're still weak and you need that shoulder looked at."

What she doesn't understand is that I do. The general isn't going to leave without me in tow. And I can't risk more blood on my hands. Not now. Not after we've come so far in freeing everyone from their restraints. I peel off my gloves and snuggly tuck them into my vest. It's time I free myself from General Onica's clutches once and for all.

CHAPTER 31

I have no idea what I'm walking into. But I do know that no matter what happens, I refuse to return to Castle Forge.

Inside, the village is quiet. There's a faint odor of something burning, but no sign of smoke. Ignoring the pain in my shoulder and the exhaustion feuding with my consciousness, I push on toward Goslings. I wish I had my bow, but my knife and hands will make do. Hopefully, the general will come to her senses and leave peacefully—eh, who am I kidding? That woman will plow over the innocent to get what she wants.

Limping along the road, through the run-down village, I search the shadows for villagers in hiding. The ground has more mud than brown grass, and the wood siding on the homes and shops is gray and withered. Even the clear blue sky and high sun aren't enough to breach the dreariness the village has succumbed to all these years. I can only hope now that Merigoth is imprisoned that it'll have a chance to heal.

As I approach the tavern, a figure emerges out the open front door. It's General Onica. Her cloak, the color of wine…or blood…sways against her legs. Beneath the cloak, she's wearing a tarnished gold breastplate. One of her gloved hands rests on the hilt of her broadsword, strapped to her waist. She descends the porch steps at a leisurely pace, taking in my condition. Even with her head held high, her short hair, the color of coal, hangs low over her eyes.

Cocking her head, she tsks at me. "There you are."

"Here I am." I shift my weight from one leg to the other, trying not to show I'm in pain. "And…here you are."

She stops halfway down the steps. "What happened to you?"

"I got into a fight."

Both eyebrows rise and she chuckles. One would think it's strange for such a tyrant to ever smile, but not General Onica. She often does whenever Fayatin celebrates a victory, or when she belittles the lords, or when she's divulging secrets to her close council, though her amusement is more sinister than heartwarming.

"Oh, is that right? I'd like to meet the warrior who bested you!" She steps onto the dirt, and from the sides of the tavern, I catch movement. This is an ambush, and the general is the distraction. This isn't going to end well, for them or me.

Preparing for their attack, I muster up what little strength I have while keeping the general talking. I have to give Elijah, Kit, and Mum enough time to find the villagers and sneak them off to safety. "Who says I was defeated? I'm walking, aren't I?"

Lips pursed, she makes an *uh-hum* sound, as if she doesn't believe me. But she doesn't say any more on the matter. Instead, she raises her chin and, with a parental tone, tells me, "It's time to come home, Adele. You're a danger to these people, or anyone who crosses your path. Why do you think I kept you locked up all those years?" She stares at me, as if waiting for an answer. But I'm too tired and too annoyed to argue with her. "Do you know the damage you caused at Castle Forge?"

"Me? I wasn't the one who brought a demon spirit into the castle. You did that of your own accord."

Rolling her neck, she sighs. "Oh, Adele. You're giving away too much information. I thought I taught you better than that."

Abruptly, I replay our conversation in my head, unsure of her meaning. Did she catch me looking at the abandoned row of homes? Does she know Elijah, Kit, and my mum are here? What information did I reveal to her?

"I didn't know what 'it' was when my soldiers pulled up to the front gates. They claimed to have trapped it over here in Harvesgrove. It wasn't until your kind stormed the castle, freeing the phantom creature—or what did you call it…a demon spirit—that I realized you are not unique. There are others like you. Tell me…" she pauses, eyes burrowing into mine, "How long have you known there were others like you or that these phantom creatures existed? Were you plotting to use them against me?"

I let her babble on about her ridiculous assumptions because that faint smell of smoke and something burning fills my nose again. Looking to the sky, there's no sign of a fire. But that pungent smell…it's vaguely familiar.

"Did you hear me?" she snaps.

"What? Yeah, I heard you. I had nothing to do with your captured demon spirit or the invaders that attacked Castle Forge." I think I've kept her talking long enough. Pulling out my knife from my waistband, I hold it up and aim it at her. "I'm not going anywhere with you. So, call out your soldiers and let's get this over with!"

Her fingers rap along the steel hilt of her sword. One of her many prized possessions forged from the iron ore mined from the Crescent Mountains. Narrowing her dark eyes, she responds, "No. I don't think I will." Then, looking out to the village, she adds, "Do you know I've been meaning to come to Harvesgrove and visit the quaint villages for some time now?"

Ugh, more talking. But I let her go on in case it gives Mum and the others more time to rescue the villagers. I hold my stance, even though every muscle in my body aches and demands rest. But it's coming—the barrage of soldiers. The general is just toying with me.

"This country lacks proper leadership," she bellows out as if she's addressing all the people of Harvesgrove. "This country has no sovereign rulers or lords, just small pathetic villages waiting to be conquered. It's quite sad, actually. I don't know how anyone survives here without a ruling order to oversee everything."

I don't like where this is going. Inhaling a deep breath, I push through the fatigue. "And I suppose you're that person to bring order to these lands?"

Her smile widens. "I would've proclaimed Alister the ruler of this country, but since you killed him—"

"I did not kill Alister."

"I saw you two out in the bailey courtyard. You killed him!"

There's no point in arguing with this crazed woman, and I'm tired and want to rest. "I think we're done here."

"We are far from done." She withdraws her broadsword and holds it out to her side. Then, from the sides of the buildings, the Fayatin soldiers scramble out into the open. Metal swords clanking against their metal armor. Boots pounding the dry dirt, kicking up wafts of dust.

"You know," General Onica says, moving out of the way so her soldiers can close in on me. "Dear, dear Selene isn't looking so good."

Selene. Oh, no. Glancing over the general's shoulder, up at the tavern door. It's wide open. A bleak darkness looming inside.

The distraction is exactly what they needed to strike. I don't see the fist until it connects with my face. I fall hard on my backside. The air forced from my lungs. I struggle to inhale while rubbing the sore spot on my cheek. Rolling to one side, I'm able to get to my knees, but a second soldier rushes at me and throws a powerful punch—this time to my injured shoulder. I scream from the pain spiking deep within the healed wound. Once again, I'm lying on the ground, curling in on myself. Cursing, I swear to the stars I'm going to kill every single one of them.

I try to grab whatever hand or foot comes at me, but I'm losing my strength and I can't keep up with their punches and kicks.

"That's enough!" the general shouts. The guards recede and part, allowing the general to come closer. She points the tip of her sword at my head and says, "Submit and come with me peacefully. No one will be harmed if you comply. I know the villagers are hiding, and there're only so many places they can hide before I find them all."

I spit blood onto the dirt, then wipe my mouth with the back of my hand. "I'm not going with you." Gasping for air, I wince as something inside my body stabs at my lungs. Oh, man. There's got to be at least one or two broken ribs in there. With one arm wrapping my waist, I shake my head and say with haggard breaths, "You're going to have to kill me." The words cause more aches to my lungs, but I endure because they needed to be said.

"How about I don't…and kill someone else instead?" She waves a hand high over her head, and a guard drags a young girl out from Goslings. The girl's kicking and screaming, trying to break free from his hold.

It's Magdala.

"Let her go!" I yell, wincing while staggering up from the ground to my knees. I try to get to my feet, but the piercing pain in my chest is too great. "She's only a child!"

"Return home with me."

"No!" I yell. My gaze drifting to the ground. I need to stay conscious. Lifting my head, I tell the general, "I'll never let anyone control me ever again."

"So be it." The guard pushes Magdala forward, and she lands on the ground in front of me. I try and scoot closer. A string of groans accompanies each move. I need to get to her so I can put myself between her and the impending blade. She's an innocent child and doesn't deserve to die like this. Tears well under my eyes as my arms drag my weakened body forward along the dirt road to Magdala.

But I'm not close enough.

General Onica swings her steel sword high into the air, then brings it down, except the blade doesn't connect with the girl's flesh. A thick cloud of dust forms, engulfing everyone in the area. A loud *clang* of metal against metal reverberates across the village. When the dust settles, Aunt Lauren stands in front of the girl with massive, light-gray feathered wings spread wide. The general's sword has connected with the shiniest piece of metal I've ever seen, covering Lauren's forearm.

General Onica's eyes are wide and frantically taking in the otherworldly creature before her. Staggering back, she holds her sword up. "What in the stars are you?"

"You will leave this place and never return," Aunt Lauren commands, slowly drawing in her wings.

Aunt Lauren is an angel. That's why her blood healed that boy in Noviska, like Rune's blood healed the villagers.

The silence lingering in the air lasts several heart beats, making me wonder if the general will concede, but who am I kidding? That power-hungry woman never takes orders or advice from anyone but herself.

"Attack!" General Onica commands with her sword pointing at Aunt Lauren. The army of Fayatin soldiers close in, blades swinging at my poor aunt. But she evades their strikes and flies up into the sky, taking Magdala with her. The soldiers redirect their attention from the flying angel to me. Their battle cries might be the last thing I ever hear in this world.

One man closes in fast, and before he's able to strike, an arrow zooms by my head and plunges into the man's chest. Glancing over my shoulder, Elijah's running into the village. He's got his bow in hand. Kit is by his side, swinging her shortsword. The villagers must all be out.

Even Mum has joined them, geared up with two daggers, one in each hand, confronting one soldier after another. Her fighting skills are impressive. She's swift on her feet and knows exactly where to strike to make them fall with one or two blows. How had I never seen this side of her before?

That strange, acrid-smoky scent returns. It's much stronger now. I slide my legs along the dirt road, trying to avoid being trampled. When a soldier comes up from behind, I roll out of the way, then sweep my leg under his legs, causing him to fall face-first onto the ground. Scrambling to my knees, I muster enough energy to crawl over to him, ignoring the pain in my lungs. With one bare hand, I grab the nape of his neck. Normally, I'd trap him in his own mind—that way he's not a threat to me—but instead I take all the anger rolling inside my core and use it to command him to protect me.

I don't know if it works, and when I let go of him, I drop to my side again. My muscles are drained and fatigued. And when another Fayatin soldier rushes at me, I don't even have the strength to lift up my arm and block his blow. But thank the stars, I don't have to. The man I compelled acts, blocking the guard's sword from killing me. He quickly gets to his feet and fights off the soldier.

With his back to me, he continues to fend off any threat that comes toward me. Oh, my Stars… It worked.

The smoky smell grows stronger. Wherever it's coming from, it's close by. Something's burning, I'm sure of it.

General Onica yells in my direction, "This ends now! I can rule a country without you by my side. I've found a more powerful ally! And he will do what you—" She doesn't even have time to raise her sword to me when an axe swings through the air from behind and chops into the general's shoulder, slicing through her gold-pleated armor.

I flinch at the sight of the general stumbling about. She staggers in a circle, blood spurting from the deep slice in her flesh. "No," she whimpers. "You're supposed to obey me!" she gurgles, blood dribbles down her chin. The second the mighty General Onica topples to the ground, her killer is revealed—Alister.

"There's only one who commands me, and it isn't you," he says with an unnatural growl. Grabbing the handle of the axe, he yanks it free from the general's dead body. Then he turns to me. "We weren't done. You and me."

"You've got to be kidding me. Do you know what I've been through today?" I half jest and half plea with the oversized brute. "Alister, let's talk for a minute."

He releases an inhuman scream. The shriek of a Reborn man. Reminding me that Alister is dead. This thing is not human.

The Fayatine soldier I compelled moves between us, holding his sword up to protect me. But Alister's quick to grab him, lift him up, and then slam him to the ground. The soldier lies still, unmoving.

Alister turns his attention to me, and it doesn't take much for him to wrap his meaty hand around my neck, then lift me up until my feet are dangling. I pound my fists against his arms, but he doesn't let me go. I even try pressing my hands to his skin, but nothing happens. There's no mind to infiltrate. I continue to hit and kick him because I need to get free before he snaps my neck.

"Merigoth is dead?" the Reborn demands.

Croaking out my response, I say, "Not dead. Just taking a nap." Oh, the pungent smell of burning wood and ash is coming from him. It's so potent my eyes are watering.

He moans out a deep, guttural groan. "Humans are weak. Easily defeated."

"What about angels?" my aunt yells, flying in from the side. She straightens her legs, coming in fast, ready to slam her feet into his side, but he intercepts her efforts. He punches her legs in a downward motion, forcing them to buckle and slam hard into the ground. The top half of her continues toward Alister. He grabs her by the throat and squeezes. Her light-gray wings flap in a desperate frenzy. She's trying to escape his hold.

Now, he's got us both by the throats.

I don't know how to save her, so instead of fighting Alister, I grab hold of Aunt Lauren's flailing hand. Her wings relax and she tries to turn and look at me. I close my eyes and enter her mind. There's no resistance. She wants me to see these memories.

The first one is of her as a child, dancing in a forest similar to the one I saw in Merigoth's memory. Her wings are half the size of her body, spread wide, as another angel teaches her how to fly. Then the memory changes and she's older. Aunt Lauren is here, in Bricen, long before the Shades attacked. She's happy, living among the humans, watching over them. Then, the memory shifts again, and this time, it's my mum. She's dressed in ragged clothes. So many layers that she looks three times her size. Their voices are muted, but I can tell Mum is crying. She's begging Aunt Lauren for help, handing her a small crying bundle. This is when I realize Aunt Lauren isn't family by blood. Mum hands over a small child. I search the memory, looking for the second child mum had taken from the Under Realm, but it's just mum and the one child. Aunt Lauren kisses the top of the child's head and says, "Don't let your blood decide who you are. You, sweet Adele, are the only one who gets to make that choice." It's me she's holding.

"Adele!" Aunt Lauren's strangled voice seizes my thoughts.

When I feel her hand slip from mine, I blink open my eyes and focus on Alister's snarling face. His skin doesn't look like that of the Reborn I saw in the throne room of the Under Realm. I guess over time, his skin will start to detach from the bone and flesh beneath. For now, Alister still looks like Alister. Except for the tiny red veins sprouting out from around his black eyes.

I try and gasp for air, but he's tightened his grip on my neck. Alister stares at us, as if he were a child waiting to see what happens when you squeeze an animal too tightly. It's sickening and I want to kill him.

When the world goes dark at the edges of my vision, I fear this is finally the end. No one is coming to save us this time. I don't know if Elijah, Kit, and Mum are even alive. I will never know if Selene survived her injuries or if the general harmed her. All I know is that I'm at peace with my end. I no longer have to worry about who I'm going to be or what I'm going to do with my life. I let the void of death wash over me.

Then suddenly, I'm falling. My side slams into the ground and a sharp pain like lightning shoots through my body. I realize the pain comes from my snapped collarbone. The broken bone presses into my shoulder muscle, right where Marcellus stabbed me with his spear. The world feels as if it's slipping from me, and I barely register the two hands gripped under my arms, dragging me across the ground. Soft feathers brush against my skin. The moment my double vision settles, I blink and ask, "What happened?"

Aunt Lauren has me next to her. One wing is outstretched, supporting my back so I can sit up. She's gasping for air while making sure I'm okay. We both turn our attention to the sky where Alister's body is being carried away. Short strands of dark-brown hair flutter in the wind as vibrant brown wings soar through the air.

It's Rune.

The Reborn is struggling to break free, swinging his meaty hands up at her. With a sharp dive, she flies straight toward the ground. The Reborn is no longer trying to grab Rune but preparing for the blow. His arms shield his face as Rune stretches one hand out in front of her. With a flick of her finger, she opens a giant doorway right there in the ground…then dives through.

I crawl closer, as does Aunt Lauren, and we look through the wavering surface. Beyond is the midnight-sky world with desolate fields—the Under Realm. When Rune flies out, I shield my face from the rush of dry, hot air that trails behind. She quickly circles the sky above, then lands next to us, closing the doorway to the Under Realm.

"Rune!" I croak, my throat tight and sore from Alister's grip.

"Shh, it's okay. He's gone." She launches into the air and shouts, "Soldiers!" When the Fayatin soldiers cease their fighting, she tells them, "Your general is dead. Leave this land and never return!"

They look confused for a moment, glancing at one another. It isn't until Rune repeats her words, adding a powerful gust of air by sweeping her wings forward, that they flee the village. Rune remains in the sky until the last has left. "People of Bricen, you can come out." She slowly lands, one foot touching the ground then the other. The villagers don't start trickling in from the front gates until the last of the Fayatin soldiers have left.

"There are no more threats to your village," she announces. "The invading leader is dead." She points to General Onica lying in the dirt and continues, "And I've banished the last Reborn from this realm to the Under Realm."

Evander and a few other angels land beside Rune. He leans in and whispers something in her ear. She nods, and then before he's about to take off, she tells him, "Wait. First, we must heal the injured. See that Gianna tends to them."

Aunt Lauren stands and approaches Rune. I'm too weak to move, so I stay resting on the ground, looking up at the blue sky. Twice today I almost died. And now I want nothing more than to live.

Gianna heals the internal injury stabbing at my lungs and around my collarbone. "Thank you," I say, then slowly get to my feet. I'm still exhausted from all the blood I lost in the Under Realm, but strong enough to stand.

Mum hugs Aunt Lauren while Kit and Elijah talk with the villagers.

Before Gianna walks away, I call to her and ask her to help Selene. She nods and we slowly make our way inside of Goslings. Selene's there, lying on the floor, right where I left her before leaving with Trevor. Gianna rests her hands on my friend's stomach and heals her with a quick flash of light. Simple as that.

Agatha steps out from one of the hidden closets next to the fireplace. Tears stream down her cheeks. "I didn't want to leave her, but the Fayatins were coming. I'm so sorry, my lady."

"You're fine," I say. "I'm glad you hid. General Onica would've killed you if she'd seen you."

The castle maid thanks me and Gianna again, then goes to tend to Selene. She doesn't even question or look twice at the angel before her. But then again, the servants of Castle Forge are taught not to question anything they see or hear. Just go about your business.

Gianna nods, and I nod in return. Then she marches out of the tavern, her black feathers tucked in close along her back.

Looking down at Selene's peaceful face, knowing that she'll wake and be able to live a normal life, has me wondering if the thing holding me back from being happy hasn't been knowing the truth, but rather just believing that I can control this power within me. I'll hold on to the hope that there's a better future for all of us.

For now, the village of Bricen needs me, and I'm not planning on going anywhere anytime soon.

CHAPTER 32

ADELE

A few days later, everything's almost back to normal. Mum moved back in with Aunt Lauren, for now. She's planning on moving into one of the abandoned homes once the rest of the village is restored. Selene has woken and is doing better but remains sore and weak. Mum has fallen into the role of village leader in Trevor's absence, with Elijah, Kit, and me as her close counsel.

I think we make an excellent team.

"What are you thinking about?" Selene asks. She's resting on a blanket outside beneath the warm sun after complaining about being cooped up inside for the last few days.

"Here! I found another one of the purple flowers you like!" Magdala runs over to us and hands Selene a few freshly picked flowers.

"Thank you, my dear. These are beautiful."

Magdala beams and asks, "Can you read to me?"

"Oh," Selene says, "You have a book?"

The girl nods then takes off running toward the homes at the rear of the village.

"She's never going to let you leave, you know that, right?" I say, watching Magdala disappear into the second to last home in the short row.

"Well, let's not tell her that I plan to stay then."

Twisting on the blanket, I look at my friend. "Your uncle would never approve."

"Yes, I know. But that's a problem for another day. For now, I wish to stay." Bringing the small bouquet to her nose, she inhales. "There's something magical happening in this village, and I want to be a part of it."

We sit in silence. Selene soaks in the sun while I think about my future. I want to learn more about what I'm capable of. When I compelled that soldier to protect me, it worked. It's a dangerous ability, and I'll have to be careful with it, but that's why I plan to work hard and train with my mum. Merigoth's blood had more than just the power to extend Mum's life span; over time, she also developed the ability to enter people's minds. Despite this newfound ability, she chose to use her hands for healing rather than causing harm. During her healing seasons, she would enter the minds of those she was helping to block out the traumas and fears that haunted them. I find her selflessness inspiring, and I aspire to follow in her footsteps by using the power in my hands for good.

"What are you thinking about?" Selene repeats.

Leaning back on my hands, I tell her, "How I lost your hairpin."

"Oh, that old thing. It wasn't important."

"It was important to me."

"Well, then I'll get you another one."

The thought is nice, and I know she means well. But I want that one back. The one with the three rubies on it. It was the borrowed item that'd been with me since my escape. Shifting our conversation, I tell her, "I think I want to become a healer like my mum."

Selene lowers her hands, laying the small colorful flowers on her stomach, and smiles. "That's a wonderful idea, Adele!"

"Also, I can't help but wonder how safe Bricen really is? I mean, I know the Under Realm is closed off and that only Rune can create doorways, but what if there are other dangers? Ones we don't know about yet."

Selene brushes a strand of dark-brown hair from her eyes and tells me, "Adele, you shouldn't worry about such things until the need calls for it. Otherwise, you'll create concern where there is no concern."

"Ah, such a wise old woman you are." I clap my gloved hands together and laugh. Then, once our giggles have died, I add, "But what I mean is I also want to protect the village."

"There's no rule that says you can't do both—heal and protect." She pushes my arm, and silently I think how good it feels not to have to worry about personal space. With a playful tone, she asks, "And when are you going to take those ridiculous gloves off?"

I'm nowhere near ready to walk around without my gloves on. Not yet at least, and not while I'm around Selene. "Mum is going to help me control my abilities better. But it's going to take time."

"Hey, you two. It's time to eat!" Mum calls from the back door of Goslings.

I help Selene to her feet, and we slowly walk toward the tavern. When we reach the back door, I help her inside and to a chair. Lauren is passing out stew with two young girls following, handing out rolls and spoons.

"Can we talk?" Mum asks me, tugging gently on my shirt.

I follow her out the back. She goes straight for Trevor's old shed and opens the door. Rune is inside waiting.

"Rune! What are you doing here, and why are you lurking inside this old shed?"

She opens her arms to give me a hug but pauses. "May I?"

I answer her by pulling her into a tight embrace. "I'm happy to see you. So soon, too."

"Yes, well, Rune and I have something to give you," Mum says, then moves to the back side of the shed and pries open the wood panels to the window.

Rune moves to the window, leans close, her lips almost touching the iron bar crossing the window, and whispers words I can't hear. A few seconds later, a familiar string of *caw*s grows louder. Then, one at a time, three large crows land on the bar. I'm about to inquire about Barclay when the fourth bird flies over and perches on the bar with his siblings.

"Barclay!" I exclaim. He answers by lifting his black beak into the air before releasing a loud *caw*. I move in and carefully pet the top of his head. "It's good to see you've recovered."

He makes a chirping sound as he bobs his head.

"Now that Trevor's gone," Rune says, "these crows are your responsibility."

"What? Mine?"

Rune lifts her hand to my face but doesn't make contact. She waits until I nod, granting her permission to touch me. When I do, she presses her hand to my cheek. She whispers words of a foreign language, and light transfers from her hand to my face...into my mind. As if she's dropped a present in the middle of my consciousness. When the gift opens, I feel an invisible tether tugging at my mind.

Rune draws her hands away from me and tells Sara, "It's done."

"What's done?" I ask, rubbing my cheeks. Both Rune and my mum are beaming with delight. "Can someone please explain what you just did?"

"I gave you the ability to command Trevor's crows." Rune briefly pauses in her explanation. "Well, now your crows. Barclay, Valor, Serafina, and Olive are each special in their own way."

Mum walks out of the shed. "I need to get back inside. I'll leave you two to close up." She turns and heads back into Goslings.

"What do you mean, I can command the crows?" I knew these birds weren't normal birds.

Rune walks out of the shed, leaving the crows to perch on the iron bar. I turn to them, each one emitting a pleasant vibe that travels from them to me through our connected tethers. "I can feel what they're feeling!"

"Yes, and eventually you'll get better at communicating with them." Rune's brown wings trail down her back. They're beautiful and deadly at the same time. A trait I realize I want too. I want to help yet still be feared by those who dare to invade Bricen.

"I must return," Rune says, looking to the sky.

"You don't want to come in and sit? To see Elijah?"

"I do, but another day. Right now, Evander and I are trying to make plans for where to begin rebuilding our home. The capital is our primary focus. It's been centuries since we were taken, and nature has claimed almost every part of the city. We have a lot of work ahead of us in restoring its beauty."

"I understand. Come back and visit soon."

This time, Rune doesn't hesitate to wrap her arms around me. Then she exits the shed and flies off into the sky.

Before leaving, I look at each one of my crows and say, "We can do some real good here. Not just here in Bricen, but all over Harvesgrove, and beyond. You can be my eyes and ears and travel the lands, searching for those who need our help. As much as I want to use my ability to help others like my mum does, I can't help but enjoy bringing certain oppressors and thugs to their knees. So, between me and you, going forward, we're going to find those who prey on the weak and make them feel every bit of pain they inflict on others. Sound good?"

All four crows caw in response. I feel their excitement and eagerness to get started.

"Soon," I tell them, petting each one before commanding them to fly off.

As I close up the shed, I look forward to the days to come. Because now, I've accepted the truth that even though I'm a monster, born from a nightmare realm and created with the sole purpose of causing pain to others, I'm in control of my future. I'll decide how to use my special set of skills—for either noble reasons or for retribution. The choice is mine and mine alone.

THE HOME FOR ME
A 'SHADE OF LIGHT' SONG

Lyrics co-written by Kimberly Grymes and
Audrey Weatherstone.
Song recorded and sang by Audrey Weatherstone.

ACKNOWLEDGMENTS

Embarking on a new series, especially one that involves shifting genres, can be an overwhelming endeavor. Yet, the immense support and encouragement I've received from a remarkable network of individuals have transformed the process of crafting, refining, and preparing this story for publication into a deeply rewarding experience.

Before delving into the acknowledgments within the literary realm, I want to begin by expressing my heartfelt gratitude to my incredible family. Beyond the love and inspiration I draw from my husband and three daughters, I am truly fortunate to have an extended family and a circle of friends who continually champion and uplift my writing journey.

Now, let's delve into the incredible people within the book community who have played an instrumental role in shaping this book into its finest form.

A special mention is reserved for my dear friend, Liz Delton. Our friendship goes beyond measure; Liz has been a pillar of support, whether it's bouncing off new story ideas, sharing cover art concepts, discussing marketing strategies, or simply being there whenever I need guidance. Her early line edits and thorough proofreading of the blurb were invaluable. As we embark on this literary journey together, I eagerly anticipate the challenges and triumphs we'll face as authors.

During the initial stages of crafting this narrative, sharing chapters with a writing group offers invaluable insights. I'm incredibly grateful to have found my writing community within Sacha Black's Patreon group. Among the fantastic individuals in this group, I want to extend my gratitude to Lynn, Matthew, L.F. Wham, Mackenzie, Lovis, Holger, Verona, and CJ for their dedication in reading and providing valuable feedback on "Shade of Light." Our monthly Zoom meetings have become a source of inspiration, and I look forward to continuing to immerse myself in their stories.

A shout-out to Wes, a friend of my daughter's, who stepped in with the perfect name, "Merigoth," when I was struggling to christen a key character.

I wholeheartedly recommend working with a development editor, and Alyse Bailey from ABC Editorial stands as a testament to this. Her meticulous editorial review, coupled with comprehensive evaluations of chapters and characters, significantly influenced the book's structure and pacing. I'm eagerly anticipating our future collaborations.

My gratitude extends to the team of beta-readers: A.E. Kincaid, Liz, Gaby, Marissa, and DeAnna. Your insights and initial reactions amplified my excitement for the story's journey.

Speaking of A.E. Kincaid, her guidance and insights in our conversations about marketing and publishing have been invaluable.

Turning back to the acknowledgments, Nikki Mentges from NAM Editorial deserves a special mention. Nikki's attention to detail in content and line editing, along with her nurturing teaching approach, have not only improved my writing but also enriched my understanding of the craft. I'm looking forward to our ongoing collaboration.

Aime Sund from Red Word Editing Services played a pivotal role with her meticulous proofreading, ensuring the manuscript was impeccably polished for its release.

A special note of appreciation goes to Amanda Davidson for her exceptional work in bringing the audiobook version to life. Her professionalism and talent have truly captured the essence of the story.

I extend my heartfelt thanks to Jessie from Book Blurb Magic for her expert feedback in honing the book's blurb, a crucial component of its promotion.

Beyond the core tasks of writing and editing, numerous individuals have added layers to the story's world. Yves Muench's captivating illustrations, particularly Adele's character on the cover, have been an integral part of the book's visual identity. Collaborating with Yves has been a delight, and I'm excited to continue working together for future character artwork.

Being the first commissioned author for Angeline Trevena's Step-by-Step Worldbuilding was an honor. Her hand-drawn map of the story world is not only within the book but also graces my office wall, a constant source of motivation.

Audrey Weatherstone's remarkable contribution involved bringing my song lyrics to life with her beautiful voice, adding another dimension to the story's experience.

My gratitude extends to my dedicated street team whose unwavering support and words of encouragement have been a tremendous source of motivation. Additionally, I'm thankful for the authors who provided testimonial reviews, reflecting the strong camaraderie within our book-loving community.

Acknowledging the core of my appreciation, I want to express my immense gratitude to the readers who invest their time in my stories. Your enthusiasm and support are the driving forces behind my writing journey. Thank you for being an integral part of this incredible adventure with me.

In conclusion, the journey of crafting this book has been enriched by the collective efforts of these extraordinary individuals. To the readers, your support is the bedrock of my writing voyage. From the depths of my heart, thank you for embarking on this remarkable journey alongside me.

About The Author

Kimberly Grymes loves being sucked into science-fiction, fantasy, mystery, and paranormal worlds.

After many, *many* years of reading books and watching other people's stories on TV and film, she finally took the plunge and started writing and sharing her own stories. When she's not writing she's either hanging out with her family, watching movies or TV shows, reading a good book, or creating new designs and products for her Etsy shop.

She and her family live on the outskirts of Wichita, Kansas with their two crazy miniature pinschers, Cori and Jubilee.